Telling Tales

Edited by

Nadine Gordimer

BLOOMSBURY

First published in Great Britain 2004

Copyright in compilation and introduction © 2004 by Nadine Gordimer

The moral right of the editor has been asserted

Bloomsbury Publishing Plc, 36 Soho Square, London W1D 3QY

A CIP catalogue record for this book is available from the British Library

All papers used by Bloomsbury Publishing are natural, recyclable products made
from wood grown in well-managed forests. The manufacturing processes conform
to the environmental regulations of the country of origin.

ISBN 0 7475 7430 8
9780747574309

10 9 8

Printed in Great Britain by Clays Ltd, St Ives plc

www.bloomsbury.com

Contents

❧

Acknowledgments

❦

Many people contributed invaluably to the realisation of this anthology.

My grateful thanks to

THE AUTHORS, who contributed their stories without any fee or royalty

THE PUBLISHERS, who produced and distributed the book without any profit:
Liz Calder, Bloomsbury Publications, Britain
Jonathan Galassi, Farrar, Straus & Giroux, and Frances Coady, Picador, USA
Arnulf Conradi, Berlin Verlag, Germany
Carlo & Inge Feltrinelli, Giangiacomo Feltrinelli Editore, Italy
Ariane Fasquelle & Olivier Nora, Editions Grasset et Fasquelle, France
Yilin Press, People's Republic of China
Sophia Publishing House, Russia
Locus Publishing, Taiwan

Companhia das Letras, Brazil

Kastaniotis, Greece

Ulpius-Haz, Hungary

De Geus, the Netherlands

Miskal, Israel

and all other publishing houses who are in the process of following suit.

THE ARTISTS:

Karel Nel and Kevin Shenton, who created the jacket design from a painting by Karel Nel, without any fee.

MY LITERARY AGENTS:

Linda Shaughnessy and Teresa Nicholls, A. P. Watt Ltd., London, Timothy Seldes and Kirsten Ringer, Russell & Volkening Inc., New York, who arranged all copyrights as their contribution.

AND:

Michelle Lapautre, Agence Michelle Lapautre, Paris, for her assistance with negotiation.

Dorothy Wheeler, who word processed all the typescripts and other forms in which the stories came to me.

Verna Hunt, who assisted with correspondence and in numerous other ways.

Jean Stein, of *Grand Street*, who generously contributed to expenses.

Djibril Diallo, Director of Communication, UNDP.

Shashi Tharoor, Under-Secretary-General, Communication and Public Information, United Nations.

My special thanks to the Secretary-General of United Nations, Kofi Annan, who spontaneously proposed and generously authorised the launch of *Telling Tales* at United Nations in New York.

Introduction

❧

Gather round to enjoy the storytelling collected for your enjoyment in this book. It is going to be a unique experience in two ways.

First way. Rarely have world writers of such variety and distinction appeared on a contents list in the same anthology. Their stories capture the range of emotions and situations of our human universe: tragedy, comedy, fantasy, satire, dramas of sexual love and of war, in different continents and cultures. The reader learns about others—and about oneself, revealed as only fiction, the ancient art of storytelling can do and always has done. Along with making music, the art is the oldest form of enchantment as entertainment.

The twenty-one stories are written in different "voices"—vividly individual styles—capturing the marvellous possibilities of use of words by living writers. They include five Nobel Prize Winners in Literature. All have come together to bring the joy of reading to whoever takes up this unusual and remarkable collection of creative talent.

Second way. All twenty-one writers have given their stories—in each instance chosen by themselves as representing some of the best of their lifetime work as storytellers—without any fee or royalty. The publishers of each edition in each country where the anthology is published, have produced the book without receiving any profit or royalty.

Why have these writers agreed to grant the free gift of their talents and work?

Musicians have given their talents to jazz, pop, and classical concerts for the benefit of the 40 million worldwide men, women, and children infected with HIV/AIDS, two-thirds of whom are in Africa. We decided that we too should wish to give something of our ability, as imaginative writers, to contribute in our way to the fight against this disease from which no country, no individual, is safely isolated.

All royalties and profits from the sale of *Telling Tales* worldwide will go to HIV/AIDS preventive education and for medical treatment for people living with this pandemic infection and the suffering it brings to our contemporary world. So when you buy as a gift or for your own reading pleasure this unique anthology of renowned storytellers, you are also making a gift, of the money you have paid for the book, to combat the plague of our new millenium.

The subjects of the stories are not about HIV/AIDS; but the profits go to help succour and support its victims.

—NADINE GORDIMER

Telling Tales

Bulldog

Arthur Miller

❦

He saw this tiny ad in the paper: "Black Brindle Bull puppies, $3.00 each." He had something like ten dollars from his house-painting job, which he hadn't deposited yet, but they had never had a dog in the house. His father was taking a long nap when the idea crested in his mind, and his mother, in the middle of a bridge game when he asked her if it would be all right, shrugged absently and threw a card. He walked around the house trying to decide, and the feeling spread through him that he'd better hurry, before somebody else got the puppy first. In his mind, there was already one particular puppy that belonged to him—it was his puppy and the puppy knew it. He had no idea what a brindle bull looked like, but it sounded tough and wonderful. And he had the three dollars, though it soured him to think of spending it when they had such bad money worries, with his father gone bankrupt again. The tiny ad hadn't mentioned how many puppies there were. Maybe there were only two or three, which might be bought by this time.

The address was on Schermerhorn Street, which he had never heard of. He called, and a woman with a husky voice explained how to get there and on which line. He was coming from the Midwood section, and the elevated Culver line, so he would have to change at Church Avenue. He wrote everything down and read it all back to her. She still had the puppies, thank God. It took more than an hour, but the train was almost empty, this being Sunday, and with a breeze from its open wood-framed windows it was cooler than down in the street. Below in empty lots he could see old Italian women, their heads covered with red bandannas, bent over and loading their aprons with dandelions. His Italian school friends said they were for wine and salads. He remembered trying to eat one once when he was playing left field in the lot near his house, but it was bitter and salty as tears. The old wooden train, practically unloaded, rocked and clattered lightly through the hot afternoon. He passed above a block where men were standing in driveways watering their cars as though they were hot elephants. Dust floated pleasantly through the air.

The Schermerhorn Street neighborhood was a surprise, totally different from his own, in Midwood. The houses here were made of brownstone, and were not at all like the clapboard ones on his block, which had been put up only a few years before or, in the earliest cases, in the twenties. Even the sidewalks looked old, with big squares of stone instead of cement, and bits of grass growing in the cracks between them. He could tell that Jews didn't live here, maybe because it was so quiet and unenergetic and not a soul was sitting outside to enjoy the sun. Lots of windows were wide open, with expressionless people leaning on their elbows and staring out, and cats stretched out on some of the sills, many of the women in their bras and the men in underwear trying to catch a breeze. Trickles of sweat were creeping down his back, not only from the heat but also because he realized now that he was the only one who wanted the dog, since his parents hadn't really had an opinion and his brother, who was older, had said, "What are you, crazy, spending your few dollars on a puppy? Who knows if it will be any good? And what are you going to feed it?" He thought bones, and his brother, who always knew what was right or wrong, yelled, "Bones! They have no teeth yet!" Well, maybe soup, he had mumbled. "Soup! You going to feed a puppy *soup?*" Suddenly he saw that he had arrived at the address. Standing there, he felt the bottom falling out, and he knew it was all a mistake, like one of his dreams or a lie that he had stupidly tried to defend as being real. His heart sped up and he felt he was blushing and walked on for half a block or so. He was the only one out, and people in a few of the windows were watching him on the empty street. But how could he go home after he had come so far? It seemed he'd been travelling for weeks or a year. And now to get back on the subway with nothing? Maybe he ought at least to get a look at the puppy, if the woman would let him. He had looked it up in the Book of Knowledge, where they had two full pages of dog pictures, and there had been a white English bulldog with bent front legs and teeth that stuck out from its lower jaw, and a little black-and-white Boston bull, and a long-nosed pit bull, but they had no picture of a brindle bull. When you came down to it, all he really knew about brindle bulls was that they would cost three dollars. But he had to at least get a look at him, his puppy, so he went back down the block and rang the basement doorbell, as the woman had told him to do. The sound was so loud it startled him, but he felt if he ran away and she came out in time to see him it would be even more embarrassing, so he stood there with sweat running down over his lip.

An inner door under the stoop opened, and a woman came out

and looked at him through the dusty iron bars of the gate. She wore some kind of gown, light-pink silk, which she held together with one hand, and she had long black hair down to her shoulders. He didn't dare look directly into her face, so he couldn't tell exactly what she looked like, but he could feel her tension as she stood there behind her closed gate. He felt she could not imagine what he was doing ringing her bell and he quickly asked if she was the one who'd put the ad in. Oh! Her manner changed right away, and she unlatched the gate and pulled it open. She was shorter than he and had a peculiar smell, like a mixture of milk and stale air. He followed her into the apartment, which was so dark he could hardly make out anything, but he could hear the high yapping of puppies. She had to yell to ask him where he lived and how old he was, and when he told her thirteen she clapped a hand over her mouth and said that he was very tall for his age, but he couldn't understand why this seemed to embarrass her, except that she may have thought he was fifteen, which people sometimes did. But even so. He followed her into the kitchen, at the back of the apartment, where finally he could see around him, now that he'd been out of the sun for a few minutes. In a large cardboard box that had been unevenly cut down to make it shallower he saw three puppies and their mother, who sat looking up at him with her tail moving slowly back and forth. He didn't think she looked like a bulldog, but he didn't dare say so. She was just a brown dog with flecks of black and a few stripes here and there, and the puppies were the same. He did like the way their little ears drooped, but he said to the woman that he had wanted to see the puppies but hadn't made up his mind yet. He really didn't know what to do next, so, in order not to seem as though he didn't appreciate the puppies, he asked if she would mind if he held one. She said that was all right and reached down into the box and lifted out two puppies and set them down on the blue linoleum. They didn't look like any bulldogs he had ever seen, but he was embarrassed to tell her that he didn't really want one. She picked one up and said, "Here," and put it on his lap.

He had never held a dog before and was afraid it would slide off, so he cradled it in his arms. It was hot on his skin and very soft and kind of disgusting in a thrilling way. It had gray eyes like tiny buttons. It troubled him that the Book of Knowledge hadn't had a picture of this kind of dog. A real bulldog was kind of tough and dangerous, but these were just brown dogs. He sat there on the arm of the green upholstered chair with the puppy on his lap, not knowing what to do next. The woman, meanwhile, had put herself next to him, and it felt like she had given his hair a pat, but he wasn't sure because he had very thick hair. The more seconds that ticked away the less sure he was of what to do. Then she asked if he would like some water, and he said he would, and she went to the faucet and ran water, which gave him a chance to stand up and set the puppy back in the box. She came back to him holding the glass and as he took it she let her gown fall open, showing her breasts like half-filled balloons, saying she couldn't believe he was only thirteen. He gulped the water and started to hand her back the glass, and she suddenly drew his head to her and kissed him. In all this time, for some reason, he hadn't been able to look into her face, and when he tried to now he couldn't see anything but a blur and hair. She reached down to him and a shivering started in the backs of his legs. It got sharper, until it was almost like the time he touched the live rim of a light socket while trying to remove a broken bulb. He would never be able to remember getting down on the carpet—he felt like a waterfall was smashing down on top of his head. He remembered getting inside her heat and his head banging and banging against the leg of her couch. He was

almost at Church Avenue, where he had to change for the elevated
Culver line, before realizing she hadn't taken his three dollars, and
he couldn't recall agreeing to it but he had this small cardboard box
on his lap with a puppy mewling inside. The scraping of nails on the
cardboard sent chills up his back. The woman, as he remembered
now, had cut two holes into the top of the box, and the puppy kept
sticking his nose through them.

His mother jumped back when he untied the cord and the puppy
pushed up and scrambled out, yapping. "What is he doing?" she
yelled, with her hands in the air as though she were about to be at-
tacked. By this time, he'd lost his fear of the puppy and held him in
his arms and let him lick his face, and seeing this his mother calmed
down a bit. "Is he hungry?" she asked, and stood with her mouth
slightly open, ready for anything, as he put the puppy on the floor
again. He said the puppy might be hungry, but he thought he could
eat only soft things, although his little teeth were as sharp as pins.
She got out some soft cream cheese and put a little piece of it on the
floor, but the puppy only sniffed at it and peed. "My God in Heaven!"
she yelled, and quickly got a piece of newspaper to blot it up with.
When she bent over that way, he thought of the woman's heat and
was ashamed and shook his head. Suddenly her name came to him—
Lucille—which she had told him when they were on the floor. Just as
he was slipping in, she had opened her eyes and said, "My name is
Lucille." His mother brought out a bowl of last night's noodles and
set it on the floor. The puppy raised his little paw and tipped the
bowl over, spilling some of the chicken soup at the bottom. This he
began to lick hungrily off the linoleum. "He likes chicken soup!" his
mother yelled happily, and immediately decided he would most
likely enjoy an egg and so put water on to boil. Somehow the puppy

knew that she was the one to follow and walked behind her, back and forth, from the stove to the refrigerator. "He follows me!" his mother said, laughing happily.

On his way home from school the next day, he stopped at the hardware store and bought a puppy collar for seventy-five cents, and Mr. Schweckert threw in a piece of clothesline as a leash. Every night as he fell asleep, he brought out Lucille like something from a secret treasure box and wondered if he could dare phone her and maybe be with her again. The puppy, which he had named Rover, seemed to grow noticeably bigger every day, although he still showed no signs of looking like any bulldog. The boy's father thought Rover should live in the cellar, but it was very lonely down there and he would never stop yapping. "He misses his mother," his mother said, so every night the boy started him off on some rags in an old wash basket down there, and when he'd yapped enough the boy was allowed to bring him up and let him sleep on some rags in the kitchen, and everybody was thankful for the quiet. His mother tried to walk the puppy in the quiet street they lived on, but he kept tangling the rope around her ankles, and because she was afraid to hurt him she exhausted herself following him in all his zigzags. It didn't always happen, but many times when the boy looked at Rover he'd think of Lucille and could almost feel the heat again. He would sit on the porch steps stroking the puppy and think of her, the insides of her thighs. He still couldn't imagine her face, just her long black hair and her strong neck.

One day, his mother baked a chocolate cake and set it to cool on the kitchen table. It was at least eight inches thick, and he knew it would be delicious. He was drawing a lot in those days, pictures of spoons and forks or cigarette packages or, occasionally, his mother's Chinese vase with the dragon on it, anything that had an interesting shape. So he put the cake on a chair next to the table and drew for a while and then got up and went outside for some reason and got involved with the tulips he had planted the previous fall that were just now showing their tips. Then he decided to go look for a practically new baseball he had mislaid the previous summer and which he was sure, or pretty sure, must be down in the cellar in a cardboard box. He had never really got down to the bottom of that box, because he was always distracted by finding something he'd forgotten he had put in there. He had started down into the cellar from the outside entrance, under the back porch, when he noticed that the pear tree, which he had planted two years before, had what looked like a blossom on one of its slender branches. It amazed him, and he felt proud and successful. He had paid thirty-five cents for the tree on Court Street and thirty cents for an apple tree, which he planted about seven feet away, so as to be able to hang a hammock between them someday. They were still too thin and young, but maybe next year. He always loved to stare at the two trees, because he had planted them, and he felt they somehow knew he was looking at them, and even that they were looking back at him. The back yard ended at a ten-foot-high wooden fence that surrounded Erasmus Field, where the semi-pro and sandlot teams played on weekends, teams like the House of David and the Black Yankees and the one with Satchel Paige, who was famous as one of the country's greatest pitchers except he was a Negro and couldn't play in the big leagues, obviously. The House of Davids all had long beards—he'd never understood why, but maybe they were Orthodox Jews, although they didn't look it. An extremely long foul shot over right field could drop a ball into the yard, and that was the ball it had occurred to him to search for, now that spring had come and the weather was warming up. In the basement, he found the box and was immediately surprised at how sharp his ice skates were, and recalled that he had once had a vise to clamp the skates side by side so that a stone could be rubbed on the blades. He pushed aside a torn fielder's glove, a hockey goalie's glove whose mate he knew had been lost, some pencil stubs and a package of crayons, and a little wooden man whose arms flapped up and down when you pulled a string. Then he heard the puppy yapping over his head, but it was not his usual sound—it was continuous and very sharp and loud. He ran upstairs and saw his mother coming down into the living room from the second floor, her dressing gown flying out behind her, a look of fear on her face. He could hear the scraping of the puppy's nails on the linoleum, and he rushed into the kitchen. The puppy was running around and around in a circle and sort of screaming, and the boy could see at once that his belly was swollen. The cake was on the floor, and most of it was gone. "My cake!" his mother screamed, and picked up the dish with the remains on it and held it up high as though to save it from the puppy, even though practically nothing was left. The boy tried to catch Rover, but he slipped away into the living room. His mother was behind him yelling "The carpet!" Rover kept running, in wider circles now that he had more space, and foam was forming on his muzzle. "Call the police!" his mother yelled. Suddenly, the puppy fell and lay on his side, gasping and making little squeaks with each breath. Since they had never had a dog and knew nothing about veterinarians, he looked in the phone book and found the A.S.P.C.A. number and called them. Now he was afraid to touch Rover, because the puppy snapped at his hand when it got close and he had this foam on his mouth. When the van drew up in front of the house, the boy went outside and saw a young guy removing a little cage from the back. He told him that the dog had eaten practically a whole cake, but the man had no interest and came into the house and stood for a moment looking down at Rover, who was making little yips now but was still down on his side. The man dropped some netting over him and when he slipped him into the cage, the puppy tried to get up and run. "What do you think is the matter with him?" his mother asked, her mouth turned down in revulsion, which the boy now felt in himself. "What's the matter with him is he ate a cake," the man said. Then he carried the cage out and slid it through the back door into the darkness of the van. "What will you do with him?" the boy asked. "You want him?" the man snapped. His mother was standing on the stoop now and overheard them. "We can't have him here," she called over, with fright and definiteness in her voice, and approached the young man. "We don't know how to keep a dog. Maybe somebody who knows how to keep him would want him." The young man nodded with no interest either way, got behind the wheel, and drove off.

The boy and his mother watched the van until it disappeared around the corner. Inside, the house was dead quiet again. He didn't have to worry anymore about Rover doing something on the carpets or chewing the furniture, or whether he had water or needed to eat. Rover had been the first thing he'd looked for on returning from school every day and on waking in the morning, and he had always worried that the dog might have done something to displease his mother or father. Now all that anxiety was gone and, with it, the pleasure, and it was silent in the house.

He went back to the kitchen table and tried to think of something he could draw. A newspaper lay on one of the chairs, and he opened it and inside saw a Saks stocking ad showing a woman with a gown pulled aside to display her leg. He started copying it and thought of Lucille again. Could he possibly call her, he wondered, and do what they had done again? Except that she would surely ask about Rover, and he couldn't do anything but lie to her. He remembered how she had cuddled Rover in her arms and even kissed his nose. She had really loved that puppy. How could he tell her he was gone? Just sitting and thinking of her he was hardening up like a broom handle and he suddenly thought what if he called her and said his family were thinking of having a second puppy to keep Rover company? But then he would have to pretend he still had Rover, which would mean two lies, and that was a little frightening. Not the lies so much as trying to remember, first, that he still had Rover, second, that he was serious about a second puppy, and, third, the worst thing, that when he got up off Lucille he would have to say that unfortunately he couldn't actually take another puppy because . . . Why? The thought of all that lying exhausted him. Then he visualized being in her heat again and he thought his head would explode, and the idea came that when it was over she might insist on his taking another puppy. Force it on him. After all, she had not accepted his three dollars and Rover had been a sort of gift, he thought. It would be embarrassing to refuse another puppy, especially when he had supposedly come back to her for exactly that reason. He didn't dare go through all that and gave up the whole idea. But then the thought crept back again of her spreading apart on the floor the way she had, and he returned to searching for some reason he could give for not taking another puppy after he had supposedly come all the way across Brooklyn to get one. He could just see the look on her face on his turning down a puppy, the puzzlement or, worse, anger. Yes, she could very possibly get angry and see through him, realizing that all he had come for was to get into her and the rest of it was nonsense, and she might feel insulted. Maybe even slap him. What would he do then? He couldn't fight a grown woman. Then again, it now occurred to him that by this time she might well have sold the other two puppies, which at three dollars were pretty inexpensive. Then what? He began to wonder, suppose he just called her up and said he'd like to come over again and see her, without mentioning any puppies? He would have to tell only one lie, that he still had Rover and that the family all loved him and so on. He could easily remember that much. He went to the piano and played some chords, mostly in the dark bass, to calm himself. He didn't really know how to play, but he loved inventing chords and letting the vibrations shoot up his arms. He played, feeling as though something inside him had sort of shaken loose or collapsed altogether. He was different than he had ever been, not empty and clear anymore but weighted with secrets and his lies, some told and some untold, but all of it disgusting enough to set him slightly outside his family, in a place where he could watch them now, and watch himself with them. He tried to invent a melody with the right hand and find matching chords with the left. By sheer luck, he was hitting some beauties. It was really amazing how his chords were just slightly off, with a discordant edge but still in some way talking to the right-hand melody. His mother came into the room full of surprise and pleasure. "What's happening?" she called out in delight. She could play and sight-read music and had tried and failed to teach him, because, she believed, his ear was too good and he'd rather play what he heard than do the labor of reading notes. She came over to the piano and stood beside him, watching his hands. Amazed, wishing as always that he could be a genius, she laughed.

"Are you making this up?" she almost yelled, as though they were side by side on a roller coaster. He could only nod, not daring to speak and maybe lose what he had somehow snatched out of the air, and he laughed with her because he was so completely happy that he had secretly changed, and unsure at the same time that he would ever be able to play like this again.

The Centaur

José Saramago

❧

The horse came to a halt. His shoeless hooves gripped the round, slippery stones covering the river-bed which was almost dry. Using his hands, the man cautiously pushed back the thorny branches which obstructed his view of the plain. Day was breaking. Far away, where the land rose, first in a gentle slope, for he remembered it being similar to the pass he had descended far north, before suddenly being broken up by a balsatic mountain ridge rising up in a vertical wall, stood some houses which from a distance looked quite small and low, and lights that resembled stars. Along the mountain ridge which cut out the entire horizon from that side, there was a luminous line as if someone had passed a light brushstroke over the peaks and, because still wet, the paint had gradually spread over the slope. The sun would appear from that direction. One false move as he pushed back the branches and the man grazed his hand: he muttered something to himself and put his finger to his lips to suck the blood. The horse retreated, stamping his hooves and swishing his tail over the tall grasses that absorbed the remaining moisture on the river-bank sheltered by overhanging branches forming a screen at that black hour. The river was reduced to a trickle of water running between the stones where the river-bed was deepest and at rare intervals forming puddles wherein fish struggled to survive. The humidity in the atmosphere forecast rain and tempest, perhaps not today but tomorrow, after three suns, or with the next moon. Very slowly the sky began to light up. Time to find a hiding-place in order to rest and sleep.

The horse was thirsty. He approached the stream which seemed quite still beneath the night sky, and as his front hooves met the cool water, he lay down sideways on the ground. Resting one shoulder on the rough sand, the man drank at his leisure despite feeling no thirst. Above the man and the horse, the patch of sky that was still in darkness slowly moved, trailing in its wake the palest light, still tinged with yellow, the first deceptive hint of the crimson and red about to explode over the mountain, as over so many mountains in different places or on a level with the prairie. The horse and man got up. In front stood a dense barrier of trees, with defensive brambles between the trunks. Birds were already chirping on the uppermost branches. The horse crossed the river-bed at an unsteady trot and tried to break through the entangled bushes on the right, but the man preferred an easier passage. With time, and there had been all the time in the world, he had learned how to curb the animal's impatience, sometimes opposing him with an upsurge of violence which clouded his thoughts or perhaps affected that part of his body where the orders coming from his brain clashed with the dark instincts nourished between his flanks where the skin was black; at other times he succumbed, distracted and thinking of other things, things that certainly belonged to this physical world in which he found himself, but not to this age. Fatigue had made the horse nervous: he quivered as if trying to shake off a frenzied gadfly thirsting for blood, and he stamped his hooves restlessly only to tire even more. It would have been unwise to try and force an entry through the entanglement of brambles. There were so many scars on the horse's white coat. One particular scar, which was very old, traced a broad, oblique mark on his rump. When exposed to the blazing sun or when extreme cold made the hairs of his coat stand up, it was as if the flaming blade of a sword were striking that sensitive and vulnerable scar. Although well aware that he would find nothing there except a bigger scar than the others, at such moments the man would twist his torso and look back as if staring into infinity.

A short distance away, downstream, the river-bank narrowed: in all probability there was a lagoon, or perhaps a tributary, just as dry or even more so. It was muddy at the bottom with few stones. Around this pocket as it were, a simple neck of the river that filled and emptied with it, stood tall trees, black beneath the darkness only gradually rising from the earth. If the screen formed by trunks and fallen branches were sufficiently dense, he could pass the day there, completely hidden from sight, until night returned when he could continue on his way. He drew back the cool leaves with his hands and, impelled by the strength of his hocks, he climbed on to the embankment in almost total darkness, concealed by the thick crests of the trees. Then, almost immediately, the ground sloped down again into a ditch which further on would probably run through open countryside. He had found a good spot to rest and sleep. Between the river and the mountain there was arable land, tilled fields, but that deep and narrow ditch showed no signs of being passable. He took a few more steps, now in complete silence. Startled birds were watching. He looked overhead: saw the uppermost tips of the branches bathed in light. The soft light coming from the mountain was now skimming the leafy fringe on high. The birds resumed their chirping. The light descended little by little, a greenish dust changing to pink and white, the subtle and uncertain morning mist. Against the light, the pitch-black trunks of the trees appeared to have only two dimensions as if they had been cut out of what remained of the night and were glued to a luminous transparency that was disappearing into the ditch. The ground was covered with irises. A nice, tranquil refuge where he could spend the day sleeping.

Overcome by the fatigue of centuries and millennia, the horse knelt down. Finding a position to suit both of them was always a difficult operation. The horse usually lay on his side and the man did likewise. But while the horse could spend the entire night in this position without stirring, if the man wanted to avoid getting cramp in his shoulder and all down his side, he had to overcome the resistance of that great inert and slumbering body and make him turn over on to the other side: it was always a disquieting dream. As for sleeping on foot, the horse could, but not the man. And when the hideout was too confined, changing over from one side to another became impossible and the sense of urgency all the greater. It was not a comfortable body. The man could never stretch out on the ground, rest his head on folded arms and remain there studying the ants or grains of earth, or contemplate the whiteness of a tender stalk sprouting from the dark soil. And in order to see the sky, he had to twist his neck, except when the horse reared up on his hind legs, lifting the man on high so that he could lean a little further back; then he certainly got a much better view at the great nocturnal campanula of stars, the horizontal and tumultuous meadow of clouds, or the blue, sunlit sky, the last vestiges of the first creation.

The horse fell asleep at once. With his hooves amongst the irises and his bushy tail spread out on the ground, he lay there breathing heavily at a steady rhythm. Semi-reclined and with his right shoulder pressed up against the wall of the ditch, the man broke off low-lying branches with which to cover himself. While moving he could bear the heat and cold without any discomfort, although not as well as the horse. But when asleep and lying still, he soon began to feel the cold. And so long as the heat of the sun did not become too intense, he could rest at his ease under the shade of the leaves. From this position, he perceived that the trees did not entirely shut out the sky above: an uneven strip, already a transparent blue, stretched ahead and, crossing it intermittently from one side to the other, or momentarily following in the same direction, birds were flying swiftly through the air. The man slowly closed his eyes. The smell of sap from the broken branches made him feel a little faint. He pulled one of the leafier branches over his face and fell asleep. He never dreamed like other men. Nor did he ever dream as a horse might dream. During their hours of wakefulness, there were few moments of peace or simple conciliation. But the horse's dream, along with that of the man, constituted the centaur's dream.

He was the last survivor of that great and ancient species of men-horses. He had fought in the war against the Lapithae, the first serious defeat suffered by him and his fellow-centaurs. Once they had been defeated, the centaur had taken refuge in mountains whose name he had forgotten. Until that fatal day when, protected in part by the gods, Heracles had decimated his brothers and he alone had escaped because the long, drawn-out battle between Heracles and Nessos had given him time to seek refuge in the forest. And that was the end of the centaurs. But contrary to the claims of historians and mythologists, one centaur survived, this self-same centaur who had seen Heracles crush Nessos to death with one terrible embrace and then drag his corpse along the ground as Hector would later do with the corpse of Achilles, while praising the gods for having overcome and exterminated the prodigious race of the Centaurs. Perhaps remorseful, those same gods then favoured the hidden centaur, blinding Heracles' eyes and mind for who knows what reason.

Each day the centaur dreamt of fighting and vanquishing Heracles. In the centre of the circle of gods who reunited with every dream, he would fight arm to arm, using his croup to dodge any sly move on the enemy's part, and avoid the rope whizzing between his hooves, thus forcing the enemy to fight face to face. His face, arms and trunk perspired as only a man perspires. The horse's body was covered in sweat. This dream recurred for thousands of years and always with the same outcome: he punished Heracles for Nessos' death, summoning all the strength in his limbs and muscles as both man and horse. Set firmly on his four hooves as if they were stakes embedded in the earth, he lifted Heracles into the air and tightened his grip until he could hear the first rib cracking, then another, and finally the spine breaking. Heracles' corpse slipped to the ground like a rag and the gods applauded. There was no prize for the victor. Rising from their gilt thrones, the gods moved away, the circle becoming ever wider until they disappeared into the horizon. From the door where Aphrodite entered the heavens, an enormous star continued to shine.

For thousands of years he roved the earth. For ages, so long as the world itself remained mysterious, he could travel by the light of the Sun. As he passed, people came out on to the roadside and threw garlands of flowers over the horse's back or made coronets which they placed on his head. Mothers handed him their children to lift into mid-air so that they might lose any fear of heights. And everywhere there was a secret ceremony: in the middle of a circle of trees representing the gods, impotent men and sterile women passed under the horse's belly: people believed this would promote fertility and restore virility. At certain times of the year they would bring a mare before the centaur and withdraw indoors: but one day, someone who saw the man cover the mare like a horse and then weep like a man, was struck blind for committing such a sacrilege. These unions bore no fruit.

Then the world changed. The centaur was banished and persecuted, and forced into hiding. And other creatures too: such as the unicorn, the chimera, the werewolf, men with cloven-hooves, and those ants bigger than foxes but smaller than dogs. For ten human generations, these various outcasts lived together in the wilderness. But after a time, even there they found life impossible and all of them dispersed. Some, like the unicorn, died: the chimerae mated with shrewmice which led to the appearance of bats; werewolves found their way into towns and villages and only on certain nights do they meet their fate; the cloven-footed men also became extinct; and ants grew smaller in size so that nowadays you cannot tell them apart from other small insects. The centaur was now on his own. For thousands of years, as far as the sea would permit, he roamed the entire earth. But on his journeys he would always make a detour whenever he sensed he was getting close to the borders of his native country. Time passed. Eventually there was no longer any land where he could live in safety. He began sleeping during the day and moving on at dusk. Walking and sleeping. Sleeping and walking. For no apparent reason other than the fact that he possessed legs and needed rest. He did not need food. And he only needed sleep in order to dream. And as for water, he drank simply because the water was there.

Thousands of years ought to have been thousands of adventures.

Thousands of adventures, however, are too many to equal one truly unforgettable adventure. And that explains why all of them put together did not equal that adventure, already in this last millennium, when in the midst of an arid wilderness he saw a man with lance and coat of armour, astride a scraggy horse charging an army of windmills. He saw the rider being hurled into the air and another man, short and fat and mounted on a donkey, rush to his assistance, shouting his head off. He heard them speak in a language he could not understand and then watched them go off, the thin man badly shaken, the fat one wailing, the scraggy horse limping, and the donkey impassive. He thought of going to their assistance but, on taking another look at the windmills, he galloped up to them and, coming to a halt before the first windmill, he decided to avenge the man who had been thrown from his horse. In his native tongue, he called out: 'Even if you had more arms than the giant Briareas, I'll make you pay for this outrage.' All the windmills were left with broken wings and the centaur was pursued to the frontier of a neighbouring country. He crossed desolate fields and reached the sea. Then he turned back.

The centaur, man and beast, is fast asleep. His entire body is at rest. The dream has come and gone, and the horse is now galloping within a day from the distant past, so that the man may see the mountains file past as if they were travelling with him, or he were climbing mountain paths to the summit in order to look down on the sonorous sea and the black scattered islands, the spray exploding around them as if they had just appeared from the depths and were surfacing there in wonder. This is no dream. The smell of brine comes from the open sea. The man takes a deep breath and stretches his arms upwards while the horse excitedly stamps its hooves on protruding marble stones. Already withered, the leaves that were covering the man's face have fallen away. The sun overhead casts a speckled light on the centaur. The face is not that of an old man. Nor that of a young man, needless to say, since we are talking about thousands of years. But his face could be compared with that of an ancient statue: time has eroded it but not to the extent of obliterating the features: simply enough to show they are weather-bitten. A tiny, luminous patch sparkles on his skin, slowly edging towards his mouth, bringing warmth. The man suddenly opens his eyes as a statue might. With undulating movements a snake steals off into the under-growth. The man raises a hand to his mouth and feels the sun. At that same moment the horse shakes his tail, sweeps it over his croup and chases off a gadfly feeding on the delicate skin of the great scar. The horse rises quickly to his feet accompanied by the man. The day has almost gone and soon the first shadows of night will fall, but there can be no more sleeping. The noise of the sea, which was not a dream, still resounds in the man's ears, not the real noise of the sea but rather that vision of beating waves which his eyes have trans-formed into those sonorous waves which travel over the waters and climb up rocky gorges all the way to the sun and the blue sky which is also water.

Almost there. The ditch he is following just happens to be there and could lead anywhere, the work of men and a path by which to reach other men. But it heads in a southerly direction and that is what matters. He will advance as far as possible, even in daylight, even with the sun above the entire plain and exposing everything, whether man or beast. Once more he had defeated Heracles in his dream in the presence of all the immortal gods, but once the combat was over, Zeus retreated southwards and only then did the mountains open up, and from their highest peak surmounted by white pillars, he looked down on the islands surrounded by spray. The frontier is nearby and Zeus headed south.

Walking along the deep and narrow ditch, the man can see the countryside from one end to the other. The lands now look abandoned. He no longer knows where the village he had seen at daybreak has disappeared to. The great rocky mountains have become taller or perhaps drawn closer. The horse's hooves sink into the soft earth he is gradually climbing. The man's whole trunk is clearly out of the ditch, the trees space out, and suddenly, once in open countryside, the ditch comes to an end. With a simple movement, the horse makes the final descent, and the centaur appears in full daylight. The sun is to the right and shines directly on to the scar which begins to ache and burn. The man looks back, out of habit. The atmosphere is stuffy and humid. Not that the sea is all that close. This humidity promises rain as does this sharp gust of wind. To the north, clouds are gathering.

The man wavers. For many years he has not dared to travel out in the open unless protected by the darkness of night. But today he feels as excited as the horse. He proceeds through scrubland where the wild flowers give off a strong scent. The plain has come to an end and the ground now rises in humps restricting the horizon or extending it ever more because these elevations are already hills and a screen of mountains looms up ahead. Bushes begin to appear and the centaur begins to feel less vulnerable. He feels thirsty, very thirsty, but there is no sign of water nearby. The man looks behind and sees that one half of the sky is already covered in clouds. The sun lights up the sharp edge of an enormous grey cloud that is steadily approaching.

At this moment, a dog can be heard barking. The horse trembles nervously. The centaur breaks into a gallop between the two hills, but the man does not lose his sense of direction; they must head south. The barking comes nearer, bells can be heard ringing and then a voice speaking to cattle. The centaur stopped to get his bearings, but the echoes misled him and then, suddenly, there is an unexpectedly humid and low-lying stretch of land, a herd of goats appears and in front a large dog. The centaur stopped in his tracks. Several of the ugly scars on his body had been inflicted by dogs. The shepherd cried out in terror and took to his heels as if demented. He began shouting for help: there must be a village nearby. The man ordered the horse to advance. He broke a sturdy branch from a bush in order to chase away a dog which was barking its head off in rage and terror. But fury prevailed: the dog rapidly skirted some boulders and tried to grab the centaur sideways by the belly. The man tried to look back to see where the danger was coming from, but the horse reacted first and, turning quickly on its front hooves, aimed a vicious kick which caught the dog in mid-air. The animal was dashed against some rocks and killed. The centaur had often been forced to defend himself in this way but this time the man felt humiliated. He could feel the strain of all those vibrating muscles in his own body, his ebbing strength, hear the dull thud of his hooves, but he had his back to the battle, played no part in it, a mere spectator.

The sun had disappeared. The heat suddenly abated and there was humidity in the air. The centaur cantered between the hills, still heading south. As he crossed a tiny stream he saw cultivated fields, and when he tried to get his bearings he came up against a wall. There were several houses on one side. Then a shot rang out. He could feel the horse's body twitch as if stung by a swarm of bees. People were shouting and another shot was fired. To the left, splintered branches snapped, but this time no pellets hit him. He stepped back to regain his balance, and with one mighty effort he lept over the wall. Man and horse, centaur, went flying over, four legs outstretched or drawn in, two arms raised to the sky which was still blue in the distance. More shots rang out, and then a crowd of men began chasing him through the countryside with loud cries and the barking of dogs.

The centaur's body was covered in foam and sweat. He paused for a moment to find the way. The surrounding countryside also became expectant, as if it were listening out. Then the first heavy drops of rain began to fall. But the chase went on. The dogs were following an unfamiliar scent, but that of a deadly enemy: a mixture of man and horse, assassin hooves. The centaur ran faster, and went on running until he perceived that the cries had become different and the dogs were barking out of sheer frustration. He looked back. From a fair distance he saw the men standing there and heard their threats. And the dogs which had darted ahead now returned to their masters. But no one advanced. The centaur had lived long enough to know that this was a frontier, a border. Securing their dogs, the men dared not shoot at him; a single shot was fired, but from so far away that the explosion could not even be heard. He was safe beneath the rain which was pouring down and opening up rapid currents between the stones, safe on this land where he had been born. He continued travelling southwards. The water drenched his white skin, washed away the foam, the blood and sweat, and all the accumulated grime. He was returning much aged, covered in scars, yet immaculate.

Suddenly the rain stopped. The next minute all the clouds had been brushed away and the sun shone directly on to the damp soil, its heat sending up clouds of vapour. The centaur walked slowly as if he were treading powdery snow. He did not know the whereabouts of the sea, but there stood the mountain. He felt strong. He had quenched his thirst with rain, raising his mouth to the sky and taking enormous gulps, with a torrential downpour running down his neck and all the way down his torso, making it glisten. And now he was slowly descending the southern slope of the mountain, skirting the great boulders leaning against each other. The man rested his hands on the highest rocks, where he could feel the soft mosses and rough lichens beneath his fingers, or the sheer roughness of the stone. Below, a valley stretched all the way across which, from a distance, seemed deceptively narrow. Along the valley he could see three villages a fair distance away from each other, the biggest of them in the middle where the road beyond headed south. Cutting across the valley to the right, he would have to pass close to the village. Could he pass there safely? He recalled how he had been pursued, the cries, the shots, the men on the other side of the border. That incomprehensible hatred. This land was his, but who were these men living here? The centaur continued to descend. The day was still far from over. Suffering from exhaustion, the horse trod cautiously, and the man decided it would be just as well to rest before crossing the valley. And after much thought, he decided to wait until dusk: meanwhile he must find some safe spot where he might sleep and recover his strength for the long journey ahead before reaching the sea.

He continued his descent, getting slower and slower. And just as he was finally about to settle down between two boulders, he saw the black entrance to a cave, high enough to allow the man and horse to enter. Using his arms and stepping gingerly with tender hooves on those hard stones, he entered the cave. It was not very deep, but there was enough room inside to move at one's ease. Supporting his forearms against the rocky surface of the wall, the man was able to rest his head. He was breathing deeply, trying to resist rather than accompany the horse's laboured panting. The sweat was pouring down his face. Then the horse pulled in his front hooves and allowed himself to slump to the ground which was covered with sand. Lying down or slightly raised as was his wont, the man could see nothing of the valley. The mouth of the cave only opened to the blue sky. Somewhere deep inside, water was dripping at long, regular intervals, producing an echo as if from a well. A profound peace filled the cave. Stretching one arm behind him, the man passed his hand over the horse's coat, his own skin transformed, or skin which had transformed into him. The horse quivered with pleasure, all his muscles distended, and sleep took possession of his great body. The man released his hands allowing it to slip on to the dry sand.

The setting sun began to light up the cave. The centaur dreamt neither of Heracles nor of the gods seated in a circle. Nor were there any more visions of mountains facing the sea, of islands sending up spray, or of that infinite and sonorous expanse of water. Nothing but a dull, dark wall or simply colourless and insurmountable. Meanwhile, the sun penetrated to the bottom of the cave causing all the rock crystals to sparkle, and transforming each drop of water into a crimson pearl that had become detached from the roof after swelling to an incredible size, and then traced a blazing trail three metres long before sinking into a tiny pool already plunged into darkness. The centaur was asleep. The blue sky faded, the space was flooded by the myriad of colours of the forge and evening descended slowly, dragging in the night like some weary body about to fall asleep in its turn. Cast into darkness, the cave had become enormous and the drops of water fell like round stones on to the rim of a bell. It was already darkest night when the moon appeared.

The man woke up. He felt the anguish of not having dreamt. For the first time in thousands of years he had not had a dream. Had it abandoned him the moment he had returned to the land of his birth? Why? Some omen? What oracle could tell? The horse, more remote, was still asleep but stirring restlessly. From time to time he would move his hind legs as if he were galloping in dreams, not his, for he had no brain, or only on loan, but stirred by the willpower in his muscles. Resting his hand on a protruding stone, the man raised his trunk and, as if sleep-walking, the horse followed him effortlessly, with flowing movements which seemed weightless. And the centaur emerged into the night.

The moon cast its light over the entire valley. So much light that it could not possibly be coming from that simple little moon on earth, Selene, silent and spectral, but the light of all the moons elevated above an infinite succession of nights where other suns and lands without these or any other names rotate and shine. The centaur took a deep breath through the man's nostrils: the air was soft, as if it were passing through the filter of human skin, and it had the smell of damp soil that was slowly drying out between the labyrinthine embrace of roots securing the world. He descended into the valley by an easy, almost tranquil route, his four equine limbs harmoniously swaying, swinging his two male arms, moving step by step, without disturbing a stone or risking any more cuts on some sharp ridge. And so he finally reached the valley as if this journey were part of the dream he had been deprived of while asleep. Ahead there was a wide river. On the other bank, slightly to the left, stood the largest of the villages on the southern route. The centaur advanced out into the open, followed by that singular shadow without equal in this world. He cantered through the cultivated fields, choosing beaten paths to avoid trampling the plants. Between the strip of cultivated land and the river there were scattered trees and signs of cattle. Picking up their scent, the horse became restless, but the centaur went on heading for the river. He cautiously entered the water, using his hooves to feel his way. The water became deeper until it came up to the man's chest. In the middle of the river, beneath the moonlight, another flowing river, anyone watching there would have seen a man crossing the ford with unpraised arms, his arms, shoulders and head those of a man, and with hair instead of a mane. Concealed in the water walked a horse. Roused by the moonlight, fishes swam around him and pecked his legs.

The man's entire torso emerged from the water, then the horse appeared, and the centaur mounted the river-bank. He passed underneath some trees and on the threshold of the plain stopped to get his bearings. He remembered how they had pursued him on the other side of the mountain, he recalled the dogs and shots, the men and their cries, and he felt afraid. He now wished the night were darker and would have preferred to walk under a storm like that of the previous day which forced the dogs to seek shelter and sent people scurrying indoors. The man thought everyone in those parts must already know of the centaur's existence for the news must surely have travelled across the border. He realised he could not cross the countryside in a straight line in broad daylight and slowly began following the river protected by the shade of the trees. Perhaps ahead he might find more favourable terrain where the valley narrowed and ended up compressed between two high hills. He continued to think about the sea, about the white pillars, and closing his eyes he could see once more the trail left by Zeus when he headed south.

Suddenly, he heard the lapping of water. He remained still and listened. The noise came back, died away, then returned. On the ground covered with couch grass, the horse's steps became so muffled that they could not be heard amidst the manifold murmurings of tepid night and moonlight. The man pushed back the branches and looked towards the river. There was clothing lying on the river-bank.

Someone was bathing. He pushed the branches further back and saw a woman. She emerged from the water completely naked and her white body shone beneath the moonlight. The centaur had seen women many times before, but never like this, in this river and with this moon. On other occasions he had seen swaying breasts and hips, that dark spot in the centre of their body. On other occasions he had seen tresses falling over shoulders and hands tossing them back, such a familiar gesture. But his only contact with the world of women was that which might please the horse, perhaps even the centaur, but not the man. And it was the man who looked and saw the woman retrieve her clothes; it was the man who pushed through those branches, trotted up to her and, as she screamed, lifted her into his arms.

This, too, he had done on several occasions, but they were so few over thousands of years. A futile action, merely frightening, an act which could have resulted in madness and perhaps did. But this was his land and the first woman he had seen there. The centaur ran alongside the trees, and the man knew that further ahead he would put the woman down on the ground, he frustrated, she terrified, the woman intact, he only half-man. Now a broad path came close to the trees and ahead there was a curve in the river. The woman was no longer screaming, simply sobbing and trembling. And at that moment they heard other cries. On rounding the bend, the centaur came to a halt before a small group of low houses concealed by trees. People were gathered outside. The man pressed the woman to his chest. He could feel her firm breasts, her pubes at the spot when his human body disappeared and became the horse's pectorals. Some people fled, others threw themselves forward, while others ran into their houses and reappeared carrying rifles. The horse got up on his hind legs, and reared into the air. Terrified, the woman let out another scream. Someone fired a shot into the air. The man realised the woman was protecting him. Then the centaur headed for the open countryside, avoiding any trees that might impede his movements, and, still clutching the woman in his arms, he skirted the houses and galloped off across the open fields in the direction of the two hills. He could hear shouting coming from behind. Perhaps they had decided to pursue him on horseback, but no horse could compete with the centaur, as had been demonstrated in thousands of years of constant flight. The man looked behind: the persecutors were still some way off, some considerable way off. Then, gripping the woman under her arms, he gazed at her whole body stripped naked under the moonlight and said to her in his former tongue, in the language of the forests, of honeycombs, of the white columns of the sonorous sea, of laughter on the mountains:

-Don't hate me.

He then put her down gently on the ground. But the woman did not escape. From her lips came words the man was capable of understanding:

-You're a centaur. You exist. She placed her two hands on his chest. The horse's legs trembled. Then the woman lay down and said:

-Cover me.

The man saw her from above, stretched out in the form of a cross. For a moment, the horse's shadow covered the woman. Nothing more. Then the centaur moved sideways and broke into a gallop, while the man began shouting and clenching his fists at the sky and the moon. When his pursuers finally reached the woman, she had not stirred. And when they carried her off wrapped in a blanket, the men carrying her could hear her weep.

That night, the whole country learned of the centaur's existence. What at first had been treated as some rumour from across the border to keep them amused, now had reliable witnesses, amongst them a woman who was trembling and weeping. While the centaur was crossing this other mountain, people came from the nearby villages and towns, with nets and ropes, and even with firearms, but only to scare him off. He must be captured alive, they said. The army was also put on the alert. They were waiting for daylight before sending up helicopters to search the entire region. The centaur kept under cover, but could hear the dogs barking at frequent intervals, and in the waning moonlight even caught sight of men scouring the mountains. The centaur travelled all night in a southerly direction. And when the sun came up, the centaur was standing on top of a mountain from where he could view the sea. Way in the distance, nothing but the sea, not an island in sight, and the sound of a breeze which smelt of pines, not the lashing of waves or the pungent odour of brine. The world appeared to be a wilderness waiting to be populated.

It was not a wilderness. Suddenly a shot rang out. And then, forming a wide circle, men emerged from behind the stones, making a great din, yet unable to hide their fear as they advanced with nets and ropes, nooses and staffs. The horse reared into the air, shook its front hooves and swung round in a frenzy to face his enemies. The man tried to retreat. Both of them struggled, behind and in front. And the horse's hooves slipped on the edge of the steep slope, they scrambled anxiously seeking some support, the man's hands, too, but the cumbersome body lost its footing and fell into the abyss. Twenty metres below, a jutting edge of rock, inclined at just the right angle, polished by thousands of years of cold and heat, sun and rain, and hewn by wind and snow, cut through the centaur's body at the very spot where the man's torso became that of the horse. The fall ended there. At long last the man lay stretched out on his back and looking up at the sky. An ever deepening sea overhead, a sea with tiny, motionless clouds that were islands, and immortal life. The man turned his head from one side to the other: nothing but endless sea, an interminable sky. Then he looked at his body. It was bleeding. Half a man. A man. And he saw the gods approaching. It was time to die.

translated by Giovanni Pontiero

Down the Quiet Street

Es'kia Mphahlele

❦

N adia Street was reputed to be the quietest street in Newclare. Not that it is any different from other streets. It has its own dirty water, its own flies, its own horse manure, its own pot-bellied children with traces of urine down the legs. The hawker's trolley still slogs along in Nadia Street, and the cloppity-clop from the hoofs of the over-fed mare is still part of the street.

Its rows of houses are no different, either. The roofs slant forward as if they were waiting for the next gale to rock them out of their complacency and complete the work it has already started. Braziers still line the rocky pavement, their columns of smoke curling up and settling on everything around. And stray chickens can be seen pecking at the children's stools with mute relish. Nadia Street has its lean barking mongrels and its share of police beer raids.

Yet the street still clung to the reputation of being the quietest. Things always went on in the *next* street.

Then something happened. When it did, some of the residents

shook their heads dolefully and looked at one another as if they sensed a 100 years' plague round the corner.

Old Lebona down the street laughed and laughed until people feared that his chronic bronchitis was going to strangle him. 'Look at it down the street or up the street,' he said, 'it's the same. People will always do the unexpected. Is it any wonder God's curse remains on the black men?' Then he laughed again.

'You'll see,' said Keledi, rubbing her breast with her forearm to ease the itching caused by the milk. She always said that, to arouse her listeners' curiosity. But she hardly ever showed them what they would see.

Manyeu, the widow, said to her audience: 'It reminds me of what happened once at Winburg, the Boer town down in the Free State.' She looked wistfully ahead of her. The other women looked at her and the new belly that pushed out from under the clean floral apron.

'I remember clearly because I was pregnant, expecting—who was it now? Yes, I was expecting Lusi, my fourth. The one you sent to the butcher yesterday, Kotu.'

Some people said that it happened when Constable Tefo first came to patrol Nadia Street on Sunday afternoons. But others said the 'Russians'—that clan of violent Basotho men—were threatening war. Of course, after it had happened Nadia Street went back to what its residents insisted on calling a quiet life.

If Constable Tefo ever thought that he could remain untouched by Nadia Street gossip, he was jolly well mistaken. The fact that he found it necessary to make up his mind about it indicated that he feared the possibility of being entangled in the people's private lives.

He was tall and rather good-looking. There was nothing officious about him, nothing police-looking except for the uniform. He was in many ways one of the rarest of the collection from the glass cage at

Headquarters. His bosses suspected him. He looked to them too human to be a good protector of the law. Yes, that's all he was to the people, that's what his bosses had hired him for.

The news spread that Tefo was in love. 'I've seen the woman come here at the end of every month. He always kisses her. The other day I thought he was kissing her too long.' That was Manyeu's verdict.

It did not seem to occur to anyone that the woman who was seen kissing Tefo might be his wife. Perhaps it was just as well, because it so happened that he did not have a wife. At 40 he was still unmarried.

Manyeu was struck almost silly when Constable Tefo entered her house to buy 'maheu' (sour mealie-meal drink).

'You'll see,' said Keledi, who rubbed her breast up and down to relieve the burning itch of the milk.

Still Tefo remained at his post, almost like a mountain: at once defiant, reassuring, and menacing. He would not allow himself to be ruffled by the subtle suggestions he heard, the meaningful twitch of the face he saw, the burning gaze he felt behind him as he moved about on his beat.

One day Keledi passed him with a can of beer, holding it behind her apron. She chatted with him for a while and they both laughed. It was like that often; mice playing hide and seek in the mane of the lion.

'How's business?' Tefo asked Sung Li's wife one Sunday on the stoep of their shop.

'Velly bad.'

'Why?'

'Times is bad.'

'Hm.'

'Velly beezee, you?'

'Yes, no rest, till we get over there, at Croesus Cemetery.'

She laughed, thinking it very funny that a policeman should
think of death. She told him so.

'How's China?'

'I'm not from China, he, he, he. I'm born here, he, he, he. Fun-
nee!' And she showed rusty rotten teeth when she laughed, the top
front teeth overtaking the receding lower row, not co-operating in
the least to present a good-looking jaw.

Tefo laughed loud to think that he had always thought of the
Sung Lis as people from China, which, from what he had been told
in his childhood, conjured up weird pictures of man-eating people.

When he laughed, Constable Tefo's stomach moved up and
down while he held his belt in front and his shoulders fluttered
about like the wings of a bird that is not meant to fly long distances.

When her husband within called her, Madam Sung Li turned to
go. Tefo watched her shuffling her small feet, slippers almost
screaming with the pain of being dragged like that. From behind,
the edge of the dress clung alternatively to the woollen black stock-
ings she had on. The bundle of hair at the back of her head looked
as if all the woman's fibre were knotted up in it, and that if it were
undone, Madam Sung Li might fall to pieces. Her body bent forward like a tree in the wind. Tefo observed to himself that there was
no wind.

One Sunday afternoon Tefo entered Sung Li's shop to buy a bottle of lemonade. The heat was intense. The roofs of the houses
seemed to strain under the merciless pounding of the sun. All available windows and doors were ajar and, owing to the general lack of
verandahs and the total absence of trees, the residents puffed and
sighed and groaned and stripped off some of their garments.

Madam Sung Li leaned over the counter, her elbows planted on
the top surface, her arms folded. She might have been the statue of

some Oriental god in that position but for a lazy afternoon fly that tried to settle on her face. She had to throw her head about to keep the pestilent insect away.

Constable Tefo breathed hard after every gulp as he stood looking out through the shop window, facing Nadia Street.

One thing he had got used to was the countless funeral processions that trailed on week after week. They had to pass Newclare on the way to the cemetery. Short ones, long ones, hired double deckers, cars, lorries; poor insignificant ones, rich snobbish ones. All black and inevitable.

The processions usually took the street next to Nadia. But so many people were dying that some units were beginning to spill over into Nadia.

Tefo went out to the stoep to have a little diversion; anything to get his mind off the heat. He was looking at one short procession as it turned into Nadia when a thought crossed his mind, like the shadow of a cloud that passes under the sun.

Seleke's cousin came staggering onto the stoep. His clothes looked as if he had once crossed many rivers and drained at least one. He was always referred to as Seleke's cousin, and nobody ever cared to know his name.

Seleke lived in the next street. She was the tough sort with a lashing tongue. But even she could not whip her cousin out of his perennial stupor.

Keledi's comment was: 'You'll see, one day he'll hunt mice for food. The cats won't like it.' And she rubbed her breast. But Seleke's cousin absorbed it all without the twinge of a hair.

'Ho, chief!' Seleke's cousin hailed the constable, wobbling about like a puppet on the stage. 'Watching the coffins, eh? Too many people dying, eh? Yes, too many. Poor devils.'

Tefo nodded. A lorry drove up the street, and pulled up on the side, almost opposite the Chinaman's shop.

'Dead men don't shout,' said Seleke's cousin.

'You're drunk. Why don't you go home and sleep?'

'Me drunk? Yes, yes, I'm drunk. But don't you talk to me like these pigheaded people around here. Their pink tongues wag too much. Why don't they leave me alone? There's no-one in this bloody location who can read English like I do.'

'I'm sure there isn't.' Tefo smiled tolerantly.

'I like you, chief. You're going to be a great man one of these days. Now, you're looking at these people going to bury their dead. One of these days those coffins will tell their story. I don't know why they can't leave me alone. Why can't they let me be, the lousy lot?'

A small funeral party turned into Nadia Street on a horse-drawn trolley cart. There were three women and four men on the cart, excluding the driver. A man who looked like their religious leader sang lustily, his voice quivering above the others.

The leader had on a frayed, fading, purple surplice and an off-white cassock. He looked rather too young for such a mighty responsibility as trying to direct departed souls to heaven, Tefo thought. The constable also thought how many young men were being fired with religious feelings these days . . . The trolley stopped in front of a house almost opposite Sung Li's. Tefo looked on. The group alighted and the four men lifted the coffin down.

Tefo noticed that the leader was trembling. By some miracle his hymn book stayed in the trembling hand. He wiped his forehead so many times that the constable thought the leader had a fever and could not lift the coffin further. They obviously wanted to enter the yard just behind them. He went to the spot and offered to help.

The leader's eyes were wide and they reflected a host of emotions Tefo could not understand. And then he made a surprising gesture to stop Tefo from touching the coffin. In a second he nodded his head several times, muttering something that made Tefo understand that his help would be appreciated. Whereupon the constable picked up the handle on his side, and the quartet took the corpse into the house. Soon Tefo was back on the Chinaman's stoep.

It must have been about fifteen minutes later when he heard voices bursting out in song as the party came out of the house with the coffin. Again Tefo noticed the leader was sweating and trembling. The coffin was put on the ground outside the gate. The others in the party continued to sing lustily, the men's voices beating down the courageous sopranos.

Tefo sensed that they wanted to hoist it onto the lorry. Something told him he should not go and help. One of these religious sects with queer rules he thought.

At the gate the leader of the funeral party bent forward and, with a jerky movement, he caught hold of the handle and tilted the coffin, shouting to the other men at the same time to hold the handles on their side. Tefo turned sharply to look.

A strange sound came from the box. To break the downward tilt the other men had jerked the coffin up. But a cracking sound came from the bottom; a sound of cracking wood. They were going to hoist the coffin higher, when it happened.

A miniature avalanche of bottles came down to the ground. A man jumped into the lorry, reversed it a little and drove off. The trolley cart ground its way down Nadia Street. Tefo's eyes swallowed the whole scene. He descended from the stoep as if in a trance, and walked slowly to the spot. It was a scene of liquor bottles tumbling and tinkling and bumping into one another, some breaking, and others rolling down the street in a playful manner, like children who have been let out of the classroom at playtime. There was hissing and shouting among the funeral party.

'You frightened goat!'

'Messing up the whole business!'

'I knew this would happen!'

'You'll pay for this!'

'You should have stayed home, you clumsy pumpkin!'

'We're ruined this time!'

They had all disappeared by the time it had registered on Tefo's mind that an arrest must be made. More than that: a wild mob of people was scrambling for the bottles. In a moment they also had disappeared with the bottles, the corpus delicti! A number of people gathered round the policeman.

The lousy crowd, he thought, glad that a policeman had failed to arrest! They nudged one another, and others indulged in mock pity. Manyeu came forward. 'I want the box for fire, sir constable.' He indicated impatiently with the hand that she might have it. It did not escape Keledi's attention, and she said to her neighbour, rubbing her breast that was full of milk: 'You'll see. Wait.'

'Ho, chief! Trouble here?' Seleke's cousin elbowed his way to the centre of the crowd. He had been told what had happened.

'Funerals, funerals, funerals is my backside! Too bad I'm late for the party! Hard luck to you, chief. Now listen, I trust these corpses like the lice on my shirt. But you're going to be a great man one day. Trust my word for that. I bet the lice on my body.'

Later that afternoon Constable Tefo sat in Manyeu's room, drinking 'maheu.' Keledi, rubbing her breast, was sitting on the floor with two other women. Manyeu sat on a low bench, her new belly pushing out under her floral apron like a promising melon.

Somewhat detached from the women's continuous babble, Tefo was thinking about funerals and corpses and bottles of liquor. He wondered about funeral processions in general. He remembered what Seleke's cousin had said the other day on the Chinaman's stoep. Was it an unwitting remark? Just then another procession passed down the street. Tefo stood up abruptly and went to stand at the door. If only the gods could tell him what was in that brown glossy coffin, he thought. He went back to his bench, a figure of despair.

Keledi's prophetic 'You'll see' took on a serious meaning when Tefo one day married Manyeu after her sixth had arrived. Nadia Street gasped. But then recovered quickly from the surprise, considering the reputation it had of being the quietest street in Newclare.

It added to Keledi's social stature to be able to say after the event: 'You see!' while she vigorously rubbed her breasts that itched from the milk.

The Firebird's Nest

Salman Rushdie

❧

Now I am ready to tell how bodies are changed
Into different bodies.
—Ovid, The Metamorphoses
translated by Ted Hughes

It is a hot place, flat and sere. The rains have failed so often that now they say instead, the drought succeeded. They are plainsmen, livestock farmers, but their cattle are deserting them. The cattle, staggering, migrate south and east in search of water, and rattle as they walk. Their skulls, horned mile-posts, line the route of their vain exodus. There is water to the west, but it is salt. Soon even these marshes will have given up the ghost. Tumbleweed blows across the leached grey flats. There are cracks big enough to swallow a man.

An apt enough way for a farmer to die: to be eaten by his land. Women do not die in that way. Women catch fire, and burn.

❧

Within living memory, a thick forest stood here, Mr Maharaj tells his American bride as the limousine drives towards his palace. A rare breed of tiger lived in the forest, white as salt, wiry, small. And song-birds! A dozen dozen varieties; their very nests were built of music. Half a century ago, his father riding through the forest would hum along with their arias, could hear the tigers joining in the choruses. But now his father is dead, the tigers are extinct, and the birds have all gone, except one, which never sings a note, and, in the absence of trees, makes its nest in a secret place that has not been revealed. The firebird, he whispers, and his bride, a child of a big city, a foreigner, no virgin, laughs at such exotic melodramatics, tossing her long bright hair; which is yellow, like a flame.

There are no princes now. The government abolished them decades ago. The very idea of princes has become, in our modern country, a fiction, something from the time of feudalism, of fairy-tale. Their titles, their privileges have been stripped from them. They have no power over us. In this place, the prince has become plain Mr Maharaj. He is a complex man. His palace in the city has become a casino, but he heads a commission that seeks to extirpate the public corruption that is the country's bane. In his youth he was a mighty sportsman, but since his retirement he has had no time for games. He heads an ecological institute studying, and seeking reme-dies for, the drought; but at his country residence, at the great fortress-palace to which this limousine is taking him, cascades of precious water flow ceaselessly, for no other purpose than display. His library of ancient texts is the wonder of the province, yet he also controls the local satellite franchises, and profits from every new dish. The details of his finances, like those of his many rumoured romances, are obscure.

Here is a quarry. The limousine halts. There are men with pickaxes and women bearing earth in metal bowls upon their heads.
When they see Mr Maharaj they make gestures of respect, they gen-
uflect, they bow. The American bride, watching, intuits that she has
passed into a place in which that which was abolished is the truth,
and it is the government, far away in the capital, that is the fiction in
which nobody believes. Here Mr Maharaj is still the prince, and she,
his new princess. As though she had entered a fable, as though she
were no more than words crawling along a dry page, or as though
she were becoming that page itself, that surface on which her story
would be written, and across which there blew a hot and merciless
wind, turning her body to papyrus, her skin to parchment, her soul
to paper.

It is so hot. She shivers.

It is no quarry. It is a reservoir. Farmers, driven from their land by
drought, have been employed by Mr Maharaj to dig this water-hole
against the day when the rains return. In this way he can give them
some employment, he tells his bride, and more than employment:
hope. She shakes her head, seeing that this great hollow is already
full; of bitter irony. Briny, brackish, no use to man or cow.

The women in the reservoir of irony are dressed in the colours
of fire. Only the foolish, blinded by language's conventions, think of
fire as red, or gold. Fire is blue at its melancholy rim, green in its envious heart. It may burn white, or even, in its greatest rages, black.

Yesterday, the men with pickaxes tell Mr Maharaj, a woman in a
red and gold sari, a fool, ignited in the amphitheatre of the dry water-
hole. The men stood along the high rim of the reservoir, watching

her burn, shouldering arms in a kind of salute; recognizing, in the wisdom of their manhood, the inevitability of women's fate. The women, their women, screamed.

When the woman finished burning there was nothing there. Not a scrap of flesh, not a bone. She burned as paper burns, flying up to the sky and being blown into nothing by the wind.

The combustibility of women is a source of resigned wonder to the men hereabouts. They just burn too easily, what's to be done about it? Turn your back and they're alight. Perhaps it is a difference between the sexes, the men say. Men are earth, solid, enduring, but the ladies are capricious, unstable, they are not long for this world, they go off in a puff of smoke without leaving so much as a note of explanation. And in this heat, if they should spend too long in the sun! We tell them to stay indoors, not to expose themselves to danger, but you know how women are. It is their fate, their nature.

Even the demure ones have fiery hearts; perhaps the demure ones most of all, Mr Maharaj murmurs to his wife in the limousine. She is a woman of modern outlook and does not like it, she tells him, when he speaks this way, herding her sex into these crude corrals, these easy generalisations, even in jest. He inclines his head in amused apology. A firebrand, he says. I see I must mend my ways.

See that you do, she commands, and nestles comfortably under his arm. His grey beard brushes her brow.

Gossip burns ahead of her. She is rich, as rich as the old, obese Nizam of _____, who was weighed in jewels on his birthdays and so was able to increase taxes simply by putting on weight. His subjects would quake as they saw his banquets, his mighty halvas, his towering jellies, his kulfi Himalayas, for they knew that the endless avalanche of delicacies sliding down the Nizam's gullet meant that the food on their own tables would be sparse and plain, as he wept with exhausted repletion so their children would weep with hunger, his gluttony would be their famine. Yes, filthy rich, the gossip sizzles, her American father claims descent from the deposed royal family of an Eastern European state, and each year he flies the élite employees of his commercial empire by private aircraft to his lost kingdom, where by the banks of the River of Time itself he stages a four-day golf tournament, and then, laughing, contemptuous, godlike, fires the champion, destroys his life for the hubris of aspiring to glory, abandons him by the shores of Time's River, into whose tumultuous, deadly waters the champion finally dives, and is lost, like hope, like a ball.

She is rich; she is a fertile land; she will bring sons, and rain.

No, she is poor, the gossip flashes, her father hanged himself when she was born, her mother was a whore, she also is a creature of wildernesses and rocky ground, the drought is in her body, like a curse, she is barren, and has come in the hope of stealing brown babies from their homes and nursing them from bottles, since her own breasts are dry.

Mr Maharaj has searched the world for its treasures and brought back a magic jewel whose light will change their lives. Mr Maharaj has fallen into iniquity and brought Despair into his palace, has succumbed to yellow-haired doom.

So she is becoming a story the people tell, and argue over. Travelling towards the palace, she too is aware of entering a story, a group

of stories about women such as herself, fair and yellow, and the
dark men they loved. She was warned by friends at home, in her tall
city. Do not go with him, they cautioned her. If you sleep with him,
he will not respect you. He does not think of women like you as
wives. Your otherness excites him, your freedom. He will break
your heart.

Though he calls her his bride, she is not his wife. So far, she feels
no fear.

A ruined gateway stands in the wilderness, an entrance to nowhere.
A single tree, the last of all the local trees to fall, lies rotting beside it,
the exposed roots grabbing at air like a dead giant's hand. A wedding
party passes, and the limousine slows. She sees that the turbaned
groom, on his way to meet his wife, is not young and eager, but wisp-
haired, old and parched; she imagines a tale of undying love, long
denied by circumstance, overcoming adversity at last. Somewhere
an elderly sweetheart awaits her wizened amour. They have loved
each other always, she imagines, and now near their stories' conclusion they have found this happy ending. By accident she speaks these
words aloud. Mr Maharaj smiles, and shakes his head. The bridegroom's bride is young, a virgin from a distant village.

Why would a pretty young girl wish to marry an old fool?

Mr Maharaj shrugs. The old fellow will have settled for a small
dowry, he replies, and if one has many daughters such factors have
much weight. As for the oldster, he adds, in a long life there may be
more than a single dowry. These things add up.

Flutes and horns blow raucous music in her direction. A drum
crumps like cannon-fire. Transsexual dancers heckle her through
the window. Ohé, America, they screech, arré, howdy-podner, say

what? Okay, you take care now, I'm-a-yankee-doodle-dandy! Ooh, baby, wah-wah, maximum cool, Miss America, shake that thing! She feels a sudden panic. Drive faster, she cries, and the driver accelerates. Dust explodes around the wedding party, hiding it from view. Mr Maharaj is solicitude personified, but she is angry with herself. Excuse me, she mutters. It's nothing. The heat.

('America'. Once upon a time in 'America', they had shared an Indian lunch three hundred feet above street-level, at a table with a view of the vernal lushness of the park, feasting their eyes upon an opulence of vegetation which now, as she remembers it in this desiccated landscape, feels obscene. My country is just like yours, he'd said, flirting. Big, turbulent and full of gods. We speak our kind of bad English and you speak yours. And before you became Romans, when you were just colonials, our masters were the same. You defeated them before we did. So now you have more money than we do. Otherwise, we're the same. On your street corners the same bustle of differences, the same litter, the same everything-at-onceness. She guessed immediately what he was telling her: that he came from a place unlike anything she had ever experienced, whose languages she would struggle to master, whose codes she might never break and whose immensity and mystery would provoke and fulfil her greatest passion and her deepest need.

Because she was an American, he spoke to her of money. The old protectionist legislation, the outdated socialism that had hobbled the economy for so long, had been repealed and there were fortunes to be made if you had the ideas. Even a prince had to be on the ball, one step ahead of the game. He was bursting with projects, and she had a reputation in financial circles as a person who could bring together capital and ideas, who could conjure up, for her favoured projects, the monetary nourishment they required.

A 'rainmaker'.

She took him to the opera, was aroused, as always, by the power of great matters sung of in words she could not understand, whose meaning had to be inferred from the performers' deeds. Then she took him home and seduced him. It was her city, her stage, and she was confident, and young. As they began to make love, she guessed that she was about to leave behind everything she knew, all the roots of her self. Her lovemaking became ferocious, as if his body were a locked gateway to the unknown, and she must batter it down.

Not everything will be wonderful, he warned her. There is a terrible drought.)

His palace, unfortunately, is abominable. It crumbles, stinks. In her room, the curtains are tattered, the bed precarious, the pictures on the wall pornographic representations of arabesque couplings at some petty princeling's court. No way of knowing if these are her husband's ancestors or a job-lot purchased from a persuasive pedlar. Loud music plays in ill-lit corridors, but she cannot find its source. Shadows scurry from her sight. He installs her, vanishes, without an explanation. She is left to make herself at home.

That night, she sleeps alone. A ceiling fan stirs the hot, syrupy air. It simmers, like a soup. She cannot stop thinking of 'home': its nocturnal sirens, its cooling machinery. Its reification of the real. Amid that surplus of structures, of content, it is not easy for the phantasmagoric to gain the upper hand. Our entertainment is full of monsters, of the fabulous, because outside the darkened cinemas, beyond the pages of the books, away from the gothic decibels of the music, the quotidian is inescapable, omnipotent. We dream of other dimensions, of paranoid subtexts, of underworlds, because when we awake the actual holds us in its great thingy grasp and we cannot see beyond the material, the event horizon. Whereas here, caught in the empty bubbling of dry air, afraid of roaches, all your frontiers may crumble; are crumbling. The possibility of the terrible is renewed.

She has never found it easy to weep, but her body convulses. She cries dry tears, and sleeps. When she awakes there is the sound of a drum, and dancers.

In a courtyard, the women and girls are gathered, young and old. The drummer beats out a rhythm and the ladies respond in unison. Their knees bent outward, their splay-fingered hands semaphoring at the ends of peremptory arms, their necks making impossible, lateral shifts, eyes ablaze, they advance across cool stone like a syncopated army. (It is still early, and the courtyard is in shadow; the sun has not yet lent the stone its fire.) At the dancers' head, tallest of them all, fiercely erect, showing them how, is Mr Maharaj's sister, over sixty years old, but still the greatest dancer in the state. Miss Maharaj has seen the newcomer, but makes no acknowledgment. She is the mistress of the dance. Movement is all.

When it's finished, they face each other, Mr Maharaj's women: the sister, the American.

What are you doing?

A dance against the firebird. A propitiatory dance, to ward it off.

The firebird. (She thinks of Stravinsky, of Lincoln Center.)

Miss Maharaj inclines her head. The bird which never sings, she says. Whose nest is secret; whose malevolent wings brush women's bodies, and we burn.

But surely there is no such bird. It's just an old wives' tale.

Here there are no old wives' tales. Alas, there are no old wives.

Enter Mr Maharaj! Turbaned, with an embroidered cloth flung about his broad shoulders, how handsome, how manly, how winsomely apologetic!

She finds herself behaving petulantly, like a woman from another age. He woos and cajoles. He went to prepare her welcome. He hopes she will approve.

What is it?

Wait and see.

In the semi-desert beyond his stinking palace, Mr Maharaj has prepared an extravaganza. By moonlight, beneath hot stars, on great carpets from Isfahan and Shiraz, a gathering of dignitaries and nobles welcomes her, the finest musicians play their mournful, haunting flutes, their ecstatic strings, and sing the most ancient and freshest love-songs ever heard; the most succulent delicacies of the region are offered for her delight. She is already famous in the neighbourhood, a great celebrity. I invited your husband to visit us, the governor of an adjacent state guffaws, but I told him, if you don't bring your beautiful lady, don't bother to show up. A neighbouring ex-prince offers to show her the art treasures locked in his palace vaults. I take them out for nobody, he says, except Mrs Onassis, of course. For you, I will spread them in my garden, as I did for Jackie O.

While the moonlight lasts, there are camel-races and horse-races, dancing and song. Fireworks burst over their heads. She leans against Mr Maharaj, his absence long forgiven, and whispers, you have made a magic kingdom for me, or (she teases him) is this how you relax every night?

She feels him stiffen, smells the bitterness leaking from his words. It is you who have made this happen, he replies. In this ruined place you have conjured this illusion. The camels, the horses, even the food has been brought from far away. We impoverish ourselves to make you happy. How can you imagine that we are able to live like this? We protect the last fragments of what we had, and now, to please you, we plunge deeper into debt. We dream only of survival; this Arabian night is an American dream.

I asked for nothing, she said. This conspicuous consumption is not my fault. Your accusation, your diatribe, is offensive.

He has had too much to drink, and it has made him truthful. It is our obeisance, he tells us, at the feet of power. Rainmaker, bring us rain.

Money, you mean.

What else? Is there anything else?

I thought there was love, she says.

The full moon has never looked more beautiful. No music has ever sounded lovelier. No night has ever felt so cruel. She says: I have something to tell you.

She is pregnant. She dreams of burning bridges, of burning boats. She dreams of a movie she has always loved, in which a man returns to his ancestral village, and somehow slips through time, to the time of his father's youth. When he tries to flee the village, and returns to the railway station, the tracks have disappeared. There is no way home. This is where the film ends.

When she awakes from her dream, in her sweltering room, the

sheets are soaked and there is a woman sitting at her bedside. She gathers a wet sheet around her nakedness. Miss Maharaj smiles, shrugs. You have a strong body, she says. Younger, but in other ways not so unlike mine.

I would have left him. Now I just don't know.

Miss Maharaj shakes her head. In the village they say it will be a boy, she explains, and then the drought will break. Just superstition. But he can't let you leave. And afterwards, if you go, he'll keep the child.

We'll see about that! she blasts. When she is agitated her tones become nasal, unattractive even to herself. In her mind's eye the story is closing around her, the story in which she is trapped, and in which she must, if she can, find the path of action: preferably of right action, but if not, then of wrong. What cannot be tolerated is inertia. She will not fall into some tame and heat-dazed swoon. Romance has led her into errors enough. Now she will use her head.

Slowly, as the weeks unfold, she begins to see. He does not own the casino in his palace in the city, has signed a foolish contract, letting it to a consortium of alarming men. The rent they pay him is absurd, and it is stipulated in the small print that on certain high days each year he must hang around the gaming-tables, grinning ingratiatingly at the guests, lending a tone. The satellite-dish franchises are more lucrative, but this greedy old wreck of a country residence needs to eat off far richer platters if it's to be properly fed.

This rural palace is ageless: perhaps six hundred years. Most of it lacks electricity, windows, furniture. Cold in the cold season, hot in the heat, and if the rains should come, many of its staterooms would flood. All they have here is water, their inexhaustible palace spring. At the back of the palace, past the ruined zones where the bats hold sway, she picks her way through accumulated guano and sees a line form before dawn. The villagers, rendered indigent by the drought, come under cover of darkness, hiding their humiliation, filling their supplicant pitchers. Behind the line of the thirsty there stands, like a haunting, the high black shadow of a crenellated wall. A village woman with a few unaccountable words of English explains that this charred fortress was, in former days, the larger part of the prince's residence. Great treasures were lost when it burned; also, lives.

When did this happen?

In before time.

She begins to understand his bitterness. Another princess, Miss Maharaj tells her, a dowager even more destitute than we, recently ended her life by drinking fire. She crushed her heirloom diamonds in a cup and gulped them down.

So Mr Maharaj, visiting America, had turned himself into an illusion of sophistication and innovation, had won her with a desperate performance. He has learned to talk like a modern man but in truth is helpless in the face of the present. The drought, his unworldliness, the decision of history to turn away her face, these things are his undoing. In Greece, the athlete who won the Olympic race became a person of high rank in his home state. Mr Maharaj, however, rots, as does his house. Her own room begins to look like luxury's acme. Glass in the windows, the slow-turning electric fan. A telephone with, sometimes, a dialling tone. A socket for her laptop's power line, the intermittent possibility of forging a modem link with that other planet, her earlier life.

He has not taken her to his own room because he is ashamed of it.

Sensing the life growing inside her, she wants to forgive its father;

to help him out of the past, into that flowing, metamorphic present which has been her real life. She will do what she can do. She is 'America', and brings the rain.

Again and again she awakes, sweating, naked, with Miss Maharaj murmuring at her side. Yes, a fine body, it could have been a dancer's. It will burn well.

Don't touch me! (She is alarmed.)

All brides in these parts are brought from far afield. And once the men have spent their dowries, then the firebird comes.

Don't threaten me! (Perplexed.)

Do you know how many brides he has had?

Terrified, raging, bewildered, she confronts him. Is it true? Is that why your sister has never married, why she gathers under her roof, to protect them, all the spinsters of the village, young and old? That interminable dance class of lifetime virgins, too frightened to take a husband?

Is it true you burn your brides?

Ah, my mad sister has been whispering to you, he laughs. She came to your room at night, she caressed your body, she spoke of water and fire, of women's beauty and the secret, lethal nature of men. She told you about the magic bird, I suppose. The bird of death.

No, she remembers, carefully. The one who first named the firebird was you.

❦

Mr Maharaj in a fury brings her to his sister's dance class. Seeing him, the dancers stumble, their bell-braceleted feet lose the rhythm and come jangling to a halt. Why are you here, he asks them, raging. Tell my bride why you have come. Are you refugees or students? Sir, students. Are you here because you are afraid? Oh, please, sir, we are not afraid. His inquisition is relentless, bellowing, and all the while his eyes never leave his sister's. Miss Maharaj stands tall and silent.

The last question is for her. How many brides have I had? How many do you say? They are locked in each other's power, brother and sister, each other's eternal prisoners, outside history, beyond time. Miss Maharaj is the first to drop her eyes. She is the first, she says.

It's over. He turns to face his bride, and spreads his arms. You heard it with your own ears. Let's have no more of fables.

The heat is maddening. Skeletal bullocks die on the brown lawn. Some days, there are mustard-yellow clouds filling the sky, hanging over the evaporating marshes to the west. Even this hideous yellow rain would be welcome, but it does not fall.

Everyone has bad breath. All exhale serpents, dead cats, insects, fogs. Everyone's perspiration is thick, and stinks.

In spite of all her resolutions, the heat hypnotises her. The child grows. Miss Maharaj's dancers become careless about closing doors and windows. They are to be glimpsed, here and there, painting one another's bodies in hot colours and wild designs, making love, sleeping with limbs entwined. Mr Maharaj does not come to her, will not, while she is 'carrying'. But each night, Miss Maharaj comes. Since her brother's descent upon her dance class,

Miss Maharaj has barely spoken. At night she asks only to sit at the bedside, sometimes, almost primly, to touch. This, Mr Maharaj's American bride allows.

Her health fails. She begins to sweat, to shiver from a fever. Her shit is like thin mud. Only the palace spring saves her from dehydration and swift death. Miss Maharaj nurses her, brings her salt. The only physician hereabouts is an old fellow, out of touch, useless. Both women know the baby is at risk.

During these long, sick nights, quietly, absently, the sexagenarian dancer talks.

Something frightful has happened here. Some irreversible transformation. Without our noticing its beginnings, so that we did not resist until it was too late, until the new way of things was fixed, there has occurred a terrible, terminal rupture between our men and women. When men say they fear the absence of rain, when women say we fear the presence of fire, this is what we mean. Something has been unleashed in us. It's too late to tame it now.

Once upon a time there was a great prince here. The last prince, one could say. Everything about him was gigantic, mythological. The most handsome prince in the world, he married the most beautiful bride, a legendary dancer and temptress, and they had two children, a girl and a boy. As he aged, his strength ebbed, his eye dimmed, but she, the dancer, refused to fade. At the age of fifty she had the look of a young woman of twenty-one. As the prince's force faded, as that glamour which had been the heart of his power ceased to work its magic, so his jealousy increased . . .

(Miss Maharaj shrugged, moved quickly to the story's end.)

The fortress burned. They both died. He had suspected his wife of taking lovers but there had been none. The children, who had been left in the care of servants, lived. The daughter became a dancer and the son, a sportsman, and so on. And the villagers said that the old prince, consumed by rage, had been transformed into a giant bird, a bird composed entirely of flames, and that was the bird that burned the princess, and returns, these days, to turn other women to ashes at their husband's cruel command.

And you, asks the ill woman on the bed. What do you say?

Do not condescend to us in your heart, Miss Maharaj replies. Do not mistake the abnormal for the untrue. We are caught in metaphors. They transfigure us, and reveal the meaning of our lives.

The illness recedes and the baby seems also to be well. The return of health is like a curtain being lifted. She is thinking like herself again. She will keep the child, but will no longer be trapped in this place of fantasies with a man she finds she does not know. She will go to the city, fly back to America, and after the child is born, what will be, will be. A quick divorce, of course. She has no desire to prevent the father from seeing his child. Extremely free access, including trips East, will be granted. She wants that, wants the child to know both cultures. Enough! Time to behave like an adult. She may even continue to advise Mr Maharaj on his financial needs. Why not? It's her job. She tells Miss Maharaj her decision, and the old dancer winces, as if from a blow.

In the dead of night, the American is awakened by a hubbub in the palace, in its corridors and courtyard. She dresses, goes outside. A scratch armada of motor vehicles has assembled: a rusty bus, several motor-scooters, a newish Japanese people carrier, an open truck, a Jeep in camouflage. Miss Maharaj's women are piling into the vehicles, angry, singing. They have taken weapons, the domestic weapons that came to hand, sticks, garden implements, kitchen knives. At their head, revving the Jeep, shouting impatiently at her troops, is Miss Maharaj.

What's going on?

None of your business. You don't believe in fairies. You're going home.

I'm coming with you.

Miss Maharaj treats the Jeep roughly, driving it at speed over broken ground, without lights. The motley convoy jolts along behind. They drive by the light of a molten full moon.

Ahead of them stands a ruined stone arch, an entrance to nothing, beside a fallen tree. The armada halts, turns on its lights. The dance class pours through the archway, as if it were the only possible entrance to the open waste ground beyond, as if it were the portal to another world. When she, the American, does likewise, she has that feeling again: of passing through an invisible membrane, a looking glass, into another kind of truth; into fiction.

A tableau, illuminated by the lights of motor vehicles. Remember the old bridegroom, on his way to meet his young, imported bride? Here he is again, guilty, murderous, and his young wife, uncomprehending, at his side.

In the background, silhouetted, are the figures of male villagers. Facing the unhappy couple is Mr Maharaj.

The women burst shrieking upon the charmless scene, then come raggedly to a halt, intimidated by Mr Maharaj's presence. The sister faces the brother. Somebody has left their lights flashing. The siblings' faces glow white, yellow, red in the headlights. They speak in a language the American cannot understand, it is an opera without overtitles, she must infer what they are saying from their actions, from their thoughts made deeds, and so, as clearly as if she comprehended every syllable, she hears Miss Maharaj command her brother, what started between our parents stops now, and his response, a response that has no meaning in the world beyond the ruined archway, which he speaks as his body turns to fire, as the wings burst out of him, as his eyes blaze; his words hang in the air as the firebird's breath scorches Miss Maharaj, burns her to a cinder and then turns upon the dotard's shrieking bride.

I am the firebird's nest.

Something loosens within the American as she sees Miss Maharaj burn, some shackle is broken, some limit of possibility passed. Unleashed, she crashes upon Mr Maharaj like a wave, and the angry dancers pour behind her, seething, irresistible. They feel the frontiers of their bodies burst and the waters pour out, the immense crushing weight of their rain, drowning the firebird and its nest, flowing over the drought-hardened land that no longer knows how to absorb the flood which bears away the old dotard and his murderous fellows, cleansing the region of its horrors, of its archaic tragedies, of its men.

The flood waters ebb, like anger. The women become themselves again, and the universe too resumes its familiar shape. The women huddle patiently under the old stone arch, listening for helicopters, waiting to be rescued from the deluge of themselves, freed from fear. As for the American, her own shape will continue to change. Mr Maharaj's child will be born, not here but in her own country, to which she will soon return. Increasing, she caresses her swelling womb. The new life growing within her will be both fire and rain.

November, 1998.

Cell Phone

Ingo Schulze

❧

They came in the night of July 20th–21st, in the half hour after midnight. There couldn't have been many of them, five, six guys maybe. I just heard voices and the racket. They probably hadn't even noticed light in the bungalow. The sleeping area is at the back and the curtains were drawn. The first sultry night in a good while and the start of our last week of vacation. I was still reading—Stifter, *Great Grandfather's Satchel.*

Constanze had received a telegram from her newspaper in Berlin, telling her to report for work at 7:30 on Tuesday morning. Evidently her secretary had coughed up our address. The series about Fontane's favorite haunts was getting bogged down because commissioned articles hadn't come in or would be late. That's the problem when you don't go far away. We're both on the road all year more or less— I work for the sports section, Constanze for the feuilleton—and neither of us has any desire to spend our vacation in hotels or sitting around in airports. We rented the bungalow for the first time last summer—twenty marks a day, for twenty by twenty feet—in Prieros, southeast of Berlin, exactly forty-six kilometers from our front door, a corner lot with pine woods on two sides, perfect when it's hot.

It was odd being alone. Not that I was afraid, but I was aware of every falling branch, every bird hopping across the roof, every little rustle. It sounded like gunshots when they kicked in the fence boards—and then the whooping. I turned off the light, pulled on a pair of pants, went to the front—we always keep the roll-down shutters open at night. But I still couldn't see anything. Suddenly there was a hollow thud. Something heavy had been upended. They yowled. I thought of turning on the outside light, just to show that somebody was here, so that the idiots wouldn't think nobody would spot them. There were a couple more loud noises—then they moved on. I could feel sweat beading even on my legs. I washed myself for a second time. I could open the window from the bed. It had cooled off a little outside. You could just barely hear those guys now. Finally everything was quiet again.

The cell phone rang around seven in the morning. "Rang" is actually the wrong word, it was more like a "tootle-toot" that kept getting louder, but I liked its familiar sound because it meant Constanze. She was the only person who had the number. While Constanze talked about how unbearably hot Berlin was and wanted to know why I hadn't stopped her from driving back into the inhuman city, I took the cell phone with me out into the sunny, quiet morning and surveyed the damage. Three sections of fence were lying in the path. The concrete post between them had been broken off just above the ground and tipped over. Two twisted steel rods stuck up out of the stump. Out by the gate, the rowdies had turned the newspaper tube on its head. Just underneath it I discovered the roof and back wall of the birdhouse. I counted seven fence slats that had been kicked in, plus four ripped loose entirely.

Constanze said that she hadn't realized what a dirty trick that telegram was until now. I really shouldn't have let her drive back. I didn't want to worry Constanze—she's always quick to get the feeling that something is a bad omen—so I didn't mention last night's visitors. It would have been hard to interrupt her anyway. She had already laid into the people who had rented the bungalow before us for turning the power off and leaving a half-full fridge, and there hadn't been enough bed linen either. Suddenly Constanze cried that she had to go, said that she loved me, and hung up.

I crept back into bed. The damage was nothing I needed to take personally of course, and there was a relatively simple explanation, too. The half acre of land that goes with the bungalow is only leased. That will end in 2001, or 2004 at the latest, when the transitional period will be over and our acquaintances will have to leave. That's why they haven't invested anything in it for several years now. The fence is held together by wire in places where the wood is too rotten for nails. Last fall Constanze wrote an article about the New York police and their new philosophy. I remembered an example about an abandoned car that had stood on the street for weeks. Trash collected around it, yellowed fliers were wedged under the wipers. One morning a wheel was suddenly missing, two days later the license plates were gone, and the rest of the wheels. The next thing was a rock through a window, and then there was no stopping it. The car went up in flames. Conclusion: you don't let junk even start to collect. None of this would have happened if the fence were in good shape. Next thing you know they'll be throwing rocks through the window. I was glad Constanze hadn't been here. Together we would probably have done something we shouldn't, or Constanze would have been depressed for days.

Around ten I got up to clear the sections of fence from the path. The first slat I picked up broke in two. With its protruding nails it looked like a weapon from the arsenal of Thomas Müntzer. First I threw them all into a pile. Then I began dragging them to the shed. To leave them lying out where anyone could get at them seemed too dangerous. Maybe I was exaggerating. But the fact was that not even a symbolic barrier protected the bungalow now. Given the situation, it was some comfort to have a cell phone. I'd got more familiar with it over the last few days, because I'd brought the envelope that included all the instructions—which Constanze had guarded so jealously—along with me to Prieros and had finally learned how to store numbers and activate my answering machine. It was my surprise for Constanze.

The "Hello!" of a man's voice startled me. Medium build, dressed in thongs and a pullover, he was standing at the gate and asked what damage the rowdies had done at our place. His fence was missing two slats. "A hunting fence," he said. "Do you know what kind of strength that takes?" The worst thing for him was the dent in the hood of his Fiat Punto. He'd looked everywhere for whatever it was they'd thrown, but had found nothing. His crew cut arched just above his brow like a fur hat. "It always happens during summer vacation," he said. "All young kids. Always during vacation."

I led him around. He took the inspection tour very seriously, squatting down a couple of times as if searching for clues. He found more pieces of birdhouse and turned the newspaper tube back to horizontal. Then he helped me carry pieces of fence to the shed.

He had notified the police last night and evidently hadn't let them off the hook until they had promised to send someone. "You need to know one thing," he said. "This is small potatoes to them.

Undermanned like they are, totally undermanned." He was interested in what I had to say about the New York police and I promised to send him Constanze's article.

"Can you give me your cell phone number?" he suddenly asked. "My cell phone number? I don't even know it."

His frown pulled his bristly hair so deep that the first row pointed straight at me.

"I'll have to check," I said and asked what he planned to do in case these guys came back again.

"First off, get in touch," he replied curtly, as if afraid of detaining me unnecessarily.

Inside I sat down on the bed with the envelope in hand. I'd never wanted a cell phone, until Constanze came up with the idea of a one-way phone. To make calls, yes—to be called, no, with the exception of her of course. Even if I had wanted to give the number to someone, I didn't even know it, I would have had to ask Constanze. But now the envelope with all the information was no longer in her desk drawer, but here on my knees. As I copied our number I noticed that it ended in 007.

"My name's Neumann by the way," he said, holding out a store receipt on which he had scribbled his own number. In the same moment the phone rang. With a hasty goodbye he headed off.

Pretty much everything had gone wrong at the office. Constanze would have to stay in Berlin, at least until the day after tomorrow. She said that the latest deportations had also set off a row within the feuilleton staff itself. I didn't even know what deportations she was talking about. We hadn't listened to the radio because the FM button was missing. Constanze was still angry and claimed that men didn't know what to do with themselves now that the soccer world championship was over, that's why they were all carrying on like this.

I told her about last night.

She just said, "Well then come home."

"Yes," I replied, "I will, tomorrow."

I didn't want to look like a coward. Besides, it was easier to deal with the heat here. I tidied up. In case the police actually did show, I didn't want them to think it made no difference if something got kicked in here or not. And I definitely wasn't going to forget to tell them the lot itself was leased, from a "Wessi." As a final touch I swept the terrace.

That afternoon I spoke with some of the other neighbors as well. We agreed to leave on all the lights we could at night. We parked our cars with the headlights directed at the fences, so that we could suddenly blind these guys and maybe even get a picture of them. Our motto was: People, noise, light. We bungalow dwellers developed a kind of Wild-West posse mentality. No policeman ever showed his face, but we didn't waste words talking about that.

Out of a kind of gratitude I dialed Neumann's number. I had at times found it intoxicating to be connected by satellite with people anywhere in the world. That we were neighbors, not three hundred yards apart, made the idea seem even more fantastic. But instead of Neumann himself, I heard a woman who told me that my call would be transferred to an automatic voice mail. She said, "This is the voice mail of . . ." followed by a pause, and then I heard a voice speak the name out of a galactic void: Harald Neumann. I felt goose bumps creep up my arm, clear to my shoulder. I could think of no other situation when I had heard someone speak his own name with such despondency. Of course even friends usually sound distracted or lonely on their answering machines. But Neumann didn't just sound lost or forsaken, but as if he were ashamed even to have a name.

A little later there was a brief thunderstorm. I saw Neumann coming out of the woods with a basket full of mushrooms. He called to me from a good distance. "Like carrots!" he said, meaning that in this weather you could gather mushrooms the way you could harvest carrots. He invited me to help him eat them.

In comparison to our little shack, his bungalow was a small palace, with a television and stereo, leather chairs, and two barstools. Neumann served red wine and French bread with the mushrooms. After that we played chess and smoked a whole pack of cigarettes between us. There seemed to be no connection between the Neumann here before me and the man who spoke his name for his voice mail. All the same, I felt shy about asking him about his family or occupation. And he didn't offer anything on his own.

The clouds above the lake turned pink toward evening. I laid my big flashlight and Neumann's number where they were handy. By ten o'clock the lightning was flashing with the regularity of a lighthouse. A cloudburst followed. By then it was clear to me that no one would be coming tonight.

The next morning I packed everything up, did a last dusting, and said goodbye to my neighbors. I didn't find Neumann at home. Presumably he was in the woods again. I don't think that the people here got the idea that I was a coward. They realized that Constanze was no longer here, so that what I told them was probably true. The telephone call with our acquaintances, our landlords, proved more difficult. They wanted me to do something about the fence, said that there were still some posts in the shed. But that refrigerator alone had cost us a whole morning—that was quite enough.

In late September the cell phone rang in the middle of the night. In the first moment I thought it was the peep it makes when the battery is low. But the tootle-toot got louder each time. I groped for it on Constanze's vanity. I traced the tip of my forefinger across the keys— I needed the middle one in the second row from the top. The signal was now insufferably loud.

"Those guys are back again. They're really raising a racket!" he shouted. And then after a brief pause: "Hello! This is Neumann! What a racket! Do you hear it?"

"But I'm not there anymore," I finally said.

"They're just banging away!"

The light on Constanze's side went on. She was sitting on the edge of the bed, shaking her head.

With my free hand I covered the speaker. "A neighbor from Prieros." I could feel sweat in every pore. I had never mentioned exchanging phone numbers—we wouldn't be going to Prieros again anyway, at least not to the bungalow.

"Are you alone?"

"Somebody has to hold down the fort," Neumann said, "don't they?"

"Are you alone?"

"You mean has something happened? I wouldn't be calling otherwise. . . . They're breaking down my fence, the bastards," he shouted.

"Have you called the police?"

Neumann gave a laugh, then took a drink and swallowed wrong. "That's funny . . ."

I had never sent him Constanze's article about New York. "What is it you want?" I asked.

"Just listen to that racket!"

I pressed the phone tight to my ear, but it made no difference.

"Now they're at the mailbox," he shouted. "They'll have to sweat and strain at that. Even two of them won't be able to manage that, the stupid shits. I'll show them. They've gone too far . . ."

"Stay where you are!" I shouted.

Constanze was standing in the door, tapping a finger at her forehead. She said something from the next room that I didn't understand.

"Hello?" Neumann called.

"Yes," I said. Or did he mean those guys at the fence. "Stay inside. Don't try to be a hero."

"They're gone," he said in amazement. "Nobody in sight . . ." It sounded as if he took another sip. "So how are you doing?" he asked.

"Stay in the house," I said. "You shouldn't even be out at the lake, do you hear? Weekends maybe, but not during the week."

"When are you coming back? We still have a game we haven't finished. Or would you like to play by mail? You want to give me your address? I've got some dried mushrooms, a whole sack of mushrooms."

"Herr Neumann," I said, and didn't know what else to say.

"The garbage can," he suddenly bellowed. "My garbage can!"

"Calm down," I said. I called out "Hello?" and "Herr Neumann," a few more times. Then there was only the dial tone, and the display read: "Call ended."

Constanze came back into the room, laid down on her side, facing the wall and pulling the blanket up over her shoulders. I tried to explain the whole thing to her, how I'd hesitated at first, but then had actually been glad that I could call a neighbor for help in an emergency. Constanze didn't stir. I said I was worried about Neumann, but that I didn't have his phone number, had left it at the bungalow, in the bowl with the keys.

"Maybe he'll call back," she replied. "This is going to be happening fairly often now. But you never give anybody the number."

I think at moments like this we're both so disappointed with ourselves that we hate each other. I went to my study to get the recharger for the cell phone.

When I came back she said, "Why don't you call information?"

"I don't even know Neumann's first name." I wasn't lying. But in the next moment I could clearly hear that awful voice repeating the name for his voice mail: Harald Neumann.

"And what if he passes your number on?" Constanze turned over and propped herself up.

"Why would he do that?"

"But just imagine if he does!"

"Constanze," I said. "That's nonsense."

"You need to think about it!" The strap of her nightgown had slipped off her shoulder, and she pulled it back up. But it didn't stay. "Think of all those people who could call now," she said. "All those neighbors."

"Our number's in the book, a perfectly normal number. Anybody can call us."

"That's not what I mean. A building is on fire or gets bombed and somebody runs out with nothing but his cell phone, because it happens to be in his jacket or his pants pocket. You can talk with somebody like that now."

I plugged the recharger into the wall socket beside the bed.

"It can very well happen," Constanze said. Her voice now had that "teacher" tone of hers. "Somebody calls you up from Kosovo or Afghanistan or from wherever that tsunami was. Or one of those guys that froze up on Mount Everest. You can talk with him to the bitter end. No one can help him, but you hear his last words." Braced on her elbow, one shoulder still bare, she went on talking while she stared at the tip of her pillow, which was propped up a little. "Just imagine who all you'll be dealing with now. Nobody has to be alone anymore."

It was pointless to call information, because it was pointless to call Neumann. Besides, I was afraid that woman's voice would answer, and then Neumann would speak his name again. The cell phone display showed the symbol for recharging: the outline of a little battery, with a slanted bar marching across three positions. It was the last thing I saw before I turned out the light.

In the dark Constanze said, "I think I'm going to get a divorce."

I listened to her breathing, her moving, and waited for the tootle-toot.

The shutters on the newspaper kiosk had already rattled when our hands accidentally touched. It took another eternity before we risked moving closer to one another. Then we started to devour each other in a way we hadn't done for ages, as if sleeplessness had made us crazy. I don't know when the tootle-toot began. It came from somewhere faraway, like the signal of an airplane or a ship maybe, soft and indistinct at first. Gradually it grew louder, came closer, louder and louder, drowning out everything else, until for a moment it seemed as if Constanze and I were moving without making any sound at all. The only thing we could hear was that tootle-toot—until it suddenly stopped, ceased to bother us, and was as silent as we were.

translated by John E. Woods

Death Constant Beyond Love

Gabriel García Márquez

❧

S enator Onésimo Sánchez had six months and eleven days to go before his death when he found the woman of his life. He met her in Rosal del Virrey, an illusory village which by night was the furtive wharf for smugglers' ships, and on the other hand, in broad daylight looked like the most useless inlet on the desert, facing a sea that was arid and without direction and so far from everything no one would have suspected that someone capable of changing the destiny of anyone lived there. Even its name was a kind of joke, because the only rose in that village was being worn by Senator Onésimo Sánchez himself on the same afternoon when he met Laura Farina.

It was an unavoidable stop in the electoral campaign he made every four years. The carnival wagons had arrived in the morning. Then came the trucks with the rented Indians who were carried into the towns in order to enlarge the crowds at public ceremonies. A short time before eleven o'clock, along with the music and rockets and jeeps of the retinue, the ministerial automobile, the color of strawberry soda, arrived. Senator Onésimo Sánchez was placid and weatherless inside the air-conditioned car, but as soon as he opened the door he was shaken by a gust of fire and his shirt of pure silk was soaked in a kind of light-colored soup and he felt many years older and more alone than ever. In real life he had just turned forty-two, had been graduated from Göttingen with honors as a metallurgical engineer, and was an avid reader, although without much reward, of badly translated Latin classics. He was married to a radiant German woman who had given him five children and they were all happy in their home, he the happiest of all until they told him, three months before, that he would be dead forever by next Christmas.

While the preparations for the public rally were being completed, the senator managed to have an hour alone in the house they had set aside for him to rest in. Before he lay down he put in a glass of drinking water the rose he had kept alive all across the desert, lunched on the diet cereals that he took with him so as to avoid the repeated portions of fried goat that were waiting for him during the rest of the day, and he took several analgesic pills before the time prescribed so that he would have the remedy ahead of the pain. Then he put the electric fan close to the hammock and stretched out naked for fifteen minutes in the shadow of the rose, making a great effort at mental distraction so as not to think about death while he dozed. Except for the doctors, no one knew that he had been sentenced to a fixed term, for he had decided to endure his secret all alone, with no change in his life, not because of pride but out of shame.

He felt in full control of his will when he appeared in public again at three in the afternoon, rested and clean, wearing a pair of coarse linen slacks and a floral shirt, and with his soul sustained by the anti-pain pills. Nevertheless, the erosion of death was much more pernicious than he had supposed, for as he went up onto the platform he felt a strange disdain for those who were fighting for the good luck to shake his hand, and he didn't feel sorry as he had at other times for the groups of barefoot Indians who could scarcely bear the hot saltpeter coals of the sterile little square. He silenced the applause with a wave of his hand, almost with rage, and he began to speak without gestures, his eyes fixed on the sea, which was sighing with heat. His measured, deep voice had the quality of calm water, but the speech that had been memorized and ground out so many times had not occurred to him in the nature of telling the truth, but, rather, as the opposite of a fatalistic pronouncement by Marcus Aurelius in the fourth book of his *Meditations*.

'We are here for the purpose of defeating nature,' he began, against all his convictions. 'We will no longer be foundlings in our own country, orphans of God in a realm of thirst and bad climate, exiles in our own land. We will be different people, ladies and gentlemen, we will be a great and happy people.'

There was a pattern to his circus. As he spoke his aides threw clusters of paper birds into the air and the artificial creatures took on life, flew about the platform of planks, and went out to sea. At the same time, other men took some prop trees with felt leaves out of the wagons and planted them in the saltpeter soil behind the crowd. They finished by setting up a cardboard façade with make-believe houses of red brick that had glass windows, and with it they covered the miserable real-life shacks.

The senator prolonged his speech with two quotations in Latin in order to give the farce more time. He promised rainmaking machines, portable breeders for table animals, the oils of happiness which would make vegetables grow in the saltpeter and clumps of pansies in the window boxes. When he saw that his fictional world was all set up, he pointed to it. 'That's the way it will be for us, ladies and gentlemen,' he shouted. 'Look! That's the way it will be for us.'

The audience turned around. An ocean liner made of painted paper was passing behind the houses and it was taller than the tallest houses in the artificial city. Only the senator himself noticed that since it had been set up and taken down and carried from one place to another the superimposed cardboard town had been eaten away by the terrible climate and that it was almost as poor and dusty as Rosal del Virrey.

For the first time in twelve years, Nelson Farina didn't go to greet the senator. He listened to the speech from his hammock amidst the remains of his siesta, under the cool bower of a house of unplaned boards which he had built with the same pharmacist's hands with which he had drawn and quartered his first wife. He had escaped from Devil's Island and appeared in Rosal del Virrey on a ship loaded with innocent macaws, with a beautiful and blasphemous black woman he had found in Paramaribo and by whom he had a daughter. The woman died of natural causes a short while later and she didn't suffer the fate of the other, whose pieces had fertilized her own cauliflower patch, but was buried whole and with her Dutch name in the local cemetery. The daughter had inherited her color and her figure along with her father's yellow and astonished eyes, and he had good reason to imagine that he was rearing the most beautiful woman in the world.

Ever since he had met Senator Onésimo Sánchez during his first electoral campaign, Nelson Farina had begged for his help in getting a false identity card which would place him beyond the reach of the law. The senator, in a friendly but firm way, had refused. Nelson Farina never gave up, and for several years, every time he found the chance, he would repeat his request with a different recourse. But this time he stayed in his hammock, condemned to rot alive in that burning den of buccaneers. When he heard the final applause, he lifted his head, and looking over the boards of the fence, he saw the back side of the farce: the props for the buildings, the framework of the trees, the hidden illusionists who were pushing the ocean liner along. He spat without rancor.

'*Merde,*' he said. '*C'est le Blacamén de la politique.*'

After the speech, as was customary, the senator took a walk through the streets of the town in the midst of the music and the rockets and was besieged by the townspeople, who told him their troubles. The senator listened to them good-naturedly and he always found some way to console everybody without having to do them any difficult favors. A woman up on the roof of a house with her six youngest children managed to make herself heard over the uproar and the fireworks.

'I'm not asking for much, Senator,' she said. 'Just a donkey to haul water from Hanged Man's Well.'

The senator noticed the six thin children. 'What became of your husband?' he asked.

'He went to find his fortune on the island of Aruba,' the woman answered good-humoredly, 'and what he found was a foreign woman, the kind that put diamonds on their teeth.'

The answer brought on a roar of laughter.

'All right,' the senator decided, 'you'll get your donkey.'

A short while later an aide of his brought a good pack donkey to the woman's house and on the rump it had a campaign slogan written in indelible paint so that no one would ever forget that it was a gift from the senator.

Along the short stretch of street he made other, smaller gestures, and he even gave a spoonful of medicine to a sick man who had had his bed brought to the door of his house so he could see him pass.

At that last corner, through the boards of the fence, he saw Nelson Farina in his hammock, looking ashen and gloomy, but nonetheless the senator greeted him, with no show of affection.

'Hello, how are you?'

Nelson Farina turned in his hammock and soaked him in the sad amber of his look.

'Moi, vous savez,' he said.

His daughter came out into the yard when she heard the greeting. She was wearing a cheap, faded Guajiro Indian robe, her head was decorated with colored bows, and her face was painted as protection against the sun, but even in that state of disrepair it was possible to imagine that there had never been another so beautiful in the whole world. The senator was left breathless. 'I'll be damned!' he breathed in surprise. 'The Lord does the craziest things!'

That night Nelson Farina dressed his daughter up in her best clothes and sent her to the senator. Two guards armed with rifles who were nodding from the heat in the borrowed house ordered her to wait on the only chair in the vestibule.

The senator was in the next room meeting with the important people of Rosal del Virrey, whom he had gathered together in order to sing for them the truths he had left out of his speeches. They looked so much like all the ones he always met in all the towns in the desert that even the senator himself was sick and tired of that perpetual nightly session. His shirt was soaked with sweat and he was trying to dry it on his body with the hot breeze from an electric fan that was buzzing like a horse fly in the heavy heat of the room.

'We, of course, can't eat paper birds,' he said. 'You and I know that the day there are trees and flowers in this heap of goat dung, the day there are shad instead of worms in the water holes, that day neither you nor I will have anything to do here, do I make myself clear?'

No one answered. While he was speaking, the senator had torn a sheet off the calendar and fashioned a paper butterfly out of it with his hands. He tossed it with no particular aim into the air current coming from the fan and the butterfly flew about the room and then went out through the half-open door. The senator went on speaking with a control aided by the complicity of death.

'Therefore,' he said, 'I don't have to repeat to you what you already know too well: that my reelection is a better piece of business for you than it is for me, because I'm fed up with stagnant water and Indian sweat, while you people, on the other hand, make your living from it.'

Laura Farina saw the paper butterfly come out. Only she saw it because the guards in the vestibule had fallen asleep on the steps, hugging their rifles. After a few turns, the large lithographed butterfly unfolded completely, flattened against the wall, and remained stuck there. Laura Farina tried to pull it off with her nails. One of the guards, who woke up with the applause from the next room, noticed her vain attempt.

'It won't come off,' he said sleepily. 'It's painted on the wall.'

Laura Farina sat down again when the men began to come out of the meeting. The senator stood in the doorway of the room with his hand on the latch, and he only noticed Laura Farina when the vestibule was empty.

'What are you doing here?'

'*C'est de la part de mon père,*' she said.

The senator understood. He scrutinized the sleeping guards, then he scrutinized Laura Farina, whose unusual beauty was even more demanding than his pain, and he resolved then that death had made his decision for him.

'Come in,' he told her.

Laura Farina was struck dumb standing in the doorway to the

room: thousands of bank notes were floating in the air, flapping like the butterfly. But the senator turned off the fan and the bills were left without air and alighted on the objects in the room.

'You see,' he said, smiling, 'even shit can fly.'

Laura Farina sat down on a schoolboy's stool. Her skin was smooth and firm, with the same color and the same solar density as crude oil, her hair was the mane of a young mare, and her huge eyes were brighter than the light. The senator followed the thread of her look and finally found the rose, which had been tarnished by the saltpeter.

'It's a rose,' he said.

'Yes,' she said with a trace of perplexity. 'I learned what they were in Riohacha.'

The senator sat down on an army cot, talking about roses as he unbuttoned his shirt. On the side where he imagined his heart to be inside his chest he had a corsair's tattoo of a heart pierced by an arrow. He threw the soaked shirt to the floor and asked Laura Farina to help him off with his boots.

She knelt down facing the cot. The senator continued to scrutinize her, thoughtfully, and while she was untying the laces he wondered which one of them would end up with the bad luck of that encounter.

'You're just a child,' he said.

'Don't you believe it,' she said. 'I'll be nineteen in April.'

The senator became interested.

'What day?'

'The eleventh,' she said.

The senator felt better. 'We're both Aries,' he said. And smiling, he added:

'It's the sign of solitude.'

Laura Farina wasn't paying attention because she didn't know what to do with the boots. The senator, for his part, didn't know what to do with Laura Farina, because he wasn't used to sudden love affairs and, besides, he knew that the one at hand had its origins in indignity. Just to have some time to think, he held Laura Farina tightly between his knees, embraced her about the waist, and lay down on his back on the cot. Then he realized that she was naked under her dress, for her body gave off the dark fragrance of an animal of the woods, but her heart was frightened and her skin disturbed by a glacial sweat.

'No one loves us,' he sighed.

Laura Farina tried to say something, but there was only enough air for her to breathe. He laid her down beside him to help her, he put out the light and the room was in the shadow of the rose. She abandoned herself to the mercies of her fate. The senator caressed her slowly, seeking her with his hand, barely touching her, but where he expected to find her, he came across something iron that was in the way.

'What have you got there?'

'A padlock,' she said.

'What in hell!' the senator said furiously and asked what he knew only too well. 'Where's the key?'

Laura Farina gave a breath of relief.

'My papa has it,' she answered. 'He told me to tell you to send one of your people to get it and to send along with him a written promise that you'll straighten out his situation.'

The senator grew tense. 'Frog bastard,' he murmured indignantly. Then he closed his eyes in order to relax and he met himself in the darkness. *Remember,* he remembered, *that whether it's you or someone else, it won't be long before you'll be dead and it won't be long before your name won't even be left.*

He waited for the shudder to pass.

'Tell me one thing,' he asked then. 'What have you heard about me?'

'Do you want the honest-to-God truth?'

'The honest-to-God truth.'

'Well,' Laura Farina ventured, 'they say you're worse than the rest because you're different.'

The senator didn't get upset. He remained silent for a long time with his eyes closed, and when he opened them again he seemed to have returned from his most hidden instincts.

'Oh, what the hell,' he decided. 'Tell your son of a bitch of a father that I'll straighten out his situation.'

'If you want, I can go get the key myself,' Laura Farina said.

The senator held her back.

'Forget about the key,' he said, 'and sleep awhile with me. It's good to be with someone when you're so alone.'

Then she laid his head on her shoulder with her eyes fixed on the rose. The senator held her about the waist, sank his face into woods-animal armpit, and gave in to terror. Six months and eleven days later he would die in that same position, debased and repudiated because of the public scandal with Laura Farina and weeping with rage at dying without her.

translated by Gregory Rabassa

The Age of Lead

Margaret Atwood

❧

The man has been buried for a hundred and fifty years. They
dug a hole in the frozen gravel, deep into the permafrost, and
put him down there so the wolves couldn't get to him. Or that is the
speculation.

When they dug the hole the permafrost was exposed to the air,
which was warmer. This made the permafrost melt. But it froze again
after the man was covered up, so that when he was brought to the surface he was completely enclosed in ice. They took the lid off the coffin and it was like those maraschino cherries you used to freeze in
ice-cube trays for fancy tropical drinks: a vague shape, looming
through a solid cloud.

Then they melted the ice and he came to light. He is almost the
same as when he was buried. The freezing water has pushed his lips
away from his teeth into an astonished snarl, and he's a beige colour,
like a gravy stain on linen, instead of pink, but everything is still
there. He even has eyeballs, except that they aren't white but the

light brown of milky tea. With these tea-stained eyes he regards
Jane: an indecipherable gaze, innocent, ferocious, amazed, but con-
templative, like a werewolf meditating, caught in a flash of lightning
at the exact split second of his tumultuous change.

Jane doesn't watch very much television. She used to watch it more.
She used to watch comedy series, in the evenings, and when she was
a student at university she would watch afternoon soaps about hospi-
tals and rich people, as a way of procrastinating. For a while, not so
long ago, she would watch the evening news, taking in the disasters
with her feet tucked up on the chesterfield, a throw rug over her legs,
drinking a hot milk and rum to relax before bed. It was all a form of
escape.

But what you can see on the television, at whatever time of day, is
edging too close to her own life; though in her life, nothing stays put
in those tidy compartments, comedy here, seedy romance and sentimental tears there, accidents and violent deaths in thirty-second
clips they call *bites,* as if they were chocolate bars. In her life, everything is mixed together. *Laugh, I thought I'd die,* Vincent used to
say, a very long time ago, in a voice imitating the banality of mothers;
and that's how it's getting to be. So when she flicks on the television
these days, she flicks it off again soon enough. Even the commer-
cials, with their surreal dailiness, are beginning to look sinister, to
suggest meanings behind themselves, behind their façade of cleanli-
ness, lusciousness, health, power, and speed.

Tonight she leaves the television on, because what she is seeing is
so unlike what she usually sees. There is nothing sinister behind this
image of the frozen man. It is entirely itself. *What you sees is what
you gets,* as Vincent also used to say, crossing his eyes, baring his

teeth at one side, pushing his nose into a horror-movie snout. Although it never was, with him.

The man they've dug up and melted was a young man. Or still is: it's difficult to know what tense should be applied to him, he is so insistently present. Despite the distortions caused by the ice and the emaciation of his illness, you can see his youthfulness, the absence of toughening, of wear. According to the dates painted carefully onto his nameplate, he was only twenty years old. His name was John Torrington. He was, or is, a sailor, a seaman. He wasn't an able-bodied seaman though; he was a petty officer, one of those marginally in command. Being in command has little to do with the ableness of the body.

He was one of the first to die. This is why he got a coffin and a metal nameplate, and a deep hole in the permafrost—because they still had the energy, and the piety, for such things, that early. There would have been a burial service read over him, and prayers. As time went on and became nebulous and things did not get better, they must have kept the energy for themselves; and also the prayers. The prayers would have ceased to be routine and become desperate, and then hopeless. The later dead ones got cairns of piled stones, and the much later ones not even that. They ended up as bones, and as the soles of boots and the occasional button, sprinkled over the frozen stony treeless relentless ground in a trail heading south. It was like the trails in fairy tales, of bread crumbs or seeds or white stones. But in this case nothing had sprouted or lit up in the moonlight, forming a miraculous pathway to life; no rescuers had followed. It took ten years before anyone knew even the barest beginnings of what had been happening to them.

❧

All of them together were the Franklin Expedition. Jane has seldom paid much attention to history except when it has overlapped with her knowledge of antique furniture and real estate—"19th C. pine harvest table," or "Prime location Georgian centre hall, impeccable reno"—but she knows what the Franklin Expedition was. The two ships with their bad-luck names have been on stamps—the *Terror,* the *Erebus.* Also she took it in school, along with a lot of other doomed expeditions. Not many of those explorers seemed to have come out of it very well. They were always getting scurvy, or lost.

What the Franklin Expedition was looking for was the Northwest Passage, an open seaway across the top of the Arctic, so people, merchants, could get to India from England without going all the way around South America. They wanted to go that way because it would cost less and increase their profits. This was much less exotic than Marco Polo or the headwaters of the Nile; nevertheless, the idea of exploration appealed to her then: to get onto a boat and just go somewhere, somewhere mapless, off into the unknown. To launch yourself into fright; to find things out. There was something daring and noble about it, despite all of the losses and failures, or perhaps because of them. It was like having sex, in high school, in those days before the Pill, even if you took precautions. If you were a girl, that is. If you were a boy, for whom such a risk was fairly minimal, you had to do other things: things with weapons or large amounts of alcohol, or high-speed vehicles, which at her suburban Toronto high school, back then at the beginning of the sixties, meant switchblades, beer, and drag races down the main streets on Saturday nights.

Now, gazing at the television as the lozenge of ice gradually melts and the outline of the young sailor's body clears and sharpens, Jane remembers Vincent, sixteen and with more hair then, quirking one eyebrow and lifting his lip in a mock sneer and saying, "Franklin, my dear, I don't give a damn." He said it loud enough to be heard, but the history teacher ignored him, not knowing what else to do. It was hard for the teachers to keep Vincent in line, because he never seemed to be afraid of anything that might happen to him.

He was hollow-eyed even then; he frequently looked as if he'd been up all night. Even then he resembled a very young old man, or else a dissipated child. The dark circles under his eyes were the ancient part, but when he smiled he had lovely small white teeth, like the magazine ads for baby foods. He made fun of everything, and was adored. He wasn't adored the way other boys were adored, those boys with surly lower lips and greased hair and a studied air of smouldering menace. He was adored like a pet. Not a dog, but a cat. He went where he liked, and nobody owned him. Nobody called him Vince.

Strangely enough, Jane's mother approved of him. She didn't usually approve of the boys Jane went out with. Maybe she approved of him because it was obvious to her that no bad results would follow from Jane's going out with him: no heartaches, no heaviness, nothing burdensome. None of what she called *consequences*. Consequences: the weightiness of the body, the growing flesh hauled around like a bundle, the tiny frill-framed goblin head in the carriage. Babies and marriage, in that order. This was how she understood men and their furtive, fumbling, threatening desires, because Jane herself had been a consequence. She had been a mistake, she had been a war baby. She had been a crime that had needed to be paid for, over and over.

By the time she was sixteen, Jane had heard enough about this to last her several lifetimes. In her mother's account of the way things were, you were young briefly and then you fell. You plummeted downwards like an overripe apple and hit the ground with a squash; you fell, and everything about you fell too. You got fallen arches and a fallen womb, and your hair and teeth fell out. That's what having a baby did to you. It subjected you to the force of gravity.

This is how she remembers her mother, still: in terms of a pendulous, drooping, wilting motion. Her sagging breasts, the downturned lines around her mouth. Jane conjures her up: there she is, as usual, sitting at the kitchen table with a cup of cooling tea, exhausted after her job clerking at Eaton's department store, standing all day behind the jewellery counter with her bum stuffed into a girdle and her swelling feet crammed into the mandatory medium-heeled shoes, smiling her envious, disapproving smile at the spoiled customers who turned up their noses at pieces of glittering junk she herself could never afford to buy. Jane's mother sighs, picks at the canned spaghetti Jane has heated up for her. Silent words waft out of her like stale talcum powder: *What can you expect,* always a statement, never a question. Jane tries at this distance for pity, but comes up with none.

As for Jane's father, he'd run away from home when Jane was five, leaving her mother in the lurch. That's what her mother called it—"running away from home"—as if he'd been an irresponsible child. Money arrived from time to time, but that was the sum total of his contribution to family life. Jane resented him for it, but she didn't blame him. Her mother inspired in almost everyone who encountered her a vicious desire for escape.

Jane and Vincent would sit out in the cramped backyard of Jane's house, which was one of the squinty-windowed little stuccoed wartime bungalows at the bottom of the hill. At the top of the hill were the richer houses, and the richer people: the girls who owned cash-mere sweaters, at least one of them, instead of the Orlon and lambs-wool so familiar to Jane. Vincent lived about halfway up the hill. He still had a father, in theory.

They would sit against the back fence, near the spindly cosmos flowers that passed for a garden, as far away from the house itself as they could get. They would drink gin, decanted by Vincent from his father's liquor hoard and smuggled in an old military pocket flask he'd picked up somewhere. They would imitate their mothers.

"I pinch and I scrape and I work my fingers to the bone, and what thanks do I get?" Vincent would say peevishly. "No help from you, Sonny Boy. You're just like your father. Free as the birds, out all night, do as you like and you don't care one pin about anyone else's feelings. Now take out that garbage."

"It's love that does it to you," Jane would reply, in the resigned, ponderous voice of her mother. "You wait and see, my girl. One of these days you'll come down off your devil-may-care high horse." As Jane said this, and even though she was making fun, she could picture love, with a capital L, descending out of the sky towards her like a huge foot. Her mother's life had been a disaster, but in her own view an inevitable disaster, as in songs and movies. It was Love that was responsible, and in the face of Love, what could be done? Love was like a steamroller. There was no avoiding it, it went over you and you came out flat.

Jane's mother waited, fearfully and uttering warnings, but with a sort of gloating relish, for the same thing to happen to Jane. Every time Jane went out with a new boy her mother inspected him as a po-tential agent of downfall. She distrusted most of these boys; she dis-trusted their sulky, pulpy mouths, their eyes half-closed in the up-drifting smoke of their cigarettes, their slow, sauntering manner of walking, their clothing that was too tight, too full: too full of their bodies. They looked this way even when they weren't putting on the sulks and swaggers, when they were trying to appear bright-eyed and industrious and polite for Jane's mother's benefit, saying goodbye at the front door, dressed in their shirts and ties and their pressed heavy-date suits. They couldn't help the way they looked, the way they were. They were helpless; one kiss in a dark corner would reduce them to speechlessness; they were sleepwalkers in their own liquid bodies. Jane, on the other hand, was wide awake.

Jane and Vincent did not exactly go out together. Instead they made fun of going out. When the coast was clear and Jane's mother wasn't home, Vincent would appear at the door with his face painted bright yellow, and Jane would put her bathrobe on back to front and they would order Chinese food and alarm the delivery boy and eat sitting cross-legged on the floor, clumsily, with chopsticks. Or Vincent would turn up in a threadbare thirty-year-old suit and a bowler hat and a cane, and Jane would rummage around in the cupboard for a discarded church-going hat of her mother's, with smashed cloth violets and a veil, and they would go downtown and walk around, making loud remarks about the passers-by, pretending to be old, or poor, or crazy. It was thoughtless and in bad taste, which was what they both liked about it.

Vincent took Jane to the graduation formal, and they picked out her dress together at one of the second-hand clothing shops Vincent frequented, giggling at the shock and admiration they hoped to cause. They hesitated between a flame-red with falling-off sequins and a backless hip-hugging black with a plunge front, and chose the black, to go with Jane's hair. Vincent sent a poisonous-looking lime-green orchid, the colour of her eyes, he said, and Jane painted her eyelids and fingernails to match. Vincent wore white tie and tails, and a top hat, all frayed Sally-Ann issue and ludicrously too large for him. They tangoed around the gymnasium, even though the music was not a tango, under the tissue-paper flowers, cutting a black swath through the sea of pastel tulle, unsmiling, projecting a corny sexual menace, Vincent with Jane's long pearl necklace clenched between his teeth.

The applause was mostly for him, because of the way he was adored. Though mostly by the girls, thinks Jane. But he seemed to be popular enough among the boys as well. Probably he told them dirty jokes, in the proverbial locker room. He knew enough of them.

As he dipped Jane backwards, he dropped the pearls and whispered into her ear, "No belts, no pins, no pads, no chafing." It was from an ad for tampons, but it was also their leitmotif. It was what they both wanted: freedom from the world of mothers, the world of precautions, the world of burdens and fate and heavy female constraints upon the flesh. They wanted a life without consequences. Until recently, they'd managed it.

The scientists have melted the entire length of the young sailor now, at least the upper layer of him. They've been pouring warm water over him, gently and patiently; they don't want to thaw him too abruptly. It's as if John Torrington is asleep and they don't want to startle him.

Now his feet have been revealed. They're bare, and white rather than beige; they look like the feet of someone who's been walking on a cold floor, on a winter day. That is the quality of the light that they reflect: winter sunlight, in early morning. There is something intensely painful to Jane about the absence of socks. They could have left him his socks. But maybe the others needed them. His big toes are tied together with a strip of cloth; the man talking says this was to keep the body tidily packaged for burial, but Jane is not convinced. His arms are tied to his body, his ankles are tied together. You do that when you don't want a person walking around.

This part is almost too much for Jane; it is too reminiscent. She reaches for the channel switcher, but luckily the show (it is only a show, it's only another show) changes to two of the historical experts, analyzing the clothing. There's a close-up of John Torrington's shirt, a simple, high-collared, pin-striped white-and-blue cotton, with mother-of-pearl buttons. The stripes are a printed pattern, rather than a woven one; woven would have been more expensive. The trousers are grey linen. Ah, thinks Jane. Wardrobe. She feels better: this is something she knows about. She loves the solemnity, the reverence, with which the stripes and buttons are discussed. An interest in the clothing of the present is frivolity, an interest in the clothing of the past is archaeology; a point Vincent would have appreciated.

After high school, Jane and Vincent both got scholarships to university, although Vincent had appeared to study less, and did better. That summer they did everything together. They got summer jobs at the same hamburger heaven, they went to movies together after work, although Vincent never paid for Jane. They still occasionally dressed up in old clothes and pretended to be a weird couple, but it no longer felt careless and filled with absurd invention. It was beginning to occur to them that they might conceivably end up looking like that.

In her first year at university Jane stopped going out with other boys: she needed a part-time job to help pay her way, and that and the schoolwork and Vincent took up all her time. She thought she might be in love with Vincent. She thought that maybe they should make love, to find out. She had never done such a thing, entirely; she had been too afraid of the untrustworthiness of men, of the gravity of love, too afraid of consequences. She thought, however, that she might trust Vincent.

But things didn't go that way. They held hands, but they didn't hug; they hugged, but they didn't pet; they kissed, but they didn't neck. Vincent liked looking at her, but he liked it so much he would never close his eyes. She would close hers and then open them, and there would be Vincent, his own eyes shining in the light from the streetlamp or the moon, peering at her inquisitively as if waiting to see what odd female thing she would do next, for his delighted amusement. Making love with Vincent did not seem altogether possible.

(Later, after she had flung herself into the current of opinion that had swollen to a river by the late sixties, she no longer said "making love"; she said "having sex." But it amounted to the same thing. You had sex, and love got made out of it whether you liked it or not. You woke up in a bed or more likely on a mattress, with an arm around you, and found yourself wondering what it might be like to keep on doing it. At that point Jane would start looking at her watch. She had no intention of being left in any lurches. She would do the leaving herself. And she did.)

Jane and Vincent wandered off to different cities. They wrote each other postcards. Jane did this and that. She ran a co-op food store in Vancouver, did the financial stuff for a diminutive theatre in Montreal, acted as managing editor for a small publisher, ran the publicity for a dance company. She had a head for details and for adding up small sums—having to scrape her way through university had been instructive—and such jobs were often available if you didn't demand much money for doing them. Jane could see no reason to tie herself down, to make any sort of soul-stunting commitment, to anything or anyone. It was the early seventies; the old heavy women's world of girdles and precautions and consequences had been swept away. There were a lot of windows opening, a lot of doors: you could look in, then you could go in, then you could come out again.

She lived with several men, but in each of the apartments there were always cardboard boxes, belonging to her, that she never got around to unpacking; just as well, because it was that much easier to move out. When she got past thirty she decided it might be nice to have a child, some time, later. She tried to figure out a way of doing this without becoming a mother. Her own mother had moved to Florida, and sent rambling, grumbling letters, to which Jane did not often reply.

Jane moved back to Toronto, and found it ten times more interesting than when she'd left it. Vincent was already there. He'd come back from Europe, where he'd been studying film; he'd opened a design studio. He and Jane met for lunch, and it was the same: the same air of conspiracy between them, the same sense of their own potential for outrageousness. They might still have been sitting in Jane's garden, beside the cosmos flowers, drinking forbidden gin and making fun.

Jane found herself moving in Vincent's circles, or were they orbits? Vincent knew a great many people, people of all kinds; some were artists and some wanted to be, and some wanted to know the ones who were. Some had money to begin with, some made money; they all spent it. There was a lot more talk about money, these days, or among these people. Few of them knew how to manage it, and Jane found herself helping them out. She developed a small business among them, handling their money. She would gather it in, put it away safely for them, tell them what they could spend, dole out an allowance. She would note with interest the things they bought, filing their receipted bills: what furniture, what clothing, which *objets*. They were delighted with their money, enchanted with it. It was like milk and cookies for them, after school. Watching them play with their money, Jane felt responsible and indulgent, and a little matronly. She stored her own money carefully away, and eventually bought a townhouse with it.

All this time she was with Vincent, more or less. They'd tried being lovers but had not made a success of it. Vincent had gone along with this scheme because Jane had wanted it, but he was elusive, he would not make declarations. What worked with other men did not work with him: appeals to his protective instincts, pretences at jealousy, requests to remove stuck lids from jars. Sex with him was more like a musical workout. He couldn't take it seriously, and accused her of being too solemn about it. She thought he might be gay, but was afraid to ask him; she dreaded feeling irrelevant to him, excluded. It took them months to get back to normal.

He was older now, they both were. He had thinning temples and a widow's peak, and his bright inquisitive eyes had receded even further into his head. What went on between them continued to look like a courtship, but was not one. He was always bringing her things: a new, peculiar food to eat, a new grotesquerie to see, a new piece of gossip, which he would present to her with a sense of occasion, like a flower. She in her turn appreciated him. It was like a yogic exercise, appreciating Vincent; it was like appreciating an anchovy, or a stone. He was not everyone's taste.

There's a black-and-white print on the television, then another: the nineteenth century's version of itself, in etchings. Sir John Franklin, older and fatter than Jane had supposed; the *Terror* and the *Erebus*, locked fast in the crush of the ice. In the high Arctic, a hundred and fifty years ago, it's the dead of winter. There is no sun at all, no moon; only the rustling northern lights, like electronic music, and the hard little stars.

What did they do for love, on such a ship, at such a time? Furtive solitary gropings, confused and mournful dreams, the sublimation of novels. The usual, among those who have become solitary.

Down in the hold, surrounded by the creaking of the wooden hull and the stale odours of men far too long enclosed, John Torrington lies dying. He must have known it; you can see it on his face. He turns towards Jane his tea-coloured look of puzzled reproach.

Who held his hand, who read to him, who brought him water? Who, if anyone, loved him? And what did they tell him about whatever it was that was killing him? Consumption, brain fever, Original Sin. All those Victorian reasons, which meant nothing and were the wrong ones. But they must have been comforting. If you are dying, you want to know why.

In the eighties, things started to slide. Toronto was not so much fun any more. There were too many people, too many poor people. You could see them begging on the streets, which were clogged with fumes and cars. The cheap artists' studios were torn down or converted to coy and upscale office space; the artists had migrated elsewhere. Whole streets were torn up or knocked down. The air was full of windblown grit.

People were dying. They were dying too early. One of Jane's clients, a man who owned an antique store, died almost overnight of bone cancer. Another, a woman who was an entertainment lawyer, was trying on a dress in a boutique and had a heart attack. She fell over and they called the ambulance, and she was dead on arrival. A theatrical producer died of AIDS, and a photographer; the lover of the photographer shot himself, either out of grief or because he knew he was next. A friend of a friend died of emphysema, another of viral pneumonia, another of hepatitis picked up on a tropical vacation, another of spinal meningitis. It was as if they had been weakened by some mysterious agent, a thing like a colourless gas, scentless and invisible, so that any germ that happened along could invade their bodies, take them over.

Jane began to notice news items of the kind she'd once skimmed over. Maple groves dying of acid rain, hormones in the beef, mercury in the fish, pesticides in the vegetables, poison sprayed on the fruit, God knows what in the drinking water. She subscribed to a bottled spring-water service and felt better for a few weeks, then read in the paper that it wouldn't do her much good, because whatever it was had been seeping into everything. Each time you took a breath, you breathed some of it in. She thought about moving out of the city, then read about toxic dumps, radioactive waste, concealed here and there in the countryside and masked by the lush, deceitful green of waving trees.

Vincent has been dead for less than a year. He was not put into the permafrost or frozen in ice. He went into the Necropolis, the only Toronto cemetery of whose general ambience he approved; he got flower bulbs planted on top of him, by Jane and others. Mostly by Jane. Right now John Torrington, recently thawed after a hundred and fifty years, probably looks better than Vincent.

A week before Vincent's forty-third birthday, Jane went to see him in the hospital. He was in for tests. Like fun he was. He was in for the unspeakable, the unknown. He was in for a mutated virus that didn't even have a name yet. It was creeping up his spine, and when it reached his brain it would kill him. It was not, as they said, responding to treatment. He was in for the duration.

It was white in his room, wintry. He lay packed in ice, for the pain. A white sheet wrapped him, his white thin feet poked out the bottom of it. They were so pale and cold. Jane took one look at him, laid out on ice like a salmon, and began to cry.

"Oh Vincent," she said. "What will I do without you?" This sounded awful. It sounded like Jane and Vincent making fun, of obsolete books, obsolete movies, their obsolete mothers. It also sounded selfish: here she was, worrying about herself and her future, when Vincent was the one who was sick. But it was true. There would be a lot less to do, altogether, without Vincent.

Vincent gazed up at her; the shadows under his eyes were cavernous. "Lighten up," he said, not very loudly, because he could not speak very loudly now. By this time she was sitting down, leaning forward; she was holding one of his hands. It was thin as the claw of a bird. "Who says I'm going to die?" He spent a moment considering this, revised it. "You're right," he said. "They got me. It was the Pod People from outer space. They said, 'All I want is your poddy.' "

Jane cried more. It was worse because he was trying to be funny. "But what *is* it?" she said. "Have they found out yet?"

Vincent smiled his ancient, jaunty smile, his smile of detachment, of amusement. There were his beautiful teeth, juvenile as ever. "Who knows?" he said. "It must have been something I ate."

Jane sat with the tears running down her face. She felt desolate: left behind, stranded. Their mothers had finally caught up to them and been proven right. There were consequences after all; but they were the consequences to things you didn't even know you'd done.

❧

The scientists are back on the screen. They are excited, their earnest mouths are twitching, you could almost call them joyful. They know why John Torrington died; they know, at last, why the Franklin Expedition went so terribly wrong. They've snipped off pieces of John Torrington, a fingernail, a lock of hair, they've run them through machines and come out with the answers.

There is a shot of an old tin can, pulled open to show the seam. It looks like a bomb casing. A finger points: it was the tin cans that did it, a new invention back then, a new technology, the ultimate defence against starvation and scurvy. The Franklin Expedition was excellently provisioned with tin cans, stuffed full of meat and soup and soldered together with lead. The whole expedition got lead poisoning. Nobody knew it. Nobody could taste it. It invaded their bones, their lungs, their brains, weakening them and confusing their thinking, so that at the end those that had not yet died in the ships set out in an idiotic trek across the stony, icy ground, pulling a lifeboat laden down with toothbrushes, soap, handkerchiefs, and slippers, useless pieces of junk. When they were found ten years later, they were skeletons in tattered coats, lying where they'd collapsed. They'd been heading back towards the ships. It was what they'd been eating that had killed them.

Jane switches off the television and goes into her kitchen—all white, done over the year before last, the outmoded butcher-block counters from the seventies torn out and carted away—to make herself some hot milk and rum. Then she decides against it; she won't sleep anyway. Everything in here looks ownerless. Her toaster oven, so perfect for solo dining, her microwave for the vegetables, her espresso maker—they're sitting around waiting for her departure, for this evening or forever, in order to assume their final, real appearances of purposeless objects adrift in the physical world. They might as well be pieces of an exploded spaceship orbiting the moon.

She thinks about Vincent's apartment, so carefully arranged, filled with the beautiful or deliberately ugly possessions he once loved. She thinks about his closet, with its quirky particular outfits, empty now of his arms and legs. It has all been broken up now, sold, given away.

Increasingly the sidewalk that runs past her house is cluttered with plastic drinking cups, crumpled soft-drink cans, used take-out plates. She picks them up, clears them away, but they appear again overnight, like a trail left by an army on the march or by the fleeing residents of a city under bombardment, discarding the objects that were once thought essential but are now too heavy to carry.

Witnesses of an Era

Günter Grass

❧

1914

Finally, in the Mid-Sixties, after two of my colleagues at the institute tried and failed several times, I managed to bring the two elderly gentlemen together. Perhaps I had better luck because I was a young woman, and Swiss to boot, that is, I had the bonus of neutrality. My letters, despite the dispassionate tone I used to describe the object of my research, were meant as a sensitive if not timid knock at the door. The acceptances arrived within a few days and almost simultaneously.

I characterized them to my colleagues as an impressive, if slightly fossilized pair. I had booked them quiet rooms in the Zum Storchen. We spent much of our time in the Rôtisserie there, with its view of the Limmat, the Town Hall directly opposite, and the Zum Rüden house. Herr Remarque, who was sixty-seven at the time, had come from Locarno. Clearly a bon vivant, he seemed more fragile to me than Herr Jünger, who had just turned seventy and made a sprightly, pointedly athletic impression. He lives in Württemberg, but had come to Zurich via Basel after making a foot tour through the Vosges to the Hartmannsweiler Kopf, the scene of severe fighting in 1915.

Our first session was anything but promising. The conversation of my "witnesses of an era" centered on Swiss wines, Remarque preferring Ticino vintages, Jünger those of La Dôle in the canton of Vaud. Both made a show of plying me with their well-conserved charm. I found their attempts to use *Schwyzerdütsch* amusing but tiresome. It wasn't until I quoted the opening of "The Flemish Dance of Death," an anonymous song popular during the First World War— "Death rides on a raven-black steed, / Wearing a stocking cap over his head"—that things changed. First Remarque, then Jünger hummed the haunting, melancholy melody, and both knew the lines that brought the refrain to a close: "Flanders is in danger. / Death is there no stranger." They looked off in the direction of the Cathedral, its spires towering over the houses along the embankment.

Following this meditative interlude, broken only by some clearing of throats, Remarque said that in the autumn of 1914—he was still on a school bench in Osnabrück while volunteers at Bikschote and Ieper were lying in their own blood—the Langemark legend, that is, that German soldiers had responded to English machine-gun fire by singing "Deutschland über alles," had made a great impression on him. That, together with their teachers' exhortations, had moved many a class to enlist in the war effort. Every second soldier did not return. And those who did—like Remarque, who was not allowed to continue his education—were tainted to this day. He still thought of himself as one of the living dead.

Herr Jünger, who had followed his fellow writer's account of his school experiences with a delicate smile, qualified the Langemark legend as "patriotic balderdash," though he admitted that long before the war began he had been obsessed with a craving for danger, a yen for the unusual—"be it only a stint in the French Foreign Legion." "When it broke out at last, we felt we'd been fused with an enormous body. Yet even after the war showed its claws, I was fascinated, during the raiding parties I led, by the idea of battle as inner experience. Fess up, my friend. Even in *All Quiet on the Western Front,* your excellent debut, you described the camaraderie unto death among soldiers in highly moving terms."

The novel did not record what he himself had experienced, Remarque replied. It brought together the front-line experiences of a generation sent to the slaughter. "My service in the ambulance corps provided me with all the material I needed."

I wouldn't go so far as to say the gentlemen began to argue, but they made a point of showing how they differed on matters military, how opposed their very styles were, and that in other respects as well they came from opposing camps. While one of them still considered himself "an incorrigible pacifist," the other wished to be seen as an "anarch."

"Don't be silly," Remarque said at one point. "Why, in *The Storm of Steel* you were like a holy terror bent on adventure. Until Ludendorff's final offensive. You would throw together a raiding party for the bloodthirsty pleasure of taking a quick prisoner or two—and possibly a bottle of cognac . . ." But then he admitted that his colleague's diary gave a partially valid description of trench and positional warfare and of the character of the matériel battle.

Toward the end of our first round—by which time the gentlemen had emptied two bottles of red wine—Jünger returned to the issue of Flanders. "Digging trenches along the Langemark front two and a half years later, we came across belts, weapons, and cartridge cases from 1914. We even found spiked helmets, the kind worn by whole volunteer regiments marching off to war. . . ."

1915

Our next round took place at the Odeon, a café so venerable that, until the German Reich granted him safe-conduct to Russia, Lenin sat there reading the *Neue Zürcher Zeitung* and the like, secretly planning his revolution. We concentrated on the past rather than the future, though the gentlemen insisted on opening the meeting with a champagne breakfast. I was served orange juice.

They laid their evidence, their once hotly debated novels, on the marble table between the croissants and the cheese platter. *All Quiet on the Western Front* had had much larger editions than *The Storm of Steel*. "Once my book was burned publicly in '33," Remarque said, "it was out of print for a good twelve years—and not only in Germany—while your hymn to war has obviously been available everywhere and at all time."

Jünger made no response. But when I brought the conversation round to the trench war in Flanders and the chalky soil of the Champagne region and placed pictures of the areas under siege on the table, which has since been cleared, he immediately started in on the Somme offensive and counteroffensive and made a point that set the tone for the rest of the conversation: "That miserable leather spiked helmet—which you, my most worthy colleague, were spared— was replaced as early as June 1915 in our section of the front by a steel helmet. It was developed by an artillery captain named Schwerd after a number of false starts in a race with the French who were also introducing steel helmets. Since Krupp was not in a position to man-ufacture a suitable chrome alloy, contracts went to other companies, including the Thale Iron Works. By February 1916 steel helmets were in use on all fronts. Troops at Verdun and on the Somme received them first; the eastern front had to wait the longest. You have no idea, my dear Remarque, how many lives were lost to that useless leather cap, which, leather being in short supply, was actually made of felt. The losses were particularly great in positional warfare, where every well-aimed shot meant one man fewer, every bomb fragment blasted its way home."

Then he turned to me and said, "The helmet used by your Swiss police today—true, in modified form—is modeled after our steel helmet down to the pins that provide ventilation."

My response—"Fortunately our helmet has not had to stand up to the bombardments of matériel you so powerfully celebrate"—he passed over in silence, inundating instead the pointedly tight-lipped Remarque with further details, from the battle-gray finishing process used for rust protection to the neck protector in the back and the horsehair or quilted-felt lining. Then he lamented, the poor visibility in trench warfare as a result of the front rim's having to protrude enough to provide protection down to the tip of the nose. "You can be sure I found the heavy steel helmet a terrible burden while leading raids. It was admittedly frivolous of me, but I preferred my good old lieutenant's cap, which, I should add, was lined with silk." Then something else occurred to him, something he qualified as amusing. "By the way, I keep a Tommy helmet on my desk as a souvenir. It's completely different, flat as it can be. With a bullet hole in it, naturally."

After a lengthy pause—the gentlemen were having plum brandy with their coffee—Remarque said, "The M-16 steel helmets, later M-17, were much too large for the green replacement recruits; they kept slipping. All you could see of the childlike faces was a frightened

mouth and quivering chin. Comical and pitiful at once. Nor need I tell
you that infantry bullets and shrapnel could pierce even steel. . . ."

He called for another brandy. Jünger joined him. The nice Swiss
Meidschi was served another glass of freshly squeezed orange juice.

1917

Right after breakfast—nothing opulent this time, no champagne;
in fact, the gentlemen decided to accept my recommendation of
Birchermüsli—we resumed our conversation: As if talking to a school-
girl they were afraid to shock, they gave me a cautious account of
chemical warfare, that is, the deliberate use of chlorine and mustard
gas as ammunition, referring partly to their own experience but also
to secondary sources.

We had come to chemical weapons without beating around the
bush, when Remarque brought up the Vietnam War, which was going on at the time of our conversation, and called the use of napalm
and Agent Orange "criminal." "Once you drop an atom bomb," he
said, "you lose all inhibitions." Jünger condemned the systematic
defoliation of the jungle by surface poisons as a logical continuation
of the use of poison gas in World War I and agreed with Remarque
that the Americans would lose this "dirty war," which had no use for
true "soldierly behavior."

"Though we must admit," he added, "that we were the first to
use chlorine gas. In April 1915, at Ieper, against the English."

Whereupon Remarque cried out—so loud that a waitress came to
a halt not far from our table and then rushed off—"Gas attack! Gas!
Gaaas!" and Jünger imitated the ring of the alarm with a teaspoon.
Then, suddenly, as if obeying some inner command, he was serious
and to the point: "We immediately started oiling our rifle barrels and

anything made of metal. Those were our orders. Then we buckled on the gas masks. Later, in Monchy, just before the Battle of the Somme, we saw a group of gas victims writhing and moaning, water streaming from their eyes. But the main thing chlorine does is to eat away at your lungs, burn them up. I saw what it could do in enemy trenches as well. Not long thereafter the English began using phosgene on us. It had a sickly-sweet smell."

Then it was Remarque's turn: "They would retch for days, spewing out their burned-up lungs. The worst thing was when they were caught in a shell hole or funk hole during a barrage of fire, because clouds of gas would settle in any depression like jellyfish, and woe unto those who took their masks off too soon . . . The replacements, inexperienced, were always the first to go. . . . Poor young, helpless boys bumbling about . . . Baggy uniforms . . . Turnip-white faces . . . Still alive but with the deadpan gaze of dead children . . . I once saw a dugout filled with the poor beasts. . . . All blue heads and black lips . . . Taken their masks off too soon . . . Hemorrhaging to death."

They both apologized; it was too much so early in the morning. I could tell they found it odd and unpleasant for a young lady to be interested in the bestialities war naturally entailed. I assured Remarque—who, more than Jünger, saw himself as a gentleman of the old school—that he needn't worry about me: the report that Bührli has commissioned from us had to be comprehensive, after all. "I'm sure you're aware of the quality of the weapons Bührli turns out for export," I said, and asked them for more detail.

Since Herr Remarque gazed off in the direction of the Town Hall bridge and the Limmat Embankment and did not respond, Herr Jünger, more in control of himself, filled me in on the development of the gas mask and then of mustard gas, which was first used—and by the Germans—in June of 1917 during the third battle at Ieper. It formed an all but odorless, barely perceptible cloud, a kind of mist that stuck to the ground and didn't start taking effect— eating away at your cells—until three or four hours after you breathed it. Dichloroethyl sulfide, an oily compound sprayed in tiny drops. No gas mask could keep it out.

Herr Jünger went on to explain that entire trench systems would be infected with the gas, whereupon they would be evacuated without a fight. "But late in the autumn of '17," he said, "the English captured a major cache of mustard-gas grenades and immediately used them against us. Many soldiers lost their sight. . . . Tell me, Remarque, wasn't that what landed the greatest corporal of all time in sick bay at Pasewalk? Where he spent the rest of the war in safety. And where he decided to go into politics."

translated by Michael Henry Heim

The Journey to the Dead

John Updike

❧

Living alone after nearly thirty married years, Martin Fredericks
was beset with occasional importunities. A college friend of his
former wife's—a jaunty, sturdy comp.-lit. major named Arlene
Quint—telephoned him one early-spring day and asked him to drive
her to the hospital. He wasn't sure he understood. "Now?"

"Pretty soon, yeah, if you could." The plea in her voice was
braced by something firm and ceremonious he remembered from
college days. "I thought, you have that little car parked out behind
your building, and in this city when you call a taxi it takes hours and
then they drive like maniacs. I need to be driven gently."

"You do?"

"Yes, Marty," she said. "None of your sudden stops and starts."

They had recently remet, after many years, at a party in an artist's
loft a few blocks away in town; she was less surprised to see him than
he her, since she had been in touch with his former wife, Harriet,
and knew he had moved in from the suburbs. She, too, lived in town

now. She and Sherman Quint—a chem. major—had been divorced for several years. She loved being in the city, and free, Arlene told Fredericks. She looked sallow, and her pulled-back black hair had gone gray in strange distinct bands, but she seemed much as he remembered her, solid and energetic, with a certain air of benign defiance. Like his former wife, she had been a collegiate artsy type, in a pony tail and peasant skirt. Now, still pony-tailed, she sat up on a table swinging her plump legs in sheer happiness, it seemed, at being alive and single and here.

The table was a heavy harvest table that the artist, a small goateed man, worked on; it was peppered with thumbtack holes and covered with accidents of ink and paint. At Arlene's back hung tacked-up charcoal sketches of idealized male nudes. At her side, space fell away through a big steel-mullioned industrial window onto the lights of the city, amber and platinum and blurred dabs of neon red, stretching far away; the city was not New York but Boston, and nothing in this direction looked higher than their own windows, the streets and brick rows streaming beneath them like the lights of an airport during takeoff. Her happiness glowed through her not quite healthy skin and her legs kept kicking friskily—the drumstick-shaped calves, the little round-toed Capezio flats. Those shoes dated her; Fredericks' former wife, too, had worn ballerina shoes in all weathers, in rain or snow, as if life at any moment might become a dance.

The crowd at this party seemed young—young would-be artists with ugly punk haircuts, shaved above the ears and tinted in pastel tufts, boys and girls alike, wearing baggy sweaters and getting louder and shriller as they sipped wine from cheap plastic glasses. One boy took a flexible stack of these glasses and pretended to play it like an accordion. Their host's voice, nasal and gleeful, cut through the noise. Only the host, and his Japanese boy friend, seemed close to

Fredericks' age, and though this troubled him the youthfulness of
the gathering seemed to add to Arlene's happiness, her aimless,
kicking happiness like that of a little girl perched up on a high wall.
"Hey. I think I'll, as they say, split," he said at last to her, in slight
parody of her own eager assimilation to this youthful scene. "Want
to be walked home?"

Her eyes abruptly focused on him. Shadows beneath them betrayed fatigue. "Oh no, Marty, it's much too early!" Her voice came
out high and as if from far away. Her lips were slow to close back over
her teeth, which protruded a bit and were stained like a smoker's,
though she no longer smoked. "You're sweet, but I can walk alone.
This section of town is quite safe."

He was glad to be rejected; he was involved with another woman
and had made the offer in a truly protective spirit, and as an obscure
gesture toward his former wife. Because the two girls had been close,
a taboo as of incest had come between him and Arlene in college; it
was strange to feel that taboo lifted, and a queasy freedom fallen over
them all, relatively late in life. Freedom—that was what her plump
kicking legs expressed. But Americans are oversold on freedom,
Fredericks thought, and availability does not equal attractiveness.
There was a glaze of unhealth on Arlene, and she had grown thick
around the middle.

When he described the encounter to Harriet over the phone, she
told him that Arlene had had a cancer scare but the chemotherapy
seemed to have worked. The disease figured in his mind as another
reason to let Arlene alone. She was taken. It slowly ebbed from his
mind that she lived a half-mile away, working part-time in an art-
supplies store near the local university, until this sudden phone call.

It was late afternoon, becoming evening. The downtown skyscrapers visible from his window were broken into great blocks of

shadow and orange glare as the sun sank over the Fens. By the time he had made his way to his automobile—a decrepit Karmann-Ghia convertible, its left fender dented, its canvas top slashed one night by a thief looking for drugs or an expensive radio—it was dark enough to use his headlights. Irritated and flattered, he inched through the rush-hour traffic to the address Arlene had given him.

She was standing in the vestibule of her building, and came out carrying a little suitcase, walking very carefully, with short slow steps. When he jackknifed awkwardly up out of the car and moved around it to take her bag, she lifted a hand in alarm, as if fearful he would bump against her. She wore a loose heavy cloth coat, but, even so, he could see that her shape was not right—her middle was not just thick but swollen. The street lights didn't help her color; her face looked greenish, waxy, with hollows like thumb-marks in wax beneath her eyes. She smiled at the intensity of his inspection. Arlene, whose mother's parents had emigrated from Macedonia, had a certain stiff old-world mannerliness, and Fredericks sensed her determination to make this mannerliness see them through. Though his car, double-parked, forced the street's two lanes of traffic to squeeze into one, with some indignant honking, he made his own movements as unhurried as hers, and set the suitcase in the back seat as gently as if it contained her pain.

She slammed the door on her side but remained a bit hunched forward, her profile silhouetted against the side window, beneath the slashed and taped canvas: her sharp high-bridged nose, her lips' prim set over her slightly protuberant teeth. He asked, before easing in the clutch, "O.K.?"

"Just fine," she said, in a voice surprising in its normality. "You're sweet to do this, Marty."

"Not at all. Which hospital?"

She named one a mile away. The rush hour was at its worst, as darkness deepened, and there were many stops and starts. She rested a hand on the dashboard at one point, as if to brace herself, then abandoned the posture, as perhaps more uncomfortable than it was worth. The car was rusty and old and gave a jerky ride however delicately he shifted. "Sorry," he said, more than once.

"You're doing fine," she said, almost condescendingly.

He couldn't believe a taxi wouldn't have been better. It was as if she had decided to accept, now, his rejected invitation to see her home. "Sorry the car's cold; the heater should come on any minute."

"I don't feel the cold."

"Is your—is this, ah, a sudden thing?"

"It's been coming on."

"They know at the hospital you're coming?"

"Oh yes. They do."

"Is it going to be a long stay?"

"That's up to them. My assignment is to deliver the body."

The body. "I'm sorry," he said.

"About what, Marty?" They had broken free of the traffic for a block and were gliding along smoothly, between four-story bowfronts, beneath trees that in a month would have leaves.

"That your body's, uh, acting up."

The glide ended; a cross street, a principal artery, was jammed solid. "I expect it will all be all right," Arlene said, after a second of tense silence in which she saw that the stop was not going to be jarring. Her voice had the false, light tempo of someone issuing reassurances to a child.

"I do hope so," Fredericks said, feeling foolish and puny relative to the immense motions, the revolutions of mortality, taking place inside her, next to him in the shuddering, cold, slashed cave of the car.

She said, more conversationally, "You adjust. You come to terms with it."

"Really?"

"Oh yes," Arlene said simply, as if he were in on the secret now—as if he and she were now on the same side of the mystery growing within her. But he couldn't imagine death's having a human size, finite enough to come to terms with. The car heater was producing heat at last, as the hospital's lights came into sight. She directed him to a curved side street that became a ramp. As he gently pulled up at the entrance, Fredericks had the impression of bustling all-hours brightness that an airport gives, or a railroad terminal in the old days—a constant grand liveliness of comings and goings.

He said, scrambling to extricate himself from behind the wheel, "Let me get the door for you."

"I can manage." She popped the door latch and was standing at the side of the car when he came around for the suitcase. She had that waistless stiff look women of the Balkans have, in their layered peasant outfits. She was reverting. Her face was turned toward the light pouring through the glass doors of the hospital lobby.

"Shall I walk you in?"

"No." The answer was so abrupt she tried to soften it. "You can't park here. I can manage." Hearing the repetition, she insisted on it: "I want to manage. I've chosen to be on my own." She looked at him quickly, with a suspicious slide of her eyes, and gave him her gracious, buck-toothed, matter-of-fact smile. "Thanks, Marty. That was a nice ride."

"Do you want visitors?"

"I'll have plenty, thanks. All those children we had for some reason."

"Call me up when you're done and I can come for you."

Her lips slowly closed over her teeth. "I should be up to a taxi by then." There was no offer of a pecked kiss goodbye, though he would have been careful not to bump against her. But if her own body was betraying her, Fredericks thought, why should she trust him? She passed through the glass doors and did not look back. From behind, she seemed, with her little suitcase and bulky coat, an immigrant, just arrived.

Arlene was not the first dying woman his own age that Fredericks had known. In the suburb where he and Harriet had lived together, a mutual friend, the merriest wife in their circle, had a breast removed in her early forties. For years, that seemed to have solved the problem; then she raucously confided to them, outside the doors of the local supermarket, "The damn stuff's come back!" The last time they saw her, it was at a small barbecue lunch that all the guests tacitly knew, though none would admit aloud, to be a farewell to their hostess.

On that summer Sunday, as Fredericks and his wife in their car pulled into the property, a new green hose, stretched to reach a flower bed, lay across the asphalt driveway, and he braked. Their hostess, in a sun hat and gaudy muu-muu, was standing on her lawn and vigorously waving him forward onto a section of grass set aside for parking. Hesitantly he eased the car—a Volvo station wagon, which felt stiff as a truck to drive—forward into the spot she was marking, fearful his foot might slip and his front bumper strike this woman already stricken by disease.

He got out and kissed her on her upturned face, which in illness had become round and shiny, and explained that he hadn't wanted to run over the hose. "Ach, the hose!" she exclaimed with startling guttural force and a sweeping, humorous gesture. "Phooey to the hose!"

Nevertheless, Fredericks went back and moved the hose so the
next car would not run over it, at the same time trying to imagine how
these appurtenances to our daily living, as patiently treasured and
stored and coiled and repaired as if their usefulness were eternal,
must look to someone whose death is imminent. The hose. The flowers. The abandoned trowel whose canary-yellow handle winks within
weeds in the phlox border. The grass itself, and the sun and sky and
trees like massive scuffed-up stage flats—phooey to them. Their value
was about to undergo a revision so vast and crushing Fredericks
could not imagine it. Certainly he could not imagine it in relation to
the merry presence who entertained them, sitting with her guests on
the screened porch while her husband cooked at the grill outside, in a
cloud of gnats. As a concession to her debility she lay on an alu-
minum chaise longue, her feet in thick wool slipper-socks though the
day was warm, and still wearing her sun hat, perhaps to hide her
chemotherapy-blasted hair. The party, as the guests drank wine, became ever more relaxed and hilarious, the hostess urging the conversation into mundane channels—local zoning problems, and movies
they had seen. She elaborated so feelingly on the horrors of a proposed condominium development that they forgot she would not
be there to see it or to contend with the parking problems it would
pose. When another woman objected that all the movies seemed to
be about—with emphasis—*sleaze,* the dying woman quickly-joked,
"Gesundheit!" and then, merrily added, "I love sleaze. Sleaze," she
said, "is truth. Sleaze," she went on, excited to a crescendo by the
laughter surrounding her, "shall set us free!"

A season later, attending her funeral, trying to picture her moving somewhere from strength to strength as the service claimed,
Fredericks wondered that none of them that afternoon had been
able to find a topic more elevated, more affectionately valedictory,

than condominiums and sleazy movies, and wondered where that
garden hose of which he had been so solicitous now lay coiled.

The dying, he marvelled, do not seem to inhabit a world much
different from ours. His elderly neighbors in this suburb plucked
with rakes at the leaves on their lawn, walked their old lame dogs, and
talked of this winter's scheduled trip to Florida as if in death's very
gateway there was nothing to do but keep living, living in the same
old rut. They gossiped, they pottered, they watched television. No
radical insights heightened their conversation, though Fredericks listened expectantly. In college he had been a classics major, and dimly
recalled the section of *The Odyssey* in which the dead stare mutely at
Odysseus, unable to speak until they have drunk of the sheep's blood
with which the hero has filled, by Circe's prescription, a pit a cubit
square and a cubit deep. The hero's own mother, Anticleia, crouches
wordless and distraught until he allows her to drink "the storm-dark
blood." The dead in Homer feel themselves inferior, even—in the
T. E. Lawrence translation—silly. Dead Achilles tauntingly asks
Odysseus, "How will you find some madder adventure to cap this
coming down alive to Hades among the silly dead, the worn-out
mockeries of men?" And Aeneas, in Virgil's Avernus, cannot elicit a
word from angry Dido, who listens to his entreaties and apologies
with fixed eyes and a countenance of stone, and who flees still hating
him—*inimica*—back to the shadowy groves where Sychaeus, her former husband, responds to her cares and equals her love—*inimica
refugit / in nemus umbriferum coniunx ubi pristinus illi / respondet
curis aequatque Sychaeus amorem.* Virgil's version of the underworld
becomes implausibly detailed, with the future of Rome set forth at
length by Anchises, and various rings and compartments all laid out
as if in anticipation of Dante's definitive mapping. Whereas Gilgamesh, an older journeyer still, found only, as far as the broken

tablets of his tale can be deciphered, confusion and evasion at the end of his passionate quest: "Sorrow has come into my belly. I fear death; I roam over the hills. I will seize the road; quickly I will go to the house of Utnapishtim, offspring of Ubaratutu. . . ."

Utnapishtim answers Gilgamesh in broken clay, "Since there is no . . . There is no word of advice . . . From the beginning there is no permanence. . . . As for death, its time is hidden. The time of life is shown plain."

Fredericks was shy about calling Arlene, lest it seem to be a kind of courtship. Yet in decency he should ask, after their perilous ride together, how she was doing. For several weeks, her phone didn't answer; then, one day, it was picked up. "Oh," she responded, with a thoughtful, chiming, lazy lilt to her voice which seemed new, "not bad. There are good days and bad days. They have me on a mixture of things, and for a while there the mix was all wrong. But it's settled down now. I feel pretty good, Marty."

"You're home now," he said, as if to fix a fact in this flux of unimaginable therapy. The wandering drugged sound of her voice awakened firmness in his. "Are you going to work, too?"

"Yesterday, which was so sunny, I trotted over to the art store, and they were happy to see me, but I'm really not ready yet to be on my feet all day. Some afternoon next week is my goal. You learn to set goals."

"Yes." His firmness seemed to miscarry—a punch at empty air. "Well, take things a day at a time."

There was a pause. "I don't mind visitors," she said.

He thought of the artist's loft and that noisy crowd and how happy she had been to be among them, and felt spiteful. If they were all so great, where were they now? "Well, I could come by some day," he said. "If it wouldn't tire you out."

"Oh no, Marty," she said, "It would be cheery."

Fredericks felt uncomfortably obliged to set a time, late one afternoon, after his own work. He did not feel, in this single interim of his life, quite free—the woman he was involved with was possessive of his time, and kept watch on it. His life seemed destined to be never wholly his own. By his choice, of course. Arlene had told him, *I've chosen to be on my own.*

At the hour when he drove to Arlene's address, cars were leaving the streets to return to the suburbs, and he had no trouble finding an empty space at a meter. Every day, the sunlight clung to the city a few minutes longer. Her house was a bowfront brownstone, handsomer than his brick tenement, and faced not the downtown's little knot of skyscrapers but a strip of old-fashioned park, part of the Fens, with iron lamp standards and a stone footbridge arched over a marshy creek dotted with beer cans and snow-white Styrofoam takeout boxes. A wide-spreading beech tree whose roots drank at the edge of the creek was coming into bud. *The time of life is shown plain.*

Arlene greeted him at the elevator, unexpectedly, so that he nearly bumped into her. As he kissed her cheek, she stayed hunched over, so it was awkward to plant his lips. Her cheek felt dry and a bit too warm.

She was wearing a kind of navy-blue running suit, and looked much thinner. The sallow skin of her face had tightened, and her eyes—a surprising light brown, a flecked candy color—peered out of their deepened sockets suspiciously, around a phantom corner. Hunched and shuffling her feet, she led him toward the front room and its view of the park. From her windows he could see through the budding beech a diagonal path and, in the middle distance, an iron bandstand. Her apartment was on a higher floor than his own, though not so high as the artist's loft, and abundantly furnished with surprisingly expensive furniture: loot from her marriage, he thought. She let Fredericks make himself a drink while she lay on a brocaded sofa, with her feet up, and sipped Perrier water. "What a *lovely* place," he said, and then feared that his emphasis betrayed his assumption that she lived shabbily, in bohemian style.

"I missed it those weeks I was away. My plants were so happy to see me. A cyclamen died, though I had asked the super's wife to come in twice a week and water."

"Has Harriet ever been here?"

"Oh yes—a number of times. She likes it. She says she hates being stuck out there in that big rambling place of yours. I mean, that the two of you had."

"The children aren't quite flown. And if she moves into town, too, we'll have an overpopulation problem."

"Oh, Marty, you know she never will. Harriet needs all that showy country space. She needs animals."

The conversation began to excite him. He sat in a chair so unexpectedly soft he nearly spilled his drink. From the low angle, Arlene's front windows were full of sky, sky only, with white spring clouds set close as flagstones and hurrying thus close-packed in a direction that made the room itself seem to be travelling, smoothly pulling its walls and furniture and late-afternoon shadows backward, toward the past, toward the time when they were all in college and young and freshly acquainted, and the elms weren't blighted and cars were enormous and the Army-McCarthy hearings fascinatingly droned over the radio into the spring afternoons when they should have been studying Chaucer. And then later, still keeping in touch, Arlene and Sherman and Harriet and Martin shared the astounding feat of making babies—creating new people, citizens, out of nothing but their own bodies—and the scarcely less marvellous accomplishments of owning houses, and tending them, and having friends who were sometimes wicked, and giving cocktail parties. Though they lived in different towns, in different circles, they had occasionally entertained each other. The Quints had installed a pool, and Fredericks remembered Sunday cookouts on the patchy lawn where the recent excavation had left scars, beneath a sky marred by charcoal smoke and the lazy *bop-pop* of tennis drifting in from their neighbor's clay court. The sun of youth dappled their reminiscences, as Arlene stiffly adjusted her legs on the sofa from time to time and Fredericks sank lower into the chair and into alcoholic benignity, and the sky with its travelling clouds sank into evening blue. Arlene's voice had a high distant quality as if she were reading words from a card held almost out of eyesight. "Harriet took a shine to our minister," she said, Fredericks having recalled the cookouts.

"She did?" Though he had become adept at receiving the signals women sent out, he had never thought of Harriet as sending out any.

Arlene laughed, on a high thin prolonged note, and then her lips closed slowly over her prominent teeth. She said, "Reverend Propper—not that he *was* so proper, it turned out. He was a Unitarian, of course. Harriet even in college liked that kind of boy—a *serious* boy. You weren't *serious* enough for her, Marty."

"She did? I wasn't?" He blamed himself for their breakup, and was pleasantly startled to hear that the rejection hadn't been all on his side.

"Not really. She adored idealists. Union leaders and renegade priests and Erik Erikson—these healer types. That's what drew her to Sherm, before she discovered he was just one more chem. nerd. I guess we didn't have the word 'nerd' then, did we?"

"I had forgotten that she went out with him for a little while."

"A little while! The whole sophomore year. That's how I met him, through her."

"Did I know that?"

"You must have, Marty. She used to say she loved the way his hair was going thin even in college. She thought that was a sign of seriousness. It showed his brain was working to save mankind. All those soc.-rel. majors wanted to save the world."

He had even forgotten that Harriet had majored in social relations—not forgotten, exactly, but not had the fact brought back to life. There had been a time, in those Fifties, when sociology, combining psychology, anthropology, history, and statistics, seemed likely to save the world from those shaggy old beasts tribalism and religion. Harriet had been, with her pearly shy smile and pony tail and tatty tennis sneakers, an apostle of light, in those unfocused pre-protest days. "I hadn't realized that she and Sherm had been that serious."

"*Serious.* You said it. He never smiled, unless you told him something was a joke. God, it was good to get away at last. It was *such* bliss, Marty—and yet there really was almost nothing to complain of about the man."

He didn't want to talk about Sherman. "Did you ever notice," he asked, "how white Harriet's teeth were?"

"I *did.* She knew it, too. She used to tell me I was staining my teeth with my cigarettes. Maybe I should have listened. Nobody believed in cancer in those days."

The word was especially shocking, coming from her. He said, "But it isn't your lungs . . ."

"Oh, it's all related, don't you think?" Arlene said breezily. "And probably basically psychosomatic. I was too happy, being out from under Sherm. My body couldn't handle my happiness. It freaked out."

Fredericks laughed, trying to push up out of his soft, unresisting chair. "Remember how they used to tell us smoking stunted your growth? Listen, Arlene, I must run. Somebody's expecting me to check in. This has been lovely, though. Maybe I could swing by again."

"Please do," the woman said, squinting off as if to read an especially distant prompt card. "I'll be here."

But sometimes when he called she was absent—at the art-supplies store, perhaps, or visiting her children, who were adult, and living within a fifty-mile radius. Or else she was too sick to answer the phone. She had ups and downs, but the trend seemed down. Perhaps he saw her six or seven times in the course of the summer; each time, there was something of the initial enchantment—the day changing tone through the big windows, her thin and distant but agile voice evoking those old days, those Fifties and early Sixties when you moved toward your life with an unstressed freedom no one could understand, now, who had not been young then. There was less outside to that world—less money, fewer cars and people and buildings—and more inside, more blood and hopefulness. Nothing, really, had cost much, relative to now, and nothing, not love or politics, was half so hyped as now. There was a look, of Capezios in the slush, that summed up for Fredericks a careless and unpremeditated something, a bland grace, from those years. There were names he had all but forgotten, until Arlene would casually mention them. "And then Brett Helmerich, the section man in Chaucer, he was another Harriet had her eye on. . . ."

"She did? Brett . . . Helmerich. Wait. I *do* remember him. Leather elbow patches, and always wore a long red muffler wrapped a couple times around his neck, and a red nose like Punch's, sort of."

She softly nodded, looking off in her far-gazing way, her jaundiced face half in window light. Her feet, in thick, striped athletic socks, rested on a pillow, her knees up. Her ankles and wrists and face had been swollen at one phase of her body's struggles with its invader, and then her frame had subsided toward emaciation. She moved more and more stiffly, hunched over. While he drank whiskey or gin, she sipped at a cup of tea so weak as to be mere water turning tepid. But her mention of Brett Helmerich would conjure up the vanished throngs that once stampeded in and out of the Chaucer lectures, given by a wall-eyed professor who over the decades of teaching this course had become more and more medieval, more gruff and scatological and visionary. "You really think she had her eye on Brett? But he was ten years older than we were, with a wife and babies."

"Other people's babies aren't very real to you, until you've had some of your own. Or wives, even, until you've been one. Even then . . . Ex-wives are the worst, the way they hang on to the men's heads."

Arlene on the subject of Harriet fascinated Fredericks, as if his former wife could be displayed to him in a whole new light— resurrected, as it were, by a fresh perspective. She who had seemed to him so shy and sexually clumsy in fact had juggled a number of relationships and flirtations in those college years, and in the years of their young marriage had not been entirely preoccupied by him and their dear babies. Fredericks asked, "There really was something between her and Reverend Propper?"

Arlene's mouth opened wide but her laugh was inaudible, like a bat's cry. "Oh, I don't know if it ever got to the physical stage, but didn't you ever wonder why she would drive twenty-five miles each way to sing in our little off-key choir?"

"I thought it was because of her friendship for you—it gave her a chance to keep in touch with you."

"She kept in touch with me when it suited her," Arlene said, and sipped her weak cold tea, and made a small thrusting gesture with her lips as if to register an unquenchable dryness of mouth. "And still does."

"Harriet's in touch?"

"She calls. Often enough."

"Often enough for what?"

"To hear about you."

"Me? No!"

"Yes."

"But she's so happily remarried."

"I suppose. But a woman is like a spider, Marty. She has her web. She likes to feel the different threads vibrate."

Her phone rang, on the table a few feet from her head, but Arlene let it ring until, at last, the ringing stopped. He wondered how often he had been the person on the other end, assuming she was out or too sick to reach for the phone. Several times when she did answer, her voice croaked and dragged, and he knew that he had pulled her from a narcotic sleep. He would apologize and offer to call again, but she would say it was *cheery* to hear from him, and her voice would slowly clear into animation.

Just before Labor Day, though, she answered on the ring when he had been about to hang up, and he could hear her gasp for breath after each phrase. The medicine she had been taking had "gone crazy." Two days ago her daughter had driven in from a far suburb and gotten her to the hospital just in time. "Scary." Arlene had never

before mentioned fear to Fredericks. He asked her if she would like
him to swing around for a quick visit.

She said, almost scoldingly, "Marty, I just can't do Harriet for
you today. I'm too tired and full of pills. I'm worn out."

Do Harriet? Hanging up, he marvelled that that was what he had
been having her do. Harriet when young, and that whole vast kingdom of the dead, including himself when young. His face felt hot
with embarrassment, and a certain anger at Arlene's rebuff and its
tone. It was not as if he had nothing else to do but pay sick calls.

It was Harriet who told him, over the phone, that Arlene had had a
stroke and was in the hospital.

"For good?"

"It looks like for that."

"Have you seen her?"

"Once. I should go in more, but . . ." She didn't need to explain;
he understood. She lived too far away, the living are busier than the
dying, it was scary.

He, too, did not want to visit Arlene in the hospital; her
apartment—its air of shadowy expectant luxury, like a theatre where
a performance was arranged for him—had been one of the attrac-
tions. But Harriet urged him to go, "for the both of us," and so he
found himself making his way out of a great damp concrete edifice
full of inclined ramps and parked cars. He rode down in an elevator
whose interior was painted red, and followed yellow arrows through
murky corridors of cement and tile. Emerging briefly aboveground,
he recognized that curved stretch of side street to which, six months
ago, Arlene had guided his Karmann-Ghia. The car since then had
fallen apart, its body so rusted he could see the asphalt skimming by

beneath his feet, but the cavernous hospital lobby still radiated its look of sanitary furor, of well-lit comings and goings, of immigrants arriving on a bustling shore.

Fredericks pushed through the glass doors, made inquiries, and tried to follow directions. He threaded his way through corridors milling with pale spectres—white-clad nurses in thick-soled shoes, doctors with cotton lab coats flapping, unconscious patients pushed on gurneys like boats with IV poles for masts, stricken visitors clinging to one another in family clumps and looking lost and pasty in the harsh fluorescent light. *There beset me ten thousand seely ghosts, crying inhumanly.* Though the hospital was twelve stories tall, it all felt underground, mazelike. He passed flower shops, stores stocking magazines and candy and droll get-well cards, a cafeteria entrance, endless numbered doors, and several sighing, clanking elevator banks. He entered an elevator, and was crushed against his fellow-passengers by the entry, at the next floor, of a person in a wheelchair, a shrivelled man with a tube in his nose, pushed by an obese orderly. On the eleventh floor, stepping into a bewildering confusion of desks, he asked for Arlene. He was told a number and pointed in a direction.

The door was ajar. He pushed it open lightly, and saw first an empty bed and a big metal-framed window overlooking the city from a height even greater than that of the artist's loft many months ago. But the prospect was dominated by a great ugly iron bridge spotted with red rustproofing paint and crawling with cars.

She was around the edge of the door, sitting in a chair by the bed. Her close-cut hair seemed mostly white, and a catastrophe had overtaken her face: one side of it, eyelid and mouth-corner, had been pulled sharply down. Her Macedonian eyes burned at him from within a startled, stony fury. She could not speak. The stroke had taken away her nimble power of speech. In her lap and scattered on the bed were a number of children's books and some handmade cards each holding a letter of the alphabet.

Fredericks understood. She was trying to learn to read, to express herself. Her children—parents, now, with children of their own— had lovingly made the alphabet cards, and provided the books. He understood all this but he could not speak, either. His tongue froze after a few words, much too loud, of greeting, and when she held up some of the letters as if to indicate words, he could not make out what she was spelling.

Frantically he tried to make conversation for them both. "Harriet told me you were here. I'm so sorry. It must be—it must be hard. When will you be getting out? You have a terrific view."

In an attempt to respond to his question—he blushed at his own stupidity in asking a question she must try to answer—she pointed at the clock on her bedside table, and then shuffled the cards in her lap, looking for one she could not find. She held one up the wrong way around, and then with a grimace on the side of her mouth that was not dead she flipped it away. He remembered the gesture. *Phooey.*

In a virtual panic, blushing and stammering, he talked inanely, finding, when he reached into himself for a subject that he and Arlene had in common, only the hospital itself, its complexity and strangeness to him, and the grim comedy of being crushed in the elevator by the wheelchair and the pushing fat man. "We all could have been squeezed to death. One girl had a cardboard tray full of coffee cups and had to hold it up toward the ceiling." He imitated the heroic, Statue of Liberty–like pose, and then lowered his arm, shamed by the shining unblinking fury of Arlene's eyes, one eye half shut. The dead hate us, and we hate the dead. *I went pale with fear, lest awful Persephone send me from Hades the Gorgon's head, that fabulous horror.* Standing, he felt some liquid otherworldly element spill from him rapidly, cooling the skin of his legs. "I'm afraid I have to, as they say, split." Fredericks wondered if she would remember his saying that long ago, with faint sarcasm, and try to smile. Arlene unsmilingly stared. *None of your sudden stops and starts.* He promised, insincerely, to come again, and, like heroes before him, fled.

Sugar Baby

Chinua Achebe

❧

I caught the fierce expression on his face in the brief impulsive moment of that strange act; and I understood. I don't mean the symbolism such as it was; that, to me, was pretty superficial and obvious. No. It was rather his deadly earnestness.

It lasted no more than a second or two. Just as long as it took to thrust his hand into his sugar bowl, grasp a handful and fling it out of the window, his squarish jaw set viciously. Then it crumbled again in the gentle solvent of a vague smile.

"Ah-ah; why?" asked one of the other two present, or perhaps both, taken aback and completely mystified.

"Only to show sugar that today I am greater than he, that the day has arrived when I can afford sugar and, if it pleases me, throw sugar away."

They roared with laughter then. Cletus joined them but laughing only moderately. Then I joined too, meagrely.

"You are a funny one, Cletus," said Umera, his huge trunk shaking with mirth and his eyes glistening.

Soon we were drinking Cletus's tea and munching chunks of bread. Smeared thickly with margarine.

"Yes," said Umera's friend whose name I didn't catch, "may bullet crack sugar's head!"

"Amen."

"One day soon it will be butter's turn," said Umera. "Please excuse my bad habit." He had soaked a wedge of bread in his tea and carried it dripping into his enormous mouth, his head thrown back. "That's how I learnt to eat bread," he contrived out of a full, soggy mouth. He tore another piece—quite small this time—and threw it out of the window. "Go and meet sugar, and bullet crack both your heads!"

"Amen."

"Tell them about me and sugar, Mike, tell them," said Cletus to me.

Well, I said, there was nothing really to tell except that my friend Cletus had what our English friends would call a sweet tooth. But of course the English, a very moderate race, couldn't possibly have a name for anything like Cletus and his complete denture of thirty-two sweet teeth.

It was an old joke of mine but Umera and his friend didn't know it and so graced it with more uproarious laughter. Which was good because I didn't want to tell any of the real stories Cletus was urging. And fortunately too Umera and his friend were bursting to tell more and more of their own hardship stories; for most of us had become in those days like a bunch of old hypochondriac women vying to recount the most lurid details of their own special infirmities.

And I found it all painfully, unbearably pathetic. I never possessed some people's ability (Cletus's, for example) to turn everything to good account. Pain lasts far longer on me than on him even when—strange to say—it is his own pain. It wouldn't have occurred to me, not in a thousand years, to enact that farcical celebration of victory over sugar. Simply watching it I felt bad. It was like a man standing you a drink because some fellow who once seduced his wife had just died, according to the morning's papers. The drink would stick in my throat because my pity and my contempt would fall on the celebrator and my admiration on the gallant man who once so justly cuckolded him.

For Cletus sugar is not simply sugar. It is what makes life bearable. We lived and worked together in the last eighteen months of the war and so I was pretty close to his agony, to his many humiliating defeats. I never could understand nor fully sympathise with his addiction. As long as I had my one gari meal in the afternoon I neither asked for breakfast nor dinner. At first I had suffered from the lack of meat or fish and worst of all salt in the soup, but by the second year of the war I was noticing it less and less. But Cletus got more obsessively hinged to his sugar and tea every single day of deprivation, a dangerous case of an appetite growing on what it did not feed on. How he acquired such an alien taste in the first place I have not even bothered to investigate; it probably began like a lone cancer cell in lonely winter days and nights in the black belt of Ladbroke Grove.

Other tea and coffee drinkers, if they still found any to drink at all, had learnt long ago to take it black and bitter. Then some unrecognized genius had lightened their burden further with the discovery that the blackest coffee taken along with a piece of coconut lost a good deal of its bitter edge. And so a new, sustaining *petit déjeuner* was born. But Cletus like a doomed man must have the proper thing or else nothing at all. Did I say I lost patience with him? Well, sometimes. In more charitable and more thoughtful moments I felt sorrow for him rather than anger, for could one honestly say that an addiction to sugar was any more irrational than all the other many addictions going at the time? No. And it constituted no threat to anybody else, which you couldn't say for all those others.

One day he came home in very high spirits. Someone recently returned from abroad had sold him two-dozen tablets of an artificial sweetener for three pounds. He went straight to the kitchen to boil water. Then he brought out from some secure corner of his bag his old tin of instant coffee—he no longer had tea—which had now gone solid. "Nothing wrong with it," he assured me again and again though I hadn't even said a word. "It's the humidity; the smell is quite unimpaired." He sniffed it and then broke off two small rock-like pieces with a knife and made two cups of coffee. Then he sat back with a song in his face.

I could barely stand the taste of the sweetener. It larded every sip with a lingering cloyingness and siphoned unsuspected wells of saliva into my mouth. We drank in silence. Then suddenly Cletus jumped up and rushed outside to give way to a rasping paroxysm of vomiting. I stopped then trying to drink what was left in my cup.

I told him sorry when he came back in. He didn't say a word. He went straight to his room and fetched a cup of water and went out again to rinse his mouth. After a few gargles he tipped the remaining water into a cupped hand and washed down his face. I said sorry again and he nodded.

Later he came where I sat. "Do you care for these?" He held out the little tablets with palpable disgust. Strange how even one attack of vomiting could so utterly reduce a man. "No, not really. But keep them. I'm sure we won't need to go far to find friends who do."

He either was not listening or else he simply could not bring himself to live with the things another minute. He made his third trip outside and threw them into the same wild plot of weeds which had just received his vomit.

He must have worked himself to such a pitch of expectation over the wretched sugar substitute that he now plummeted headlong into near nervous collapse. For the next two days he kept to his bed, neither showing up in the morning at the Directorate where we worked nor going in the evening as was his custom to see his girl friend, Mercy.

On the third day I really lost patience with him and told him a few harsh things about fighting a war of survival, calling to my aid more or less the rhetoric for which his radio scripts were famous. "Fuck your war! Fuck your survival!" he shouted at me. All the same he got better soon afterwards and suitably shamefaced. Then I relented somewhat myself and began privately to make serious inquiries about sugar on his behalf.

Another friend at the Directorate told me about a certain Father Doherty who lived ten miles away and controlled Caritas relief stores for the entire district. A well-known and knowing Roman Catholic, my friend, he warned me that Father Doherty, though a good and generous man, was apt to be somewhat unpredictable and had become particularly so lately since a shrapnel hit him in the head at the airport.

Cletus and I made the journey on the following Saturday and found Father Doherty in a reasonably good mood for a man who had just spent six nights running at the airport unloading relief planes in pitch darkness under fairly constant air bombardment and getting home at seven every morning to sleep for two hours. He waved our praises aside saying he only did it on alternate weeks. "After tonight I can have my beauty sleep for seven whole days."

His sitting-room reeked of stockfish, powdered milk, powdered egg yolk and other relief odours which together can make the air of a place uninhalable. Father Doherty rubbed his eyes with the back of his hand and said what could he do for us. But before either of us could begin he got up sleepily and reached for a big thermos flask atop an empty bookcase harbouring just one tiny crucifix, and asked if we cared for coffee. We said yes thinking that in this very home and citadel of Caritas whose very air reeked solid relief one could be sure that coffee would mean with sugar and milk. And I thought too that we were doing excellently with Father Doherty and set it down to our earlier politic admiration of his dedication and courage in the service of our people, for although he had seemed to wave it aside, judicious praise (if not flattery) was still a weapon which even saints might be vulnerable to. He disappeared into a room and brought back three mean-looking fading-blue plastic cups and poured the coffee, a little on his little finger first, into the cups apologising for the incompetence of his old flask.

I began politely to swallow mine and watched Cletus with the corner of my eye. He took a little birdlike sip and held it in his mouth.

Now, what could he do for us, asked Father Doherty again covering three quarters of an enormous yawn with the back of his hand. I spoke up first. I had a problem with hay fever and would like some antihistamine tablets if he had any in stock. "Certainly," he said, "most certainly. I have the very thing for you. Father Joseph has the same complaint, so I always keep some." He disappeared again and I could hear him saying: "Hay fever, hay fever, hay fever" like a man looking for a title in a well-stocked bookshelf, and then: "There we are!" Soon he emerged with a small bottle. "Everything here is in German," he said, studying the label with a squint. "Do you read German?"

"No."

"Nor do I. Try taking one thrice daily and see how you feel."

"Thank you, Father."

"Next!" he said jovially.

His short absence to get the tablets had enabled Cletus to trans-
fer most of the coffee from his cup to his mouth and, moving smartly
to the low window behind him and putting out his neck, disgorge it
quickly outside.

"Name your wish. Joost wun wish, remember," said Father Doherty, now really gay.

"Father," said Cletus almost solemnly, "I need a little sugar."

I had been worrying since we got here how he was going to put
that request across, what form of words he would use. Now it came
out so pure and so simple like naked truth from the soul. I admired
him for that performance for I knew I could never have managed it.
Perhaps Father Doherty himself had unconsciously assisted by
lending the circumstance, albeit jovially, a stark mythological sim-
plicity. If so he now demolished it just as quickly and thoroughly as
a capricious child might kick back into sand the magic castle he had
just created. He seized Cletus by the scruff of his neck and shouting
"Wretch! Wretch!" shoved him outside. Then he went for me; but I
had already found and taken another exit. He raved and swore and
stamped like a truly demented man. He prayed God to remember
this outrage against His Holy Ghost on Judgement Day. "Sugar!
Sugar!! Sugar!!!" he screamed in hoarse crescendo. Sugar when
thousands of God's innocents perished daily for lack of a glass of
milk! Worked up now beyond endurance by his own words he
rushed out and made for us. And there was nothing for it but run,
his holy imprecations ringing in our ears.

We spent a miserable, tongue-tied hour at the road-junction trying to catch a lift back to Amafo. In the end we walked the ten miles
again but now in the withering heat and fear of midday air raid.

❧

That was one story that Cletus presumably wanted me to tell to celebrate our first tea party. How could I? I couldn't see it as victory in retrospect, only as defeat. And there were many, the ugliest yet to come.

Not long after our encounter with Father Doherty I was selected by the Foreign Affairs people "to go on a mission." Although it was a kind of poor man's mission lasting just a week and taking me no farther than the offshore Portuguese island of São Tomé I was nevertheless overjoyed because abroad was still abroad and I had never stepped out of Biafra since the war began—a fact calculated to dismiss one outright in the opinion of his fellows as a man of no consequence, but more important, which meant that one never had a chance to bask in the glory of coming back with those little amenities that had suddenly become marks of rank and good living, like bath soap, a towel, razor blades, etc.

On the last day before my journey, close friends and friends not so close, mere acquaintances and even complete strangers and near enemies came to tell me their wishes. It had become a ritual, almost a festival whose ancient significance was now buried deep in folkmemory. Some lucky fellow was going on a mission to an almost mythical world long withdrawn beyond normal human reach where goods abounded still and life was safe. And everyone came to make their wishes. And to every request the lucky one answered: "I will try, you know the problem . . ."

"Oh yes I know, but just try . . ." No real hope, no obligation or commitment.

Occasionally, however, a firm and serious order was made when one of the happier people came. For this, words were superfluous.

Just a slip of paper with "foreign exchange" pinned to it. Some wanted salt which was entirely out because of the weight. Many wanted underwear for themselves or their girls and some wretch even ordered contraceptives which I told him I assumed was for office (as against family) planning, to the great arousement of my crowd. I bustled in and out of my room gaily with my notepaper saying: "Joost wun wish!"

Yes, near enemies came too. Like our big man across the road, a one-time Protestant clergyman they said, now unfrocked, a pompous ass if ever there was one, who had early in the war wangled himself into the venal position of controlling and dispensing scarce materials imported by the government, especially women's fabrics. He came like a Nichodemus as I was about to turn in. I wouldn't have thought he knew the likes of us existed. But there he came nodding in his walk like an emir on horseback and trailing the aroma of his Erinmore tobacco. He wondered if I could buy him two bottles of a special pomade for dying grey hair and held out a five-dollar bill. This was the wretch who once asked my girlfriend when she went to file an application to buy a bra to spend a weekend with him in some remote village!

By forgoing lunch daily in São Tomé I was able at the end of the week to save up from my miserable allowance enough foreign exchange to buy myself a few things including those antihistamine tablets (for I had abandoned in our hasty retreat the bottle that Father Doherty gave me). For Cletus—and this gave me the greatest happiness of all—I bought a tin of Lipton's tea and two half-pound packets of sugar. Imagine then my horrified fury when one of the packets was stolen on my arrival home at the airport while (my eyes turned momentarily away from my baggage) I was put through make-believe immigration. Perhaps if that packet had not been stolen Cletus might have been spared the most humiliating defeat that sugar was yet to inflict on him.

Mercy came to see him (and me) the day I returned from São Tomé. I had a tablet of Lux soap for her and a small tube of hand cream. She was ecstatic.

"Would you like some tea?" asked Cletus.

"Oh yes," she said in her soft, purring voice. "Do you have tea? Great! And sugar too! Great! Great! I must take some."

I wasn't watching but I think she thrust her hand into the opened packet of sugar and grabbed a handful and was about to put it into her handbag. Cletus dropped the kettle of hot water he was bringing in and pounced on her. *That* I saw clearly. For a brief moment she must have thought it was some kind of grotesque joke. I knew it wasn't and in that moment I came very near to loathing him. He seized her hand containing the sugar and began to prize it open, his teeth clenched.

"Stop it, Cletus!" I said.

"Stop, my arse," he said. "I am sick and tired of all these grab-grab girls."

"Leave me alone," she cried, sudden tears of anger and shame now running down her face. Somehow she succeeded in wrenching her hand free. Then she stepped back and threw the sugar full in his face, snatched her handbag and ran away, crying. He picked up the sugar, about half-a-dozen cubes.

"Sam!" shouted Cletus across to his houseboy. "Put some more water on the fire." And then turning to me he said again, his eyes glazed in crazy reminiscence: "Mike, you must tell them the battle I waged with sugar."

"He was called Sugar Baby at school," I said, dodging again.

"Oh, Mike, you're no bloody good with stories. I wonder who ever recommended you for the Propaganda Directorate." The other two laughed. Beads of perspiration trembled on his forehead. He was desperate. He was on heat begging, pleading, touting for the sumptuous agony of flagellation.

"And he lost his girlfriend," I said turning brutal. "Yes, he lost a nice, decent girl because he wouldn't part with half-a-dozen cubes of the sugar I bought him."

"You know that's not fair," he said turning on me sharply. "Nice girl indeed! Mercy was just a shameless grabber like all the rest of them."

"Like all the rest of us. What interests me, Cletus, is that you didn't find out all those months you went with her and slept with her until I brought you a packet of sugar. Then your eyes were opened."

"We know *you* brought it, Mike. You've told us already. But that's not the point . . ."

"What then is the point?" Then I realized how foolish it was and how easy, even now, to slip back into those sudden irrational acrimonies of our recent desperate days when an angry word dropping in unannounced would start a fierce war like the passage of Esun between two peace-loving friends. So I steered myself to a retrieving joke, retrieving albeit with a razor-edge.

"When Cletus is ready to marry," I said, "they will have to devise a special marriage vow for him. With all my worldly goods—except my Tate and Lyle—I thee honour. Father Doherty if they ever let him back in the country will no doubt understand."

Umera and his friend laughed again.

The Way of the Wind

Amos Oz

❧

1

Gideon Shenhav's last day began with a brilliant sunrise.

The dawn was gentle, almost autumnal. Faint flashes of light flickered through the wall of cloud that sealed off the eastern horizon. Slyly the new day concealed its purpose, betraying no hint of the heat wave that lay enfolded in its bosom.

Purple glowed on the eastern heights, fanned by the morning breeze. Then the rays pierced through the wall of cloud. It was day. Dark loopholes blinked awake at daylight's touch. Finally the incandescent sphere rose, assaulted the mountains of cloud, and broke their ranks. The eastern horizon was adazzle. And the soft purple yielded and fled before the terrible crimson blaze.

The camp was shaken by reveille a few minutes before sunrise. Gideon rose, padded barefoot out of his hut, and, still asleep, looked at the gathering light. With one thin hand he shaded his eyes, still yearning for sleep, while the other automatically buttoned up his battle dress. He could already hear voices and metallic sounds; a few eager boys were cleaning their guns for morning inspection. But Gideon was slow. The sunrise had stirred a weary restlessness inside him, perhaps a vague longing. The sunrise was over, but still he stood there drowsily, until he was pushed from behind and told to get cracking.

He went back into the hut, straightened his camp bed, cleaned his submachine gun, and picked up his shaving kit. On his way, among whitewashed eucalyptus trees and clustering notices commending tidiness and discipline, he suddenly remembered that today was Independence Day, the Fifth of Iyar. And today the platoon was to mount a celebratory parachute display in the Valley of Jezreel. He entered the washroom and, while he waited for a free mirror, brushed his teeth and thought of pretty girls. In an hour and a half the preparations would be complete and the platoon would be airborne, on its way to its destination. Throngs of excited civilians would be waiting for them to jump, and the girls would be there, too. The drop would take place just outside Nof Harish, the kibbutz that was Gideon's home, where he had been born and brought up until the day he joined the army. The moment his feet touched the ground, the children of the kibbutz would close around him and jump all over him and shout, "Gideon, look, here's our Gideon!"

He pushed in between two much bigger soldiers and began to lather his face and try to shave.

"Hot day," he said.

One of the soldiers answered, "Not yet. But it soon will be."

And another soldier behind him grumbled. "Hurry it up. Don't spend all day jawing."

Gideon did not take offense. On the contrary, the words filled him with a surge of joy for some reason. He dried his face and went out onto the parade ground. The blue light had changed meanwhile to gray-white, the grubby glare of a *khamsin*.

2

Shimshon Sheinbaum had confidently predicted the previous night that a *khamsin* was on its way. As soon as he got up he hurried over to the window and confirmed with calm satisfaction that he had been right yet again. He closed the shutters, to protect the room from the hot wind, then washed his face and his shaggy shoulders and chest, shaved, and prepared his breakfast, coffee with a roll brought last night from the dining hall. Shimshon Sheinbaum loathed wasting time, especially in the productive morning hours: you go out, walk to the dining hall, have a chat, read the paper, discuss the news, and that's half the morning gone. So he always made do with a cup of coffee and a roll, and by ten past six, after the early news summary, Gideon Shenhav's father was sitting at his desk. Summer and winter alike, with no concessions.

He sat at his desk and stared for a few minutes at the map of the country that hung on the opposite wall. He was straining to recapture a nagging dream which had taken hold of him in the early hours, just before he had awakened. But it eluded him. Shimshon decided to get on with his work and not waste another minute. True, today was a holiday, but the best way to celebrate was to work, not to slack off. Before it was time to go out and watch the parachutists— and Gideon, who might actually be among them and not drop out at the last minute—he still had several hours of working time. A man of seventy-five cannot afford to squander his hours, especially if there are many, painfully many, things he must set down in writing. So little time.

The name of Shimshon Sheinbaum needs no introduction. The Hebrew Labor Movement knows how to honor its founding fathers, and for decades now Shimshon Sheinbaum's name has been invested with a halo of enduring fame. For decades he has fought body and soul to realize the vision of his youth. Setbacks and disappointments have not shattered or weakened his faith but, rather, have enriched it with a vein of wise sadness. The better he has come to understand the weakness of others and their ideological deviations, the more ferociously he has fought against his own weaknesses. He has sternly eliminated them, and lived according to his principles, with a ruthless self-discipline and not without a certain secret joy.

At this moment, between six and seven o'clock on this Independence Day morning, Shimshon Sheinbaum is not yet a bereaved father. But his features are extraordinarily well suited to the role. A solemn, sagacious expression, of one who sees all but betrays no reaction, occupies his furrowed face. And his blue eyes express an ironic melancholy.

He sits erect at his desk, his head bent over the pages. His elbows are relaxed. The desk is made of plain wood, like the rest of the furniture, which is all functional and unembellished. More like a monastic cell than a bungalow in a long-established kibbutz.

This morning will not be particularly productive. Time and again his thoughts wander to the dream that flickered and died at the end of the night. He must recapture the dream, and then he will be able to forget it and concentrate on his work. There was a hose, yes, and some sort of goldfish or something. An argument with someone. No connection. Now to work. The Poalei Zion Movement appears to have been built from the start on an ideological contradiction that could never be bridged, and which it only succeeded in disguising by means of verbal acrobatics. But the contradiction is only apparent, and anyone who hopes to exploit it to undermine or attack the movement does not know what he is talking about. And here is the simple proof.

Shimshon Sheinbaum's rich experience of life has taught him how arbitrary, how senseless is the hand that guides the vagaries of our fate, that of the individual and that of the community alike. His sobriety has not robbed him of the straightforwardness which has animated him since his youth. His most remarkable and admirable characteristic is his stubborn innocence, like that of our pure, pious forebears, whose sagacity never injured their faith. Sheinbaum has never allowed his actions to be cut loose from his words. Even though some of the leaders of our movement have drifted into political careers and cut themselves off completely from manual labor, Sheinbaum has never abandoned the kibbutz. He has turned down all outside jobs and assignments, and it was only with extreme reluctance that he accepted nomination to the General Workers' Congress. Until a few years ago his days were divided equally between physical and intellectual work: three days gardening, three days theorizing. The beautiful gardens of Nof Harish are largely his handiwork. We can remember how he used to plant and prune and lop, water and hoe, manure, transplant, weed, and dig up. He did not permit his status as the leading thinker of the movement to exempt him from the duties to which every rank-and-file member is liable: he served as night watchman, took his turn in the kitchens, helped with the harvest. No shadow of a double standard has ever clouded the path of Shimshon Sheinbaum's life; he is a single complex of vision and execution, he has known no slackness or weakness of will—so the secretary of the movement wrote about him in a magazine a few years ago, on the occasion of his seventieth birthday.

True, there have been moments of stabbing despair. There have been moments of deep disgust. But Shimshon Sheinbaum knows how to transform such moments into secret sources of furious energy. Like the words of the marching song he loves, which always inspires him to a frenzy of action: *Up into the mountains we are climbing, Climbing up toward the dawning day; We have left all our yesterdays behind us, But tomorrow is a long long way away.* If only that stupid dream would emerge from the shadows and show itself clearly, he could kick it out of his mind and concentrate at last on his work. Time is slipping by. A rubber hose, a chess gambit, some goldfish, a great argument, but what is the connection?

For many years Shimshon Sheinbaum has lived alone. He has channeled all his vigor into his ideological productions. To this life's work he has sacrificed the warmth of a family home. He has managed, in exchange, to retain into old age a youthful clarity and cordiality. Only when he was fifty-six did he suddenly marry Raya Greenspan and father Gideon, and after that he left her and returned to his ideological work. It would be sanctimonious to pretend, however, that before his marriage Shimshon Sheinbaum maintained a monastic existence. His personality attracted women just as it attracted disciples. He was still young when his thick mop of hair turned white, and his sunbeaten face was etched with an appealing pattern of lines and wrinkles. His square back, his strong shoulders, the timbre of his voice—always warm, skeptical, and rather ruminative—and also his solitude, all attracted women to him like fluttering birds. Gossip attributes to his loins at least one of the urchins of the kibbutz, and elsewhere, too, stories are current. But we shall not dwell on this.

At the age of fifty-six Shimshon Sheinbaum decided that it befitted him to beget a son and heir to bear his stamp and his name into the coming generation. And so he conquered Raya Greenspan, a diminutive girl with a stammer who was thirty-three years his junior. Three months after the wedding, which was solemnized before a restricted company, Gideon was born. And before the kibbutz had recovered from its amazement, Shimshon sent Raya back to her former room and rededicated himself to his ideological work. This episode caused various ripples, and, indeed, it was preceded by painful heart-searchings in Shimshon Sheinbaum himself.

Now let's concentrate and think logically. Yes, it's coming back. She came to my room and called me to go there quickly to put a stop to that scandal. I didn't ask any questions, but hurried after her. Someone had had the nerve to dig a pond in the lawn in front of the dining hall, and I was seething because no one had authorized such an innovation, an ornamental pond in front of the dining hall, like some Polish squire's château. I shouted. Who at, there is no clear picture. There were goldfish in the pond. And a boy was filling it with water from a black rubber hose. So I decided to put a stop to the whole performance there and then, but the boy wouldn't listen to me. I started walking along the hose to find the faucet and cut off the water before anybody managed to establish the pond as a *fait accompli*. I walked and walked until I suddenly discovered that I was walking in a circle, and the hose was not connected to a faucet but simply came back to the pond and sucked up water from it. Stuff and nonsense. That's the end of it. The original platform of the Poalei Zion

Movement must be understood without any recourse to dialectics, it must be taken literally, word for word.

3

After his separation from Raya Greenspan, Shimshon Sheinbaum did not neglect his duties as his son's mentor, nor did he disclaim responsibility. He lavished on him, from the time the boy was six or seven, the full warmth of his personality. Gideon, however, turned out to be something of a disappointment, not the stuff of which dynasties are founded. As a child he was always sniveling. He was a slow, bewildered child, mopping up blows and insults without retaliating, a strange child, always playing with candy wrappers, dried leaves, silkworms. And from the age of twelve he was constantly having his heart broken by girls of all ages. He was always lovesick, and he published sad poems and cruel parodies in the children's newsletter. A dark, gentle youth, with an almost feminine beauty, who walked the paths of the kibbutz in obstinate silence. He did not shine at work; he did not shine in communal life. He was slow of speech and no doubt also of thought. His poems seemed to Shimshon incorrigibly sentimental, and his parodies venomous, without a trace of inspiration. The nickname Pinocchio suited him, there is no denying it. And the infuriating smiles he was perpetually spreading on his face seemed to Shimshon a depressingly exact replica of the smiles of Raya Greenspan.

And then, eighteen months before, Gideon had amazed his father. He suddenly appeared and asked for his written permission to enlist in the paratroopers—as an only son this required the written consent of both parents. Only when Shimshon Sheinbaum was convinced that this was not one of his son's outrageous jokes did he agree to give his consent. And then he gave it gladly: this was surely an encouraging turn in the boy's development. They'd make a man of him there. Let him go. Why not.

But Raya Greenspan's stubborn opposition raised an unexpected obstacle to Gideon's plan. No, she wouldn't sign the paper. On no account. Never.

Shimshon himself went to her room one evening, pleaded with her, reasoned with her, shouted at her. All in vain. She wouldn't sign. No reason, she just wouldn't. So Shimshon Sheinbaum had to resort to devious means to enable the boy to enlist. He wrote a private letter to Yolek himself, asking a personal favor. He wished his son to be allowed to volunteer. The mother was emotionally unstable. The boy would make a first-rate paratrooper. Shimshon himself accepted full responsibility. And incidentally, he had never before asked a personal favor. And he never would again. This was the one and only time in his whole life. He begged Yolek to see what he could do.

At the end of September, when the first signs of autumn were appearing in the orchards, Gideon Shenhav was enrolled in a parachute unit.

From that time on, Shimshon Sheinbaum immersed himself more deeply than ever in ideological work, which is the only real mark a man can leave on the world. Shimshon Sheinbaum has made a mark on the Hebrew Labor Movement that can never be erased. Old age is still far off. At seventy-five he still has hair as thick as ever, and his muscles are firm and powerful. His eyes are alert, his mind attentive. His strong, dry, slightly cracked voice still works wonders on women of all ages. His bearing is restrained, his manner modest. Needless to say, he is deeply rooted in the soil of Nof Harish. He loathes assemblies and formal ceremonies, not to mention commissions and official appointments. With his pen alone he has inscribed his name on the roll of honor of our movement and our nation.

4

Gideon Shenhav's last day began with a brilliant sunrise. He felt he could even see the beads of dew evaporating in the heat. Omens blazed on the mountain peaks far away to the east. This was a day of celebration, a celebration of independence and a celebration of parachuting over the familiar fields of home. All that night he had nestled in a half-dream of dark autumnal forests under northern skies, a rich smell of autumn, huge trees he could not name. All night long pale leaves had been dropping on the huts of the camp. Even after he had awakened in the morning, the northern forest with its nameless trees still continued to whisper in his ears.

Gideon adored the delicious moment of free fall between the jump from the aircraft and the unfolding of the parachute. The void rushes up toward you at lightning speed, fierce drafts of air lick at your body, making you dizzy with pleasure. The speed is drunken, reckless, it whistles and roars and your whole body trembles to it, red-hot needles work at your nerve ends, and your heart pounds. Suddenly, when you are lightning in the wind, the chute opens. The straps check your fall, like a firm, masculine arm bringing you calmly under control. You can feel its supporting strength under your armpits. The reckless thrill gives way to a more sedate pleasure. Slowly your body swings through the air, floats, hesitates, drifts a little way on the slight breeze, you can

never guess precisely where your feet will touch ground, on the slope
of that hill or next to the orange groves over there, and like an exhausted migrating bird you slowly descend, seeing roofs, roads, cows
in the meadow, slowly as if you have a choice, as if the decision is entirely yours.

And then the ground is under your feet, and you launch into the
practiced somersault which will soften the impact of landing. Within
seconds you must sober up. The coursing blood slows down. Dimensions return to normal. Only a weary pride survives in your heart
until you rejoin your commanding officer and your comrades and
you're caught up in the rhythm of frenzied reorganization.

This time it is all going to happen over Nof Harish.

The older folk will raise their clammy hands, push back their
caps, and try to spot Gideon among the gray dots dangling in the
sky. The kids will rush around in the fields, also waiting excitedly
for their hero to touch down. Mother will come out of the dining
hall and stand peering upward, muttering to herself. Shimshon will
leave his desk for a while, perhaps take a chair out onto his little
porch and watch the whole performance with pensive pride.

Then the kibbutz will entertain the unit. Pitchers of lemonade
glistening with chilly perspiration will be set out in the dining hall,
there will be crates of apples, or perhaps cakes baked by the older
women, iced with congratulatory phrases.

By six-thirty the sun had grown out of its colorful caprice and
risen ruthlessly over the eastern mountain heights. A thick heat
weighed heavily on the whole scene. The tin roofs of the camp huts
reflected a dazzling glare. The walls began to radiate a dense, oppres-
sive warmth into the huts. On the main road, which passed close to

the perimeter fence, a lively procession of buses and trucks was already in motion: the residents of the villages and small towns were streaming to the big city to watch the military parade. Their white shirts could be discerned dimly through the clouds of dust, and snatches of exuberant song could be caught in the distance.

The paratroopers had completed their morning inspection. The orders of the day, signed by the Chief of Staff, had been read out and posted on the bulletin boards. A festive breakfast had been served, including a hard-boiled egg reposing on a lettuce leaf ringed with olives.

Gideon, his dark hair flopping forward onto his forehead, broke into a quiet song. The others joined him. Here and there someone altered the words, making them comical or even obscene. Soon the Hebrew songs gave way to a guttural, almost desperate Arabic wail. The platoon commander, a blond, good-looking officer whose exploits were feted around the campfires at night, stood up and said: That's enough. The paratroopers stopped singing, hastily downed the last of their greasy coffee, and moved toward the runways. Here there was another inspection; the commanding officer spoke a few words of endearment to his men, calling them "the salt of the earth," and then ordered them into the waiting aircraft.

The squadron commanders stood at the doors of the planes and checked each belt and harness. The CO himself circulated among the men, patting a shoulder, joking, predicting, enthusing, for all the world as though they were going into battle and facing real danger. Gideon responded to the pat on his shoulder with a hasty smile. He was lean, almost ascetic-looking, but very suntanned. A sharp eye, that of the legendary blond commander, could spot the blue vein throbbing in his neck.

Then the heat broke into the shady storage sheds, mercilessly flushing out the last strongholds of coolness, roasting everything with a gray glow. The sign was given. The engines gave a throaty roar. Birds fled from the runway. The planes shuddered, moved forward heavily, and began to gather the momentum without which takeoff cannot be achieved.

5

I must get out and be there to shake his hand.

Having made up his mind, Sheinbaum closed his notebook. The months of military training have certainly toughened the boy. It is hard to believe, but it certainly looks as though he is beginning to mature at last. He still has to learn how to handle women. He has to free himself once and for all from his shyness and his sentimentality: he should leave such traits to women and cultivate toughness in himself. And how he has improved at chess. Soon he'll be a serious challenge to his old father. May even beat me one of these days. Not just yet, though. As long as he doesn't up and marry the first girl who gives herself to him. He ought to break one or two of them in before he gets spliced. In a few years he'll have to give me some grandchildren. Lots of them. Gideon's children will have two fathers: my son can take care of them, and I'll take care of their ideas. The second generation grew up in the shadow of our achievements; that's why they're so confused. It's a matter of dialectics. But the third generation will be a wonderful synthesis, a successful outcome: they will inherit the spontaneity of their parents and the spirit of their grandparents. It will be a glorious heritage distilled from a twisted pedigree. I'd better jot that phrase down, it will come in handy one of these days. I feel so sad when I think of Gideon and his friends: they exude such an air of shallow despair, of nihilism, of cynical mockery. They can't love wholeheartedly, and they can't hate wholeheartedly, either. No enthusiasm, and no loathing. I'm not one to deprecate despair per se. Despair is the eternal twin of faith, but that's real despair, virile and passionate, not this sentimental, poetic melancholy. Sit still, Gideon, stop scratching yourself, stop biting your nails. I want to read you a marvelous passage from Brenner. All right, make a face. So I won't read. Go outside and grow up to be a Bedouin, if that's what you want. But if you don't get to know Brenner, you'll never understand the first thing about despair or about faith. You won't find any soppy poems here about jackals caught in traps or flowers in the autumn. In Brenner, everything is on fire. Love, and hatred as well. Maybe you yourselves won't see light and darkness face to face, but your children will. A glorious heritage will be distilled from a twisted pedigree. And we won't let the third generation be pampered and corrupted by sentimental verses by decadent poetesses. Here come the planes now. We'll put Brenner back on the shelf and get ready to be proud of you for a change, Gideon Sheinbaum.

6

Sheinbaum strode purposefully across the lawn, stepped up onto the concrete path, and turned toward the plowed field in the southwest corner of the kibbutz, which had been selected for the landing. On his way he paused now and again at a flower bed to pull up a stray weed skulking furtively beneath a flowering shrub. His small blue eyes had always been amazingly skillful at detecting weeds. Admittedly, because of his age he had retired a few years previously from his work in the gardens, but until his dying day he would not cease to scan the flower beds mercilessly in search of undesirable intruders. At such moments he thought of the boy, forty years his junior, who had succeeded him as gardener and who fancied himself as the local water-colorist. He had inherited beautifully tended gardens, and now they were all going to seed before our very eyes.

A gang of excited children ran across his path. They were fiercely absorbed in a detailed argument about the types of aircraft that were circling above the valley. Because they were running, the argument was being carried out in loud shouts and gasps. Shimshon seized one of them by the shirttail, forcibly brought him to a halt, put his face close to the child's, and said:

"You are Zaki."

"Leave me alone," the child replied.

Sheinbaum said: "What's all this shouting? Airplanes, is that all you've got in your heads? And running across the flower beds like that where it says Keep Off, is that right? Do you think you can do whatever you like? Are there no rules any more? Look at me when I'm speaking to you. And give me a proper answer, or . . ."

But Zaki had taken advantage of the flood of words to wriggle out of the man's grasp and tear himself free. He slipped in among the bushes, made a monkey face, and stuck out his tongue.

Sheinbaum pursed his lips. He thought for an instant about old age, but instantly thrust it out of his mind and said to himself: All right. We'll see about that later. Zaki, otherwise Azariah. Rapid calculation showed that he must be at least eleven, perhaps twelve already. A hooligan. A wild beast.

Meanwhile the young trainees had occupied a vantage point high up on top of the water tower, from which they could survey the length and breadth of the valley. The whole scene reminded Shein-baum of a Russian painting. For a moment he was tempted to climb up and join the youngsters on top of the tower, to watch the display comfortably from a distance. But the thought of the manly hand-shake to come kept him striding steadily on, till he reached the edge of the field. Here he stood, his legs planted well apart, his arms folded on his chest, his thick white hair falling impressively over his forehead. He craned his neck and followed the two transport planes with steady gray eyes. The mosaic of wrinkles on his face en-riched his expression with a rare blend of pride, thoughtfulness, and a trace of well-controlled irony. And his bushy white eyebrows suggested a saint in a Russian icon. Meanwhile the planes had com-pleted their first circuit, and the leading one was approaching the field again.

Shimshon Sheinbaum's lips parted and made way for a low hum. An old Russian tune was throbbing in his chest. The first batch of men emerged from the opening in the plane's side. Small dark shapes were dotted in space, like seeds scattered by a farmer in an old pio-neering print.

Then Raya Greenspan stuck her head out of the window of the kitchen and gesticulated with the ladle she was holding as though ad-monishing the treetops. Her face was hot and flushed. Perspiration stuck her plain dress to her strong, hairy legs. She panted, scratched at her disheveled hair with the fingernails of her free hand, and suddenly turned and shouted to the other women working in the kitchens:

"Quick! Come to the window! It's Gidi up there! Gidi in the sky!"
And just as suddenly she was struck dumb.

While the first soldiers were still floating gently, like a handful of feathers, between heaven and earth, the second plane came in and dropped Gideon Shenhav's group. The men stood pressed close together inside the hatch, chest against back, their bodies fused into a single tense, sweating mass. When Gideon's turn came he gritted his teeth, braced his knees, and leapt out as though from the womb into the bright hot air. A long wild scream of joy burst from his throat as he fell. He could see his childhood haunts rushing up toward him as he fell he could see the roofs and treetops and he smiled a frantic smile of greeting as he fell toward the vineyards and concrete paths and sheds and gleaming pipes with joy in his heart as he fell. Never in his whole life had he known such overwhelming, spine-tingling love. All his muscles were tensed, and gushing thrills burst in his stomach and up his spine to the roots of his hair. He screamed for love like a madman, his fingernails almost drawing blood from his clenched palms. Then the straps drew taut and caught him under the armpits. His waist was clasped in a tight embrace. For a moment he felt as though an invisible hand were pulling him back up toward the plane into the heart of the sky. The delicious falling sensation was replaced by a slow, gentle swaying, like rocking in a cradle or floating in warm water. Suddenly a wild panic hit him. How will they recognize me down there. How will they manage to identify their only son in this forest of white parachutes. How will they be able to fix me and me alone with their anxious, loving gaze. Mother and Dad and the pretty girls and the little kids and everyone. I mustn't just get lost in the crowd. After all, this is me, and I'm the one they love.

That moment an idea flashed through Gideon's mind. He put his hand up to his shoulder and pulled the cord to release the spare chute, the one intended for emergencies. As the second canopy opened overhead he slowed down as though the force of gravity had lost its hold on him. He seemed to be floating alone in the void, like a gull or a lonely cloud. The last of his comrades had landed in the soft earth and were folding up their parachutes. Gideon Shenhav alone continued to hover as though under a spell with two large canopies spread out above him. Happy, intoxicated, he drank in the hundreds of eyes fixed on him. On him alone. In his glorious isolation.

As though to lend further splendor to the spectacle, a strong, almost cool breeze burst from the west, plowing through the hot air, playing with the spectators' hair, and carrying slightly eastward the last of the parachutists.

7

Far away in the big city, the massed crowds waiting for the military parade greeted the sudden sea breeze with a sigh of relief. Perhaps it marked the end of the heat wave. A cool, salty smell caressed the baking streets. The breeze freshened. It whistled fiercely in the treetops, bent the stiff spines of the cypresses, ruffled the hair of the pines, raised eddies of dust, and blurred the scene for the spectators at the parachute display. Regally, like a huge solitary bird, Gideon Shenhav was carried eastward toward the main road.

The terrified shout that broke simultaneously from a hundred throats could not reach the boy. Singing aloud in an ecstatic trance, he continued to sway slowly toward the main electric cables, stretched between their enormous pylons. The watchers stared in horror at the suspended soldier and the powerlines that crossed the valley with unfaltering straightness from west to east. The five parallel cables, sagging with their own weight between the pylons, hummed softly in the gusty breeze.

Gideon's two parachutes tangled in the upper cable. A moment later his feet landed on the lower one. His body hung backward in a slanting pose. The straps held his waist and shoulders fast, preventing him from falling into the soft plowland. Had he not been insulated by the thick soles of his boots, the boy would have been struck dead at the moment of impact. As it was, the cable was already protesting its unwonted-burden by scorching his soles. Tiny sparks flashed and crackled under Gideon's feet. He held tight with both hands to the buckles on the straps. His eyes were open wide and his mouth was agape.

Immediately a short officer, perspiring heavily, leapt out of the petrified crowd and shouted:

"Don't touch the cables, Gidi. Stretch your body backward and keep as clear as you can!"

The whole tightly packed, panic-stricken crowd began to edge slowly in an easterly direction. There were shouts. There was a wail. Sheinbaum silenced them with his metallic voice and ordered everyone to keep calm. He broke into a fast run, his feet pounding on the soft earth, reached the spot, pushed aside the officers and curious bystanders, and instructed his son:

"Quickly, Gideon, release the straps and drop. The ground is soft here. It's perfectly safe. Jump."

"I can't."

"Don't argue. Do as I tell you. Jump."

"I can't, Dad, I can't do it."

"No such thing as can't. Release the straps and jump before you electrocute yourself."

"I can't, the straps are tangled. Tell them to switch off the current quickly, Dad, my boots are burning."

Some of the soldiers were trying to hold back the crowd, discourage well-meaning suggestions, and make more room under the powerlines. They kept repeating, as if it were an incantation, "Don't panic please don't panic."

The youngsters of the kibbutz were rushing all around, adding to the confusion. Reprimands and warnings had no effect. Two angry paratroopers managed to catch Zaki, who was idiotically climbing the nearest pylon, snorting and whistling and making faces to attract the attention of the crowd.

The short officer suddenly shouted: "Your knife. You've got a knife in your belt. Get it out and cut the straps!"

But Gideon either could not or would not hear. He began to sob aloud.

"Get me down, Dad, I'll be electrocuted, tell them to get me down from here, I can't get down on my own."

"Stop sniveling," his father said curtly. "You've been told to use your knife to cut the straps. Now, do as you've been told. And stop sniveling."

The boy obeyed. He was still sobbing audibly, but he groped for the knife, located it, and cut the straps one by one. The silence was total. Only Gideon's sobbing, a strange, piercing sound, was to be heard intermittently. Finally one last strap was left holding him, which he did not dare to cut.

"Cut it," the children shrilled, "cut it and jump. Let's see you do it."

And Shimshon added in a level voice, "Now what are you waiting for?"

"I can't do it," Gideon pleaded.

"Of course you can," said his father.

"The current." the boy wept. "I can feel the current. Get me down quickly."

His father's eyes filled with blood as he roared:

"You coward! You ought to be ashamed of yourself!"

"But I can't do it, I'll break my neck, it's too high."

"You can do it and you must do it. You're a fool, that's what you are, a fool and a coward."

A group of jet planes passed overhead on their way to the aerial display over the city. They were flying in precise formation, thundering westward like a pack of wild dogs. As the planes disappeared, the silence seemed twice as intense. Even the boy had stopped crying. He let the knife fall to the ground. The blade pierced the earth at Shimshon Sheinbaum's feet.

"What did you do that for?" the short officer shouted.

"I didn't mean it," Gideon whined. "It just slipped out of my hand."

Shimshon Sheinbaum bent down, picked up a small stone, straightened up, and threw it furiously at his son's back.

"Pinocchio, you're a wet rag, you're a miserable coward!"

At this point the sea breeze also dropped.

The heat wave returned with renewed vigor to oppress both men and inanimate objects. A red-haired, freckled soldier muttered to himself, "He's scared to jump, the idiot, he'll kill himself if he stays up there." And a skinny, plain-faced girl, hearing this, rushed into the middle of the circle and spread her arms wide:

"Jump into my arms, Gidi, you'll be all right."

"It would be interesting," remarked a veteran pioneer in working clothes, "to know whether anyone has had the sense to phone the electric company to ask them to switch off the current." He turned and started off toward the kibbutz buildings. He was striding quickly, angrily, up the slight slope when he was suddenly alarmed by a prolonged burst of firing close at hand. For a moment he imagined he was being shot at from behind. But at once he realized what was happening: the squadron commander, the good-looking blond hero, was trying to sever the electric cables with his machine gun.

Without success.

Meanwhile, a beaten-up truck arrived from the farmyard. Ladders were unloaded from it, followed by the elderly doctor, and finally a stretcher.

At that moment it was evident that Gideon had been struck by a sudden decision. Kicking out strongly, he pushed himself off the lower cable, which was emitting blue sparks, turned a somersault, and remained suspended by the single strap with his head pointing downward and his scorched boots beating the air a foot or so from the cable.

It was hard to be certain, but it looked as though so far he had not sustained any serious injury. He swung limply upside down in space, like a dead lamb suspended from a butcher's hook.

This spectacle provoked hysterical glee in the watching children. They barked with laughter. Zaki slapped his knees, choking and heaving convulsively. He leapt up and down screeching like a mischievous monkey.

What had Gideon Shenhav seen that made him suddenly stretch his neck and join in the children's laughter? Perhaps his peculiar posture had unbalanced his mind. His face was blood-red, his tongue protruded, his thick hair hung down, and only his feet kicked up at the sky.

8

A second group of jets plowed through the sky overhead. A dozen metallic birds, sculpted with cruel beauty, flashing dazzlingly in the bright sunlight. They flew in a narrow spearhead formation. Their fury shook the earth. On they flew to the west, and a deep silence followed.

Meanwhile, the elderly doctor sat down on the stretcher, lit a cigarette, blinked vaguely at the people, the soldiers, the scampering children, and said to himself: We'll see how things turn out. Whatever has to happen will happen. How hot it is today.

Every now and again Gideon let out another senseless laugh. His legs were flailing, describing clumsy circles in the dusty air. The blood had drained from his inverted limbs and was gathering in his head. His eyes were beginning to bulge. The world was turning dark. Instead of the crimson glow, purple spots were dancing before his eyes. He stuck his tongue out. The children interpreted this as a gesture of derision. "Upside-down Pinocchio," Zaki shrilled, "why don't you stop squinting at us, and try walking on your hands instead?"

Sheinbaum moved to hit the brat, but the blow landed on thin air because the child had leapt aside. The old man beckoned to the blond commander, and they held a brief consultation. The boy was in no immediate danger, because he was not in direct contact with the cable, but he must be rescued soon. This comedy could not go on forever. A ladder would not help much: he was too high up. Perhaps

the knife could be got up to him again somehow, and he could be per-
suaded to cut the last strap and jump into a sheet of canvas. After all,
it was a perfectly routine exercise in parachute training. The main
thing was to act quickly, because the situation was humiliating. Not to
mention the children. So the short officer removed his shirt and
wrapped a knife in it. Gideon stretched his hands downward and
tried to catch the bundle. It slipped between his outstretched arms
and plummeted uselessly to the ground. The children snickered.
Only after two more unsuccessful attempts did Gideon manage to
grasp the shirt and remove the knife. His fingers were numb and
heavy with blood. Suddenly he pressed the blade to his burning
cheek, enjoying the cool touch of the steel. It was a delicious moment. He opened his eyes and saw an inverted world. Everything
looked comical: the truck, the field, his father, the army, the kids, and
even the knife in his hand. He made a twisted face at the gang of children, gave a deep laugh, and waved at them with the knife. He tried to
say something. If only they could see themselves from up here, upside down, rushing around like startled ants, they would surely laugh
with him. But the laugh turned into a heavy cough; Gideon choked
and his eyes filled.

9

Gideon's upside-down antics filled Zaki with demonic glee.

"He's crying," he shouted cruelly, "Gideon's crying, look, you
can see the tears. Pinocchio the hero, he's sniveling with fear-o. We
can see you, we can."

Once again Shimshon Sheinbaum's fist fell ineffectually on thin air.

"Zaki," Gideon managed to shout in a dull, pain-racked voice,

"I'll kill you, I'll choke you, you little bastard." Suddenly he chuckled and stopped.

It was no good. He wouldn't cut the last strap by himself, and the doctor was afraid that if he stayed as he was much longer he was likely to lose consciousness. Some other solution would have to be found. This performance could not be allowed to go on all day.

And so the kibbutz truck rumbled across the plowland and braked at the point indicated by Shimshon Sbeinbaum. Two ladders were hastily lashed together to reach the required height, and then supported on the back of the truck by five strong pairs of hands. The legendary blond officer started to climb. But when he reached the place where the two ladders overlapped, there was an ominous creak, and the wood began to bend with the weight and the height. The officer, a largish man, hesitated for a moment. He decided to retreat and fasten the ladders together more securely. He climbed down to the floor of the truck, wiped the sweat from his forehead, and said, "Wait, I'm thinking." Just then, in the twinkling of an eye, before he could be stopped, before he could even be spotted, the child Zaki had climbed high up the ladder, past the join, and leapt like a frantic monkey up onto the topmost rungs; suddenly he was clutching a knife—where on earth had he got it from? He wrestled with the taut strap. The spectators held their breath: he seemed to be defying gravity, not holding on, not caring, hopping on the top rung, nimble, lithe, amazingly efficient.

10

The heat beat down violently on the hanging youth. His eyes were growing dimmer. His breathing had almost stopped. With his last glimmer of lucidity he saw his ugly brother in front of him and felt his breath on his face. He could smell him. He could see the pointed teeth protruding from Zaki's mouth. A terrible fear closed in on him, as though he were looking in a mirror and seeing a monster. The nightmare roused Gideon's last reserves of strength. He kicked into space, flailed, managed to turn over, seized the strap, and pulled himself up. With outstretched arms he threw himself onto the cable and saw the flash. The hot wind continued to tyrannize the whole valley. And a third cluster of jets drowned the scene with its roaring.

11

The status of a bereaved father invests a man with a saintly aura of suffering. But Sheinbaum gave no thought to this aura. A stunned, silent company escorted him toward the dining hall. He knew, with utter certainty, that his place now was beside Raya.

On the way he saw the child Zaki, glowing, breathless, a hero. Surrounded by other youngsters: he had almost rescued Gideon. Shimshon laid a trembling hand on his child's head, and tried to tell him. His voice abandoned him and his lips quivered. Clumsily he stroked the tousled, dusty mop of hair. It was the first time he had ever stroked the child. A few steps later, everything went dark and the old man collapsed in a flower bed.

As Independence Day drew to a close the *khamsin* abated. A fresh sea breeze soothed the steaming walls. There was a heavy fall of dew on the lawns in the night.

What does the pale ring around the moon portend? Usually it

heralds a *khamsin*. Tomorrow, no doubt, the heat will return. It is May, and June will follow. A wind drifts among the cypresses in the night, trying to comfort them between one heat wave and the next. It is the way of the wind to come and to go and to come again. There is nothing new.

translated by Nicholas de Lange
and Philip Simpson

Warm Dogs

Paul Theroux

❧

When the broker's message came that a child was available the Raths went home and put their suits on and made love in a solemn methodical way, as though mimicking conception. Afterwards they peeled their clothes off and lay exhausted, in the bubble of the balcony Arvin and Hella themselves had designed, eagerly speculating about the broker's child. He called himself a broker. But he was probably just an opportunist who knew someone as desperate to sell a child as they were desperate to buy one.

Their bare skin was an alarming color—nothing to do with having just taken off the body suits. It was the light from the lurid sunset over the western suburbs—that distant mountain range was a mirage made of a low cloud of risen, suspended dust that turned the slipping sun into a misshapen solitaire the color of dried blood. It lighted their naked bodies with garish blooms of good health and mocked their sterility. Yet most of their friends were infected, and—though it was never simple—those people had found children for themselves. One consequence of having tested positive was that it made the Raths single-minded in their urgent search for a child.

Eight times they had been notified and so the lovemaking had become a ritual, but each time something had gone wrong. They were more hopeful, even though now the risk was great: it meant a trip across the river over that awful bridge to a neighborhood on the East Bank.

Scowling at the damp body suit that lay crumpled on the bed beside her like the pelt of a gutted animal, Hella brushed it to the floor. In a pious tone that made her nakedness pathetic, she said "God, I hope it works out," adding, like an imploring one-word prayer, "Please."

Arvin said, "We'll be fine."

Hella knew what he would say next, since he had said it so many times before.

"I can test for anything," Arvin said.

That was the challenge—one of the challenges. Children were available, but were they healthy? Some had parasites, others had drugs in their system; some were diseased or brain damaged, some were unbalanced. Many had no papers—brokers had caught twice the Raths that way, offered smuggled infants. You could not trust anyone, which was why Arvin had discreetly advertised for his own broker and ignored all the ones who had come to him through the network, having heard that the Raths were desperate.

When Hella told him that it was across the bridge, he did not wince as their friends had at the thought of the East Bank.

Hella said, "It's one of those neighborhoods."

Arvin had not said anything, so she knew he had a plan. You needed a plan. The East Bank police were private, but that was only part of the problem. Many of the neighborhoods were sealed, like fortress villages, and were dangerous to outsiders. These days only humans had money value and so some were valuable and some were cheap, and a child might cost anything.

The prospect of getting a child gave the Raths the courage to risk the bridge. They knew that what they were doing was illegal; that what they were planning was an abduction. Yet a child meant everything to them, not only because they were sterile: a child was the future.

They had not told anyone of the broker. Which of their friends knew anything about the East Bank anyway? The previous eight disappointments had been shared and piteously clucked over. Even the persistent party talk—"We got one in Poland," "The Gold-stones found one in Mexico," all that—did not draw them out. You might have thought they were talking about puppies. The Raths, who had had many, were sick of pets and were no longer comforted by warm dogs.

Nor were they dismayed by the adoption stories which had turned out badly—the Bences' Rumanian infant girl who had been diagnosed as a vector after a year, and had to be destroyed; the Feer-icks' boy Ivor, from Russia, who had shot himself in a motel on his twelfth birthday; all the tales of runaways, adoptees who had fled to places like the East Bank and lived like the drifters they called Skells, or the squatters known as Trolls.

"I can test for epilepsy, I can find viruses, I can look into hered-ity, I can diagnose depression and potential malfunction, I can do brain scans, I can isolate a vector," Arvin said. "I can find any-thing."

He had confidence in his tests, but where was the child who could pass them? His sophisticated instruments meant frequent dis-appointment. Five times he had examined infants in brokers' offices and found dysfunction or systemic problems. And there were the two without papers.

Arvin was a lighting engineer, Hella an architect. Their apartment, an entire floor of a Kingsbury tower, was vast and beautiful, it lacked a child, but that was all. They had the virus but that was no disgrace—it wasn't fatal. Half the people they knew had it. You were inconvenienced by it, you were sterile; you lost your teeth, but the new implants were less trouble.

"What was that?" Arvin asked, hurriedly putting on his robe, an instinctive defense at hearing a noise when he was naked.

Someone was calling, a piercing *peep-peep* filled the room.

"It's my phone," Hella said and slipped it over her left hand and activated it. "Hello?"

"Calling the Raths," the voice said. "This is Doc."

The broker, Hella mouthed to Arvin, and then increased the speaker volume and said, "Is it still on?"

"Sooner than I thought. Can you come first thing tomorrow. Say six?"

That threw them, and Arvin considered this, becoming so engrossed, his face seemed sculpted and pale and doubtful.

"Why so early?" Hella said, prompted by Arvin's suspicious stare.

"The bridge will be clear and it'll be easier for you to find us."

"We're not finding you," Arvin said suddenly, facing the tiny phone. "You find us—in Elmo. The station parking lot. I've got a red van."

The puzzled voice at the other end said, "A van?"

"For my instruments. I'm running some tests."

"You're better off on the surface streets."

"Elmo," Arvin said, insisting.

What followed was not so much silence as scarcely audible

consternation, like someone mumbling to himself or to another person close by—a lengthy murmuring pause.

"Okay," the man said at last.

"How do you know Elmo?" Hella asked afterwards.

"I was there about twenty years ago. We had a cleaner who lived in Elmo. It was marginal then. But can it have changed that much?"

Watching as they drove across the bridge the East Bank seemed greener, denser, less settled to him than it had all those years ago, and they were hopeful again. On the horizon ahead, the sun at dawn was the same dusty solitaire they had seen last evening from the balcony, but inverted, a great lozenge of lighted dust rising in the cloud deck that looked tainted and fatigued. But there were trees here, there was long grass, and the old style of houses, and the fences were low and unthreatening; there were empty streets where they had expected savages and Skells.

"I feel right at home," Arvin said.

It made her nervous when he tried to be funny, because it meant he wasn't paying attention.

As she spoke they cleared the end of the ramp and the whirring from the echoes of the roadside trees suddenly ceased to drum against the sides of the van, and a different muffled sound began—of the sealed windowless buildings that looked like fortress walls. Then, in a place they least expected it, near an embankment wall, and a sign directing them to Elmo, where the surface streets began, there was a checkpoint, and a policeman. Arvin slowed the car to a crawl as he approached the barrier.

"Howdy," the policeman said in a friendly way, but still he did

not raise the steel barrier. It was mesh. Such barriers had been designed to snare tanks and armored vehicles and rogue trucks.

The policeman smiled and took a step back to see the van's plates.
His nametag was printed *Seely*. He was casual in the way of contract
police. His boots weren't shined, his badge was slightly crooked.
They were all overworked, nor were they paid as well as the state
troopers. But Arvin was reassured by the policeman, particularly
when he halted the van and saw the child.

The child just inside the checkpoint booth, was sitting on a
stool, a low one but even so his feet didn't touch the ground—he was
kicking them, driving his heels against the stool's hard legs with a
sort of frenzied East Bank vitality as he stabbed at the wall writing
RONG DOGZ.

"Where you headed?"

Arvin hesitated, hating the question, but he was still smiling at
the scribbling child.

The policeman said, "I'm asking you for your own good."

"Elmo. Is there a travel advisory?"

"Not today. But you want to be real careful." Gesturing with his
weapon, he pointed to the back of the van. "You got a load?"

"We're empty," Arvin said. "See you got a little helper."

Hearing this, the small boy's fleshy lips parted and his face drew
tight as he made his teeth protrude. They were new teeth, just grown,
and bulked in his mouth looking large and unused.

"Sure do," the policeman said, and waved them on.

Soon on the surface streets they had their first sight of local people—children, probably kids of Skells and Trolls. But they were not
scavenging, as people said. They looked just like the privileged children across the river who played outside, except that these were much
younger. There were terrible stories of brokers who had snatched

such children, saying, *It's not kidnapping—it's a form of rescue*, and found themselves with vicious, diseased or uncontrollable children who had no papers and had to be impounded.

"Let's make this quick," Arvin said, when he pulled into the Elmo parking lot and saw the cluster of hurrying people.

A man wearing a khaki shirt and khaki trousers, perhaps an old army uniform, was surrounded by about ten children, mostly boys, none of them more than twelve or thirteen. Several of the children watched Arvin and Hella intently as they drew in and parked the van. The other children were playing. One boy was operating a hand-held instrument and earphones, a game perhaps. The others were shouting much too loudly, and that was how Hella had been able to tell their ages—their voices hadn't broken. And their teeth too were large and ill fitting and crooked. Nothing about these children was more upsetting to Hella than these adult-sized teeth in their small ten-year-old jaws.

Arvin loathed the sight of the man with these children, the exploiter and the urchins; yet Hella became hopeful seeing the children so closely attentive or else frisking in the way all their small dogs had done.

"I'm Doc," said the man in khaki, shuffling forward, through the crowd of children. "Can I see your IDs?"

He was older than they had imagined him—too old perhaps to be the father of any of these children; but you never knew.

As Arvin showed his ID, a boy with long stringy, green-tinted hair crept close to him and looked at the phone on his wrist. His teeth did not fit his mouth; they bulged as he stared at Arvin, who made a point of indicating his phone.

He said, "I'm on an open channel," so as to caution them all. And then, "Can we see the child? I want to run some tests."

Doc satdown on a bench and tapped his own phone. He was watched intently by several other boys, the one with long hair, perhaps the eldest—thirteen at most—wore big borrowed-looking shoes, probably expensive, though they did not fit, and a shirt that hung to his knees like a dress. A girl walked behind him and, without meeting her eye, the boy reached out and pinched her arm. He turned then and stared as though defying her to scream. But she did not cry out. She pressed her lips together and squinted in dumb suffering.

Surely Doc had seen the boy do this? But the man said nothing.

The children looked bored and impatient and captive—they did not want to be here, she could tell. They looked warm and thirsty. She now remembered the child in the at the checkpoint scribbling RONG DOGZ on the wall of the policeman's boot.

Hella said, "Are they for sale, too?"

She had spoken softly, so that only the man would hear, yet the boy had heard and he gave her a sudden look of scowling malevolence, and he hissed through his clamped-together teeth. Hella was so startled that she could not get her breath.

"Here he is," Doc said.

Hella was searching among the big-toothed children when she felt her leg being clutched and she turned to see a small bright-eyed child trying to hug her. He was bigger than she expected but still so much younger than any of these other children that he seemed charming and infantile.

"In perfect shape," Doc was saying. "Mixed race. Parents couldn't keep him. They need the money. Three isn't old."

Again she thought: *Who are we taking him from?* and she thought of the nursery, already furnished with a crib, a high chair, a scale, a cupboard of toys, sheets and pillows and stuffed animals, the rocking horse, all the accumulated paraphernalia of their many attempts to find a child. Hella knew she was being sentimental, for part of her yearning to have a child was also her fantasy of cuddling an infant, feeding it, changing it, teaching it to speak and walk. Yet there was a logic in his being three—it was as though this was the child they had begun to search for three years ago, when they discarded their last pets.

"He's very bright. You can give him any test you like," the man said. "It'll be easier, you know. Being older he'll be more cooperative."

Arvin was nodding: he accepted this as reasonable.

"He's got papers," the man said. "And if the tests don't work out you can call the whole thing off."

Arvin made a familiar gesture that meant to Hella: *What have we got to lose?*

The child was clean, he seemed affectionate; he was lightly dressed this warm morning, in a clean shirt and shorts. But he had the teeth too. Arvin stepped forward when the child kissed Hella, as though to protect her, but Hella let him kiss her, and she hugged him. She sorrowed for the child yet she refused to allow herself to feel possessive. If Arvin cleared him, then she would claim him and embrace him.

"What's his name?" Arvin asked.

Before Doc could answer, the child said, "My name is Corbin," he had heard, he understood, he was so alert. His mouth was still open, the big teeth gleaming. "I want to go home with you. I want you to be my mummy."

Hella plucked his hand away and led him to Arvin. She knew he wanted to begin the tests.

Arvin said, "He's three? He looks older—six at least."

"Big for his age," Doc said. And then, "I'm going to have to take your phones."

"Wait a minute," Arvin said and put his hand over his wrist in a protective reflex.

"Or else how about moving some money into my account?"

"What is this?" Arvin said, and fear strengthened him: something was wrong.

As a small boy gripped his wrist and snagged the phone with his fingers, Arvin turned and saw that Hella was surrounded, too, and that Doc was doing nothing except smiling, like a man whose snarling dogs are menacing a stranger.

Hella called out, "No!"—she was frantic, seeing those mouths and eyes.

Her scream seemed to work: the small, toothy children and their keeper jostled and scattered as a police car skidded towards them on the parking lot.

A voice exploded from a loudspeaker, "Stand back!"

It was the policeman, Seely, throwing open the doors of his armored car, and Arvin and Hella scrambled in. Now the policeman seemed scruffier than before, with shiny trouser knees and chipped insignia on the brim of his helmet.

"Didn't I tell you to be careful?"

Arvin said gratefully, "How did you find us?"

"You think it was hard?"

They were still thanking him as they noticed the small head of a small boy in the front seat, and as though the child knew he was being scrutinized he turned to face Arvin. He was sure when he showed his teeth that he was the boy who had been kicking the stool in the checkpoint booth.

Arvin said, "Wait. The van's back there."

But the policeman said nothing. He was driving fast down an alley between two tall buildings.

"Where are you taking us?"

Arvin was still talking, as the policeman started to say, "Listen."

The small boy beside him interrupted furiously and said, "Shut up!"

Arvin realized that he was speaking to the policeman, not to him, and he spoke with such anger that the policeman flinched and gripped the steering wheel.

"Sorry," the policeman said. "He's the boss."

He kept driving. The place was blighted. It was not just the decayed buildings and broken streets; there was not a tree, not a single green thing. The trees had been cut but in a random and wasteful way, not for fuel—the limbs were strewn about. The grass had been trampled or poisoned or built over or burned; the place had been mindlessly vandalized, as though by children.

It had the look of violence: broken signs, uprooted poles, smashed windows, the scribbled and misspelled obscenities and big bewildering scrawls: RAT ROOLZ and RONG DOGZ and YUNGSTAZ and DANJAH FREEX and NO MERSI and WORRYERZ.

When Arvin muttered them disgustedly Hella wanted him to stop.

Ahead was a warehouse, with broken windows, and there seemed to be at least one face at each window, some had more, crowding to see out.

The wide warehouse door swung open to admit the car and inside, Arvin could see the broker, Doc. He was seated on a small ridiculous chair, among the children. Doc looked the other way when the policeman entered. The car doors were snatched open and the children crowded forward with steel spears made of sharpened rods and poked at Arvin and Hella. They got out of the car protesting and pleading.

The child with stringy hair and the long dress-like shirt held a weapon and said in a quacking voice to the policeman, "Why didn't you blindfold them?"

The policeman crouched slightly and in a tone of respectful explanation, said, "Because blindfolds spook them."

"Blindfold them now!" the child said. "Wrong dogs!"

Doc said softly, as though to calm the children, "You want me to put out the ransom call?"

"Go away," the first boy said, and turned to Hella and as the stinking blindfold went over her eyes she had a last look at the big malevolent teeth that had frightened her back at the parking lot when she had asked *Are they for sale too?*

Another child began to screech, "Get out! Get out! Leave us alone! No mercy!"

In their darkness, afraid and unable to move, Arvin and Hella heard the two men leaving, muttering as they went out the door, and the large door shutting, an eclipse of light and sound that she could sense through her blindfold. The children came closer. Hella could sense their damp faces and heard them breathing eagerly through their mouths, like warm dogs.

Hella heard a child's voice say, "This one is mine," and she cried out as the small fingers tugged at her.

The Ass and The Ox

Michel Tournier

❦

THE OX

The ass is a poet, a literary sort, a chatterbox. The ox, for his part, says nothing. He is meditative, taciturn, a ruminant. He says nothing, but he thinks plenty. He reflects and he remembers. His head is as heavy and massive as a boulder, and it has age-old images knocking about in it. The most venerable of these images comes from ancient Egypt. It is the image of the Bull Apis: born of a virgin heifer impregnated by a thunderbolt; bearing a crescent on his forehead and a vulture on his back. A scarab is hidden under his tongue. He is fed in a temple. You can hardly expect an ox with all that behind him to be impressed by a god born in a stable to a maiden and the Holy Ghost!

He remembers. He sees himself as a young bull. At the center of the harvest procession in honor of the goddess Cybele, he strides forward wreathed in clusters of grapes, escorted by grape-harvesting girls and paunchy, flushed silenuses.

He remembers. Black autumn fields. The slow labor of the earth, laid open by the plowshare. The work mate that shared his yoke. The steaming warm stable.

He dreams of the cow. The mother animal par excellence. The softness of her womb. The gentle thrusts of the baby calf's head inside this living, generous horn of plenty. The clustered pink teats, the spurting milk.

The ox knows he is all that, and he knows it is incumbent on his reassuring, immovable bulk to watch over the labor of the Virgin and the birth of the Child.

THE ASS'S STORY

Don't let my white hair fool you, says the ass. I was once jet black, with just a light-colored star on my forehead, obviously a sign of my pre-destination. The star is still there, but you can't see it anymore, because my whole coat has gone white. It's like the stars of the night sky, that fade in the pale of dawn. Old age has given the whole of me the color of the star on my forehead, and there again I like to see a sign, the mark of a kind of blessing.

Because I'm old, very old. I must be almost forty, which is amazing for an ass. It wouldn't surprise me if I were the dean of asses. That, too, would be a sign.

They call me Kadi Shuya. That calls for an explanation. Even in my childhood my masters noticed an air of wisdom that distinguished me from other asses. They were impressed by the serious, subtle look in my eyes. That's why they called me Kadi, because everyone knows that in our country a kadi is both a judge and a priest, in other words, somebody remarkable for two kinds of wisdom. True, I was still an ass, the humblest and most ill-treated of animals, and they couldn't very well give me a venerable name like Kadi without downgrading it by tacking on something ridiculous. This was Shuya, which means small, insignificant, contemptible. So that made me Kadi Shuya, the no-account Kadi, whose masters sometimes called him Kadi but more often Shuya, according to their humor at the time. . . .

I'm a poor man's ass. For years I affected to be pleased about it, because I had a rich man's ass as a neighbor and confidant. My master was a small farmer. There was a beautiful estate right next to his field. A Jerusalem merchant used to spend the hottest weeks of summer there with his family. His ass was called Yawul, a magnificent animal, nearly twice as big and fat as me; his coat was a solid gray, as fine as silk. It was something to see him go out harnessed in red leather and green velvet, with his tapestry saddle and his big copper stirrups, his jiggling pompons and tinkling little bells. I pretended to find this carnival outfit ridiculous. I remembered the sufferings they had put him through in his childhood to make him into a luxury mount. I'd seen him streaming with blood after his master's initials and emblem were cut into his flesh with a razor. I'd seen the tips of his ears cruelly sewn together to make them stand up straight like horns instead of drooping pathetically to the right and left like mine, and his legs squeezed into tight bands to make them slenderer and straighter than ordinary asses' legs. That's what humans are like: they manage to inflict more pain on the creatures they love and take pride in than on ones they hate or despise.

But Yawul had compensations that were not to be sneezed at, and there was a secret envy mixed with the commiseration I felt entitled to show him. For one thing, he ate barley and oats every day in a spanking clean stall. And best of all, those mares! You won't quite get the point of this unless you know how insufferably arrogant horses are about asses. The fact is, they don't look at us at all; as far as they're concerned, we don't exist any more than mice or cockroaches. And the mares are the worst of all, haughty, unapproachable . . . great ladies! Yes, to mount a mare is an ass's dream—that's his idea of revenge on that big ninny of a stallion. But how is an ass to compete with a horse on his own ground? Well, fate has more than one card up its sleeve, and it has given certain members of the asinine nation the most amazing and amusing privilege. The key to that privilege is the mule. What is a mule? A mule is a sober, safe and surefooted mount (to these adjectives in "s" I might add "silent," "scrupulous," and "studious," but I try to keep my weakness for alliteration under control). The mule is the king of sandy trails, slippery slopes, and fords. Calm, imperturbable, indefatigable, he . . .

And what is the secret of all these virtues? The secret is that he is spared the tumult of love and the trials of procreation. The mule doesn't bear children. To make a little mule, you need a daddy ass and a mummy mare. That's why some asses—and Yawul was one of them—are selected as fathers-of-mules (the most prestigious of titles in our community) and given mares for wives.

I'm not oversexed, and if I have any ambitions, they're not in that direction. But I must confess that there were mornings when the sight of Yawul, exhausted and drunk with pleasure, staggering back from his equestrian exploits, made me doubt the justice of life. It's true that life didn't spoil me. Constantly beaten, insulted, loaded with burdens heavier than I was, fed on thistles—where, I ask you, did humans get the idea that asses dote on thistles? Couldn't they give us clover or grain just once, to let us relish the difference!—and in the end, the dread of crows, when we drop with exhaustion and wait by the roadside for merciful death to come and put an end to our sufferings! Yes, the dread of crows, because we know that when our last hour comes there's a big difference between vultures and crows. Vultures, you see, attack only corpses. As long as there's a breath of life left in you, there's no need to worry about vultures; somehow they know what's what, and wait at a respectful distance. But crows are devils; they pounce before you're half dead and eat you alive, beginning with the eyes. . . .

I had to tell you all this, because otherwise you wouldn't understand my state of mind that winter's day, when I arrived in Bethlehem—that's a small town in Judea—with my master. The whole province was in a turmoil, because the Emperor had ordered a census of the population, and everybody and his family had to go back to the place they came from to register. Bethlehem is hardly more than a big village perched on the top of a hill, the sides of which are terraced and covered with little gardens with dry-stone retaining walls. In the spring and at normal times it's probably a nice enough place to live in, but at the onset of winter and with all this census bustle, I certainly missed my stable at Djela, our home village. My master and mistress had been lucky enough to find a place for themselves and their two children in a big inn that was humming like a beehive. Alongside of the main building there was a kind of barn where they probably stored provisions. In between there was a narrow passage, leading nowhere, with a sort of thatched roof made by throwing armfuls of reeds on top of some crossbeams. Under this precarious shelter some feeding troughs had been set up and the ground had been strewn with litter for the beasts belonging to the guests at the inn. That was where they tethered me, next to an ox who had just been unharnessed from a cart. I don't mind telling you that I've always had a horror of oxen. I admit they haven't an ounce of malice in them, but unfortunately my master's brother-in-law owns one. At plowing time the two brothers-in-law help each other out, and that means harnessing us to the plow together, though it's expressly forbidden by law. That is a very wise law, because, take it from me, nothing could be ghastlier than working in that sort of team. The ox has his pace—which is slow—and his rhythm—which is steady. He pulls with his neck. The ass—like the horse—pulls with his crupper. He works spasmodically, in fits and starts. To team him up with an ox is to put a ball and chain on his legs, to curtail his energy—which he hasn't got so much of to begin with.

But that night there was no question of plowing. Travelers turned away from the inn had invaded the barn. I strongly suspected that they wouldn't leave us in peace for long. And pretty soon, true enough, a man and a woman slipped into our improvised stable. The man was an old fellow, some kind of artisan. He had kicked up a big fuss, telling everyone who would listen that if he had to register in Bethlehem for the census, it was because his family tree—twenty-seven generations no less—went back to King David, who himself had been born in Bethlehem. Everybody laughed in his face. He'd have had more chance of finding lodging if he had mentioned the condition of his very young wife, who seemed dead tired and very pregnant besides. Taking straw from the floor and hay from the feeding troughs, he put together a kind of pallet between the ox and me, and laid the young woman down on it.

Little by little, everybody found his place and the noise died down. Now and then the young woman moaned softly and that's how we found out that her husband's name was Joseph. He comforted her as best he could, and that's how we found out that her name was Mary. I don't know how many hours passed, because I must have slept. When I woke up, I had a feeling that a big change had taken place, not only in our passageway, but everywhere, even, so it seemed, in the sky, glittering tatters of which shone through our miserable roof. The great silence of the longest night of the year had fallen on the earth, and it seemed as though, for fear of breaking the silence, the earth had stopped the flow of its waters and the heavens were holding their breath. Not a bird in the trees. Not a fox in the fields. Not a mole in the grass. The eagles and the wolves, whatever had beak or claw, watched and waited, with hunger in their bellies and their eyes fixed on the darkness. Even the glowworms and fireflies masked their light. Time had given way to a sacred eternity.

Then suddenly, in less than an instant, something enormous happened. An irrepressible thrill of joy traversed heaven and earth. A rustling of innumerable wings made it plain that swarms of angelic messengers were rushing in all directions. The thatch over our heads was lit up by the dazzling train of a comet. We heard the crystalline laughter of the brooks and the majestic laughter of the rivers. In the desert of Judea swirls of sand tickled the flanks of the dunes. An ovation rose from the terebinth forests and mingled with the muffled applause of the hoot owls. All nature exulted.

What had happened? Hardly anything. A faint cry had been heard, coming from the dark, warm pallet, a cry that could not have come from a man or a woman. It was the soft wailing of a newborn babe. Just then, a column of light came to rest in the middle of the stable: the Archangel Gabriel, Jesus's guardian angel, had arrived. The moment he got there, he took charge, so to speak. At the same time, the door opened, and one of the maids from the inn came in, supporting a basin of warm water on her hip. Without hesitation she knelt down and bathed the child. Then she rubbed it with salt to toughen the skin, swaddled it, and handed it to Joseph, who set it down on his knees, in token of paternal recognition.

You have to hand it to Gabriel, his efficiency was remarkable.

Meaning no disrespect to an archangel, I have to tell you that for the past year he hadn't let any grass grow under his feet. He was the one who announced to Mary that she would be the mother of the Messiah. He was the one who set the kindly old Joseph's suspicions to rest. And it was he, later on, who would dissuade the Three Kings from making their report to Herod, and organize the little family's flight into Egypt. But that's getting ahead of my story. Just then he was playing the majordomo, the master of joyous ceremonies in that lowly place, which he transfigured, pretty much the way the sun turns the rain into a rainbow. In his very own person he went about waking the shepherds in the country nearby. At first, as you might expect, he gave them quite a turn. But then, laughing to reassure them, he announced the big news, and summoned them to the stable. Stable? That seemed strange, but it also put those simple folk at their ease.

When they started pouring in, Gabriel arranged them in a semicircle and helped them to come forward, one by one, kneel on one knee, pay their respects, and proffer their good wishes. And saying those few words was no joke for those silent men, who as a rule speak only to their dogs or the moon. Stepping up to the crib, they set down the products of their toil, clotted milk, small goat's cheeses, butter made from ewe's milk, olives from Galgala, sycamore figs, and dates from Jericho, but neither meat nor fish. They spoke of their humble sufferings, epidemics, vermin, and animal pests. Gabriel blessed them in the name of the Child, and promised them help and protection.

Neither meat nor fish, I said. But one of the last shepherds stepped forward with a little ram, barely four months old, wrapped around his neck. He knelt down, deposited his burden on the straw, then raised himself to his full height. The country people recognized

Silas the Samaritan, a shepherd, to be sure, but also a kind of hermit, reputed among the simple folk for his wisdom. He lived all alone with his dogs and his beasts, in a mountain cave near Hebron. Everyone knew that he wouldn't come down from his wilderness for nothing, and when the archangel signaled him to speak, they all listened.

"My lord," he began, "some people say I withdrew to the mountains because I hated men. That's not true. It wasn't hatred of mankind but love of animals that made me a hermit. But when someone loves animals, he has to protect them from the wickedness and greed of men. It's true, I'm not the usual kind of husbandman. I neither sell nor kill my beasts. They give me their milk. I make it into cream, butter, and cheese. I sell nothing. I use these gifts according to my needs and give the rest—the greater part—to the poor. If tonight I've obeyed the angel, who woke me and showed me the star, it's because of the rebellion in my heart, not only against the ways of my society, but worse, against the rites of my religion. Unfortunately, this thing goes back a long way, almost to the beginning of time, and it would take a great revolution to bring about a change. Has the revolution happened tonight? That's what I've come to ask you."

"It has happened tonight," Gabriel assured him.

"I'll start with Abraham's sacrifice. To test Abraham, God commanded him to offer Isaac, his only son, as a burnt offering. Abraham obeyed. He took the child and climbed a mountain in the land of Moriah. The child was puzzled: They had brought wood, they had brought the fire and the knife, but where was the lamb for the burnt offering? Wood, fire, knife . . . there, my lord, are the accursed stigmata of man's destiny!"

"There will be more," said Gabriel gloomily, thinking of the nails, the hammer, and the crown of thorns.

"Then Abraham built an altar, laid the wood in order, and bound

Isaac and laid him on the altar upon the wood. And he set his knife on the child's white throat."

"But then," Gabriel interrupted, "an angel came and stayed his arm. That was me."

"Yes, of course, good angel," said Silas. "But Isaac never recovered from the fright of seeing his own father holding a knife at his throat. The blue flash of the knife blasted his eyes; his eyesight was poor as long as he lived, and at the end he went stone blind. That's why his son Jacob was able to deceive him and pass for his brother Esan. But that's not what bothers me. Why couldn't you content yourself with stopping the child-killing? Did blood have to flow? You, Gabriel, supplied Abraham with a young ram, which was killed and offered up as a burnt offering. Couldn't God do without a death that morning?"

"I admit that Abraham's sacrifice was a failed revolution," said Gabriel. "We'll do better next time."

"Actually," said Silas, "we can go further back in sacred history and trace Yahweh's secret passion to its source. Remember Cain and Abel. The two brothers were at their devotions. Each offered up products of his labor. Cain was a tiller of the soil, he offered up fruits and grain, while Abel, who was a shepherd, offered up lambs and their fat. What happened? Yahweh turned away from Cain's offering and welcomed Abel's. Why? For what reason? I can see only one: It was because Yahweh hates vegetables and loves meat! Yes, the God we worship is hopelessly carnivorous!

"And we honor Him as such. Consider the temple at Jerusalem in its splendor and majesty, that sanctuary of the radiant divinity. Did you know that on some days it's drenched in steaming fresh blood like a slaughterhouse? The sacrificial altar is a huge block of rough-hewn stone, with hornlike protuberances at the corners and traversed with runnels to evacuate the blood of the victims. On the occasion of certain festivals the priests transform themselves into butchers and massacre whole herds of beasts. Oxen, rams, he-goats, even whole flocks of doves are shaken by the spasms of their death agony. They are dismembered on marble tables, and the entrails are thrown into a brazier. The whole city is infested with smoke. Some days, when the wind is from the north, the stench spreads as far as my mountain and my beasts are seized with panic."

"Silas the Samaritan," said Gabriel, "you have done well to come here tonight to watch over the Child and worship him. The complaints of your animal-loving heart will be heard. I've said that Abraham's sacrifice was a failed revolution. Soon the Father will sacrifice the Son again. And I swear to you that this time no angel will stay His hand. All over the world from now on, even on the smallest of islands, and at every hour of the day till the end of time, the blood of the Son will flow on altars for the salvation of mankind. This little child you see sleeping in the straw—the ox and the ass do well to warm Him with their breath, for He is in truth a lamb. From now on there will be no other sacrificial lamb, because He is the Lamb of God, who alone will be sacrificed in *saecula saeculorum.*

"Go in peace, Silas. As a symbol of life you may take with you the young ram you have brought. More fortunate than Abraham's, he will testify in your herd that from now on the blood of animals will no longer be shed on God's altars."

After this angelic speech there was a thoughtful pause that seemed to make a space around the terrible and magnificent event the angel had announced. Each in his own way and according to his powers tried to imagine what the new times would be like. But then a terrible jangling of chains and rusty pulleys was heard, accompanied by a burst of grotesque, ungainly, sobbing laughter. That was me, that was the thunderous bray of the ass in the manger. Yes, what would you expect, my patience was at an end. This couldn't go on. We'd been forgotten again; I'd listened attentively to everything that had been said, and I hadn't heard one word about asses.

Everybody laughed—Joseph, Mary, Gabriel, the shepherds, Silas the hermit, the ox, who hadn't understood one thing—and even the Child, who flailed merrily about with His four little limbs in His straw crib.

"Don't let it worry you," said Gabriel. "The asses will not be forgotten. Obviously you don't have to worry about sacrifices. Within memory of priest no one has ever seen an ass offered up on an altar. That would be too much honor for you poor humble donkeys. And yet great is your merit, beaten, starved, crushed under the weight of your burdens. But don't imagine that your miseries escape the eye of an archangel. For instance, Kadi Shuya, I distinctly see a deep, festering little wound behind your left ear. Day after day your master prods it with his goad. He thinks the pain will revive your flagging vigor. Ah, poor martyr, every time he does it, I suffer with you."

The archangel pointed a luminous finger at my right ear and instantly the deep, festering little wound that had not escaped him closed. What's more, the skin that covered it was now so hard and thick that no goad would ever make a dent in it. Then and there I tossed my mane with enthusiasm and let out a triumphant bray.

"Yes, you humble and friendly companions of man's labor," Gabriel went on, "you will have your reward and your triumph in the great story that's starting tonight.

"One day, a Sunday—which will be known as Palm Sunday—the Apostles will find a she-ass and her colt in the village of Bethany near the Mount of Olives. They will loose them and throw a cloak on the back of the foal—which no one will yet have mounted—and Jesus will ride it. And Jesus will make His solemn entry into Jerusalem, through the Golden Gate, the finest of the city's gates. The people will rejoice and acclaim the Nazarene prophet with cries of Hosannah to the Son of David! And the foal will tread a carpet of palm branches and flowers that the people will have laid over the paving stones. And the mother ass will trot in the rear of the procession, braying to all and sundry: 'That's my foal! That's my foal!' for never will a mother ass have been so proud."

So for the first time in history someone had given a thought to us asses, someone had stopped to think about our sufferings of today and joys of tomorrow. But before that could happen an archangel had to come all the way down from heaven. Suddenly I didn't feel alone anymore, I'd been adopted by the great Christmas family. I was no longer the outcast whom no one understood. What a beautiful night we could all have spent together in the warmth of our sacred poverty! How late we would have slept next morning! And what a fine breakfast we'd have had!

Too bad! The rich always have to butt in. The rich are insatiable, they want to own everything, even poverty. Who could ever have imagined that this wretched family, camping between an ox and an ass, would attract a king? Did I say a king? No, three kings, authentic sovereigns, from the Orient, what's more! And really, what an outrageous display of servants, animals, canopies. . . .

The shepherds had gone home. Once again silence enveloped that incomparable night. And suddenly the village streets were full of tumult. A clanking of bridles and stirrups and weapons; purple and gold glittered in the torchlight; shouts and commands rang out in barbarous languages. And most marvelous of all: the astonishing silhouettes of animals from the ends of the earth, falcons from the

Nile, greyhounds, green parrots, magnificent horses, camels from
the far south. Why not elephants while they were about it?

At first a lot of us went out and looked. Curiosity. There had
never been such a show in a Palestinian village. You have to hand it
to them—when it came to stealing our Christmas, the rich spared no
expense. But in the end too much is enough. We went back inside
and barricaded ourselves and some beat it across the hills and fields.
Because, you see, unimportant people like us can expect no good of
the great. Better steer clear of them. For a farthing dropped here and
there, how many whippings fall to the lot of the beggar or ass who
crosses a prince's path!

That's the way it looked to my master. Awakened by the ruckus,
he gathered up his family and belongings, and I saw him elbowing
his way into our improvised stable. My master knows his own mind,
but he's a man of few words. Without so much as opening his
mouth, he untied me and we left that noisy village before the kings
marched in.

translated by Ralph Manheim

Death of a Son

Njabulo S. Ndebele

❧

At last we got the body. Wednesday. Just enough time for a Saturday funeral. We were exhausted. Empty. The funeral still ahead of us. We had to find the strength to grieve. There had been no time for grief, really. Only much bewilderment and confusion. Now grief. For isn't grief the awareness of loss?

That is why when we finally got the body, Buntu said: "Do you realize our son is dead?" I realized. Our awareness of the death of our first and only child had been displaced completely by the effort to get his body. Even the horrible events that caused the death: we did not think of them, as such. Instead, the numbing drift of things took over our minds: the pleas, letters to be written, telephone calls to be made, telegrams to be dispatched, lawyers to consult, "influential" people to "get in touch with," undertakers to be contacted, so much walking and driving. That is what suddenly mattered: the irksome details that blur the goal (no matter how terrible it is), each detail becoming a door which, once unlocked, revealed yet another door. Without being aware of it, we were distracted by the smell of the skunk and not by what the skunk had done.

We realized something too, Buntu and I, that during the two-week effort to get our son's body, we had drifted apart. For the first time in our marriage, our presence to each other had become a matter of habit. He was there. He'll be there. And I'll be there. But when Buntu said: "Do you realize our son is dead?" he uttered a thought that suddenly brought us together again. It was as if the return of the body of our son was also our coming together. For it was only at that moment that we really began to grieve; as if our lungs had suddenly begun to take in air when just before, we were beginning to suffocate. Something with meaning began to emerge.

We realized. We realized that something else had been happening to us, adding to the terrible events. Yes, we had drifted apart. Yet, our estrangement, just at that moment when we should have been together, seemed disturbingly comforting to me. I was comforted in a manner I did not quite understand.

The problem was that I had known all along that we would have to buy the body anyway. I had known all along. Things would end that way. And when things turned out that way, Buntu could not look me in the eye. For he had said: "Over my dead body! Over my dead body!" as soon as we knew we would be required to pay the police or the government for the release of the body of our child.

"Over my dead body! Over my dead body!" Buntu kept on saying.

Finally, we bought the body. We have the receipt. The police insisted we take it. That way, they would be "protected." It's the law, they said.

I suppose we could have got the body earlier. At first I was confused, for one is supposed to take comfort in the heroism of one's man. Yet, inwardly, I could draw no comfort from his outburst. It seemed hasty. What sense was there to it when all I wanted was the body of my child? What would happen if, as events unfolded, it became clear that Buntu would not give up his life? What would happen? What would happen to him? To me?

For the greater part of two weeks, all of Buntu's efforts, together with friends, relatives, lawyers and the newspapers, were to secure the release of the child's body without the humiliation of having to pay for it. A "fundamental principle."

Why was it difficult for me to see the wisdom of the principle? The worst thing, I suppose, was worrying about what the police may have been doing to the body of my child. How they may have been busy prying it open "to determine the cause of death"?

Would I want to look at the body when we finally got it? To see further mutilations in addition to the "cause of death"? What kind of mother would not want to look at the body of her child? people will ask. Some will say: "It's grief." She is too grief-stricken.

"But still . . . ," they will say. And the elderly among them may say: "Young people are strange."

But how can they know? It was not that I would not want to see the body of my child, but that I was too afraid to confront the horrors of my own imagination. I was haunted by the thought of how useless it had been to have created something. What had been the point of it all? This body filling up with a child. The child steadily growing into something that could be seen and felt. Moving, as it always did, at that time of day when I was all alone at home waiting for it. What had been the point of it all?

How can they know that the mutilation to determine "the cause of death" ripped my own body? Can they think of a womb feeling hunted? Disgorged?

And the milk that I still carried. What about it? What had been the point of it all?

Even Buntu did not seem to sense that that principle, the "fundamental principle," was something too intangible for me at that moment, something that I desperately wanted should assume the form of my child's body. He still seemed far from ever knowing.

I remember one Saturday morning early in our courtship, as Buntu and I walked hand-in-hand through town, window-shopping. We cannot even be said to have been window-shopping, for we were aware of very little that was not ourselves. Everything in those windows was merely an excuse for words to pass between us.

We came across three girls sitting on the pavement, sharing a packet of fish and chips after they had just bought it from a nearby Portuguese cafe. Buntu said: "I want fish and chips too." I said: "So seeing is desire." I said: "My man is greedy!" We laughed. I still remember how he tightened his grip on my hand. The strength of it!

Just then, two white boys coming in the opposite direction suddenly rushed at the girls, and, without warning, one of them kicked the packet of fish and chips out of the hands of the girl who was holding it. The second boy kicked away the rest of what remained in the packet. The girl stood up, shaking her hand as if to throw off the pain in it. Then she pressed it under her armpit as if to squeeze the pain out of it. Meanwhile, the two boys went on their way laughing. The fish and chips lay scattered on the pavement and on the street like stranded boats on a river that had gone dry.

"Just let them do that to you!" said Buntu, tightening once more his grip on my hand as we passed on like sheep that had seen many of their own in the flock picked out for slaughter. We would note the event and wait for our turn. I remember I looked at Buntu, and saw his face was somewhat glum. There seemed no connection between that face and the words of reassurance just uttered. For a while, we went on quietly. It was then that I noticed his grip had grown somewhat limp. Somewhat reluctant. Having lost its self-assurance, it seemed to have been holding on because it had to, not because of a confident sense of possession.

It was not to be long before his words were tested. How could fate work this way, giving to words meanings and intentions they did not carry when they were uttered? I saw that day, how the language of love could so easily be trampled underfoot, or scattered like fish and chips on the pavement, and left stranded and abandoned like boats in a river that suddenly went dry. Never again was love to be confirmed with words. The world around us was too hostile for vows of love. At any moment, the vows could be subjected to the stress of proof. And love died. For words of love need not be tested.

On that day, Buntu and I began our silence. We talked and laughed, of course, but we stopped short of words that would demand proof of action. Buntu knew. He knew the vulnerability of words. And so he sought to obliterate words with acts that seemed to promise redemption.

On that day, as we continued with our walk in town, that Saturday morning, coming up towards us from the opposite direction, was a burly Boer walking with his wife and two children. They approached Buntu and me with an ominously determined advance. Buntu attempted to pull me out of the way, but I never had a chance. The Boer shoved me out of the way, as if clearing a path for his family. I remember, I almost crashed into a nearby fashion display window. I remember, I glanced at the family walking away, the mother and the father each dragging a child. It was for one of those children that I had been cleared away. I remember, also, that as my tears came out, blurring the Boer family and everything else, I saw and felt deeply what was inside of me: a desire to be avenged.

But nothing happened. All I heard was Buntu say: "The dog!" At that very moment, I felt my own hurt vanish like a wisp of smoke. And as my hurt vanished, it was replaced, instead, by a tormenting desire to sacrifice myself for Buntu. Was it something about the powerlessness of the curse and the desperation with which it had been made? The filling of stunned silence with an utterance? Surely it ate into him, revealing how incapable he was of meeting the call of his words.

And so it was, that that afternoon, back in the township, left to ourselves at Buntu's home, I gave in to him for the first time. Or should I say I offered myself to him? Perhaps from some vague sense of wanting to heal something in him? Anyway, we were never to talk about that event. Never. We buried it alive deep inside of me that afternoon. Would it ever be exhumed? All I vaguely felt and knew was that I had the keys to the vault. That was three years ago, a year before we married.

The cause of death? One evening I returned home from work, particularly tired after I had been covering more shootings by the police in the East Rand. Then I had hurried back to the office in Johannesburg to piece together on my typewriter the violent scenes of the day, and then to file my report to meet the deadline. It was late when I returned home, and when I got there, I found a crowd of people in the yard. They were those who could not get inside. I panicked. What had happened? I did not ask those who were outside, being desperate to get into the house. They gave way easily when they recognized me.

Then I heard my mother's voice. Her cry rose well above the noise. It turned into a scream when she saw me. "What is it, mother?" I asked, embracing her out of a vaguely despairing sense of terror. But she pushed me away with an hysterical violence that astounded me.

"What misery have I brought you, my child?" she cried. At that point, many women in the room began to cry too. Soon, there was much wailing in the room, and then all over the house. The sound of it! The anguish! Understanding, yet eager for knowledge, I became desperate. I had to hold onto something. The desire to embrace my mother no longer had anything to do with comforting her; for whatever she had done, whatever its magnitude, had become inconsequential. I needed to embrace her for all the anguish that tied everyone in the house into a knot. I wanted to be part of that knot, yet I wanted to know what had brought it about.

Eventually, we found each other, my mother and I, and clasped each other tightly. When I finally released her, I looked around at the neighbors and suddenly had a vision of how that anguish had to be turned into a simmering kind of indignation. The kind of indignation that had to be kept at bay only because there was a higher purpose at that moment: the sharing of concern.

Slowly and with a calmness that surprised me, I began to gather the details of what had happened. Instinctively, I seemed to have been gathering notes for a news report.

It happened during the day, when the soldiers and the police that had been patrolling the township in their Casspirs began to shoot in the streets at random. Need I describe what I did not see? How did the child come to die just at that moment when the police and the soldiers began to shoot at random, at any house, at any moving thing? That was how one of our windows was shattered by a bullet. And that was when my mother, who looked after her grandchild when we were away at work, panicked. She picked up the child and ran to the neighbors. It was only when she entered the neighbor's house that she noticed the wetness of the blanket that covered the child she held to her chest as she ran for the sanctuary of neighbors. She had looked at her unaccountably bloody hand, then she noted the still bundle in her arms, and began at that moment to blame herself for the death of her grandchild . . .

Later, the police, on yet another round of shooting, found people gathered at our house. They stormed in, saw what had happened. At first, they dragged my mother out, threatening to take her away unless she agreed not to say what had happened. But then they returned and, instead, took the body of the child away. By what freak of logic did they hope that by this act their carnage would never be discovered?

That evening, I looked at Buntu closely. He appeared suddenly to have grown older. We stood alone in an embrace in our bedroom. I noticed, when I kissed his face, how his once lean face had grown suddenly puffy.

At that moment, I felt the familiar impulse come upon me once more, the impulse I always felt when I sensed that Buntu was in some kind of danger, the impulse to yield something of myself to him. He wore the look of someone struggling to gain control of something. Yet, it was clear he was far from controlling anything. I knew that look. Had seen it many times. It came at those times when I sensed that he faced a wave that was infinitely stronger than he, that it would certainly sweep him away, but that he had to seem to be struggling. I pressed myself tightly to him as if to vanish into him; as if only the two of us could stand up to the wave.

"Don't worry," he said. "Don't worry. I'll do everything in my power to right this wrong. Everything. Even if it means suing the police!" We went silent.

I knew that silence. But I knew something else at that moment: that I had to find a way of disengaging myself from the embrace.

Suing the police? I listened to Buntu outlining his plans. "Legal counsel. That's what we need," he said. "I know some people in Pretoria," he said. As he spoke, I felt the warmth of intimacy between us cooling. When he finished, it was cold. I disengaged from his embrace slowly, yet purposefully. Why had Buntu spoken?

Later, he was to speak again, when all his plans had failed to work: "Over my dead body! Over my dead body!"

He sealed my lips. I would wait for him to feel and yield one day to all the realities of misfortune.

Ours was a home, it could be said. It seemed a perfect life for a young couple: I, a reporter; Buntu, a personnel officer at an American factory manufacturing farming implements. He had traveled to the United States and returned with a mind fired with dreams. We dreamed together. Much time we spent, Buntu and I, trying to make a perfect home. The occasions are numerous on which we paged through *Femina, Fair Lady, Cosmopolitan, Home Garden, Car,* as if somehow we were going to surround our lives with the glossiness in the magazines. Indeed, much of our time was spent window-shopping through the magazines. This time, it was different from the window-shopping we did that Saturday when we courted. This time our minds were consumed by the things we saw and dreamed of owning: the furniture, the fridge, TV, videocassette recorders, washing machines, even a vacuum cleaner and every other imaginable thing that would ensure a comfortable modern life.

Especially when I was pregnant. What is it that Buntu did not buy, then? And when the boy was born, Buntu changed the car. A family, he would say, must travel comfortably.

The boy became the center of Buntu's life. Even before he was born, Buntu had already started making inquiries at white private schools. That was where he would send his son, the bearer of his name.

Dreams! It is amazing how the horrible findings of my newspaper reports often vanished before the glossy magazines of our dreams, how I easily forgot that the glossy images were concocted out of the keys of typewriters, made by writers whose business was to sell dreams at the very moment that death pervaded the land. So powerful are words and pictures that even their makers often believe in them.

Buntu's ordeal was long. So it seemed. He would get up early every morning to follow up the previous day's leads regarding the body of our son. I wanted to go with him, but each time I prepared to go he would shake his head.

"It's my task," he would say. But every evening he returned, empty-handed, while with each day that passed and we did not know where the body of my child was, I grew restive and hostile in a manner that gave me much pain. Yet Buntu always felt compelled to give a report on each day's events. I never asked for it. I suppose it was his way of dealing with my silence.

One day he would say: "The lawyers have issued a court order that the body be produced. The writ of *habeas corpus*."

On another day he would say: "We have petitioned the Minister of Justice."

On yet another he would say: "I was supposed to meet the Chief Security Officer. Waited the whole day. At the end of the day they said I would see him tomorrow if he was not going to be too busy. They are stalling."

Then he would say: "The newspapers, especially yours, are raising the hue and cry. The government is bound to be embarrassed. It's a matter of time."

And so it went on. Every morning he got up and left. Sometimes alone, sometimes with friends. He always left to bear the failure alone.

How much did I care about lawyers, petitions and Chief Security Officers? A lot. The problem was that whenever Buntu spoke about his efforts, I heard only his words. I felt in him the disguised hesitancy of someone who wanted reassurance without asking for it. I saw someone who got up every morning and left not to look for results, but to search for something he could only have found with me.

And each time he returned, I gave my speech to my eyes. And he answered without my having parted my lips. As a result, I sensed, for the first time in my life, a terrible power in me that could make him do anything. And he would never ever be able to deal with that power as long as he did not silence my eyes and call for my voice.

And so, he had to prove himself. And while he left each morning, I learned to be brutally silent. Could he prove himself without me? Could he? Then I got to know, those days, what I'd always wanted from him. I got to know why I have always drawn him into me whenever I sensed his vulnerability.

I wanted him to be free to fear. Wasn't there greater strength that way? Had he ever lived with his own feelings? And the stress of life in this land: didn't it call out for men to be heroes? And should they live up to it even though the details of the war to be fought may often be blurred? They should.

Yet it is precisely for that reason that I often found Buntu's thoughts lacking in strength. They lacked the experience of strife that could only come from a humbling acceptance of fear and then, only then, the need to fight it.

Me? In a way, I have always been free to fear. The prerogative of being a girl. It was always expected of me to scream when a spider crawled across the ceiling. It was known I would jump onto a chair whenever a mouse blundered into the room.

Then, once more, the Casspirs came. A few days before we got the body back, I was at home with my mother when we heard the great roar of truck engines. There was much running and shouting in the streets. I saw them, as I've always seen them on my assignments: the Casspirs. On five occasions they ran down our street at great speed, hurling tear-gas canisters at random. On the fourth occasion, they got our house. The canister shattered another window and filled the house with the terrible pungent choking smoke that I had got to know so well. We ran out of the house gasping for fresh air.

So, this was how my child was killed? Could they have been the same soldiers? Now hardened to their tasks? Or were they new ones being hardened to their tasks? Did they drive away laughing? Clearing paths for their families? What paths?

And was this our home? It couldn't be. It had to be a little bird's nest waiting to be plundered by a predator bird. There seemed no sense to the wedding pictures on the walls, the graduation pictures, birthday pictures, pictures of relatives, and paintings of lush landscapes. There seemed no sense anymore to what seemed recognizably human in our house. It took only a random swoop to obliterate personal worth, to blot out any value there may have been to the past. In desperation, we began to live only for the moment. I do feel hunted.

It was on the night of the tear gas that Buntu came home, saw what had happened, and broke down in tears. They had long been in the coming . . .

My own tears welled out too. How much did we have to cry to re-float stranded boats? I was sure they would float again.

A few nights later, on the night of the funeral, exhausted, I lay on my bed, listening to the last of the mourners leaving. Slowly, I became conscious of returning to the world. Something came back after it seemed not to have been there for ages. It came as a surprise, as a reminder that we will always live around what will happen. The sun will rise and set, and the ants will do their endless work, until one day the clouds turn gray and rain falls, and even in the township, the ants will fly out into the sky. Come what may.

My moon came, in a heavy surge of blood. And, after such a long time, I remembered the thing Buntu and I had buried in me. I felt it as if it had just entered. I felt it again as it floated away on the surge. I would be ready for another month. Ready as always, each and every month, for new beginnings.

And Buntu? I'll be with him, now. Always. Without our knowing, all the trying events had prepared for us new beginnings. Shall we not prevail?

The Letter Scene

Susan Sontag

❦

Take a deep breath. Don't attempt anything just yet, you're not ready. When will you be ready? Never never never.

That means I must start now.

Don't start, don't even think of it, it's too difficult. No, it's too easy.

Let me start, it's already started, and I have to catch up.

Not like that, you oaf. Perched on the chair's edge, that's no way to start. Sit all the way back.

Don't cool me down, can't you see I'm already off, floated by feeling, brimming with words . . . the proper implements, pen, pencil, typewriter, computer, at hand.

You're going to wreck everything, you know. These things take time. Ground has to be prepared. The others alerted to your coming.

My intrusion, you mean. My demands, entreaties.

You have a right, I admit that. Take a deep breath.

My right to breathe? Thanks. How about my right to have

a hemorrhage? I won't be stopped, stanched, bandaged. Let me try.
Just don't pay attention while I try.

Act I, Scene 2. Brow furrowed, palms moist, Tatyana sits at the escritoire in her bedroom to write Eugene a letter. After the salutation,
she stalls. How to proceed when, after all, they have met only once, a
few evenings ago, downstairs, and from her shy vantage point at the
windowsill in the conservatory, though she followed him everywhere
with her gaze, she could hardly lift her eyes from the gleaming buttons on his jacket? That rush of warmth: she wants to declare something. She gets up and asks her nurse to prepare some tea. Nanny
brings fudge cakes, too. Tatiana frowns and sets to work again. She
pictures him against a background of air, and he becomes slimmer,
taller, more remote. It's a declaration of love she wants to declare. She
begins to sing.

While:

The wind is rattling the shutters, and Eugene's scratching quill
pen moves swiftly over the paper like a small fish waving its tiny fin.
"Dearest Father, there are many things I have long wanted to tell you
but never dared to utter to your face. Perhaps I shall find the courage
in this letter. In a letter, perhaps, I can be brave." By starting thus
Eugene would delay as long as he can what he means to say. This
will be, is trying to be, a letter of denunciation. It will be very long.
He throws some wood on the fire.

The night before Dumane's execution by hanging: after the special
meal, and to the accompaniment of the hymns and freedom songs
his comrades in neighboring cells will sing through the night to

comfort him. Dumane is sitting on the cement floor of his cell, nine by twelve, knees drawn close to his chest, paper on his knees, stump of pencil clenched between three lacerated fingers of his left hand—they have broken his right hand—laboriously printing his last written words. "When you read this I will be dead. You must be brave, I am calm. Mbangeli and I die confident that our sacrifice will not be in vain. Do not grieve too long for me. I want you to remarry. Comfort Granny. Kiss the children." There was more to it than that, eked out in tottering capitals, but these were the salient points. The letter ends, "P.S. My darling daughter, remember always that your father loves you and wants you to grow up to be just like your mother. Dearest son, please take care of your mother, who will need you, and do your best at school until you are ready to take your place in our just struggle."

Think of it, all those artless letters dashed off between bouts of tormentingly slow composition of the intricate, severe novels and essays that had made her quickly famous, and now a two-volume collection of her letters has come out, which, they say, may be the finest writing she ever did. It's not only her spirited sentences that enchant; everybody is moved by the portrait of the idyllic loving family from which she sprang. Is it possible such united families still exist? Even now? Nobody knows about the embittered letters to her sister that the widower burned in the barbecue. The world is tired of disillusionment, of unseemly revelations, the world is famished for models of probity. Our world. No one would ever know her as he did, would ever know how valiant she was during the last months of her terrible illness, when the brain tumor gnawed at her language, and he took to writing letters for her, from her, the letters she would have written if she still could. As the guardian of her reputation, now he can be inside the skin of her work in a way she had never let him while she was alive. He will be exigent, as she was. Somebody, but this professor isn't distinguished enough, has embarked on a biography: he hasn't decided whether or not to coöperate. A newspaper correspondent in the Far East writes him a maudlin letter about "the irreparable loss to literature." He replies, a correspondence ensues. Could this be an old lover of hers? From Hong Kong arrives a packet of her letters, sixty-eight of them, done up in red string. These he reads with astonishment. Posthumous shock: this is not the woman he knew.

Act I, Scene 2. Tatyana gulps down the fresh glass of tea that Nanny brings. Slipping her left hand inside her blouse, she rubs her thumb against her downy shoulder. She has barely begun the letter. The rush of ecstasy in declaring something should be its own reward, but no, there is already the need for an answer. "You didn't look at me," Tatyana has written on the first page. And in the middle of the second page, "I am writing you now to ask if you ever think of me." Then she weeps, and (not in the poem or the opera—no, in real life) begins the letter again. In the opera there is a gush of feeling that floats her through to the end.

Here I am, with my irrevocable feelings, at least they feel irrevocable, and it is clear that all this could well not have happened. We did not have to meet.

We met because there had been a fire, nothing serious, in the six-story tenement where I have the great fortune to have found a rent-stabilized apartment. A drowsy pot-smoker on the fifth floor ignited his horsehair sofa. Smoke, black acrid smoke; nothing serious. I was shivering on the street, coatless, and you were feeding nickels into the vending machine for the *Times*. Seeing me staring at you, you inquired about the fire. Nothing serious. We went past the fire engines to have coffee across the street. That was last January, now I am perishing from seriousness. Why did you leave me? Don't you mind how coldly he treats you? What is this white paper outspread on my desk? I have sat down to write you a letter, do you think you could love me again, but perhaps I won't.

The letter that was never sent, ghost of.

The letter that never arrived, two more sorts of ghosts. The letter that is lost (in the mail). The letter that was not written, but she said she wrote one and that it must have gotten lost (in the mail). You can never trust the mail. You can never never trust the mailer.

To write at all is to say . . . all. An act of ardor. That is why she hesitates, while she goes on writing letters in her head. But a letter in the head is a letter, too. It is told that Artur Schnabel used to practice in his head.

Act I, Scene 2. "I write to you," Tatyana has begun, begun again— she's found the cadence. "No more confession is needed, nothing's left to tell. I know it's now in your discretion with scorn to make my world a hell."

The taper on the escritoire is flickering. Or is it the moon, the quivering moon, becoming brighter?

Go to sleep, my darling, murmurs the old nurse.

"Oh, Nanny. Nanny!" But she will not seek consolation on her dear, kind Nanny's breast.

There, there, my darling. . . .

"Nanny, I'm stifling, open the window." The musty old crone moves to obey. "Nanny, I'm chilled, bring me a coverlet." She pauses at the window, perplexed. "No. No. Oh. . . ."

Let me sing to you, my darling.

"No, Nanny, it is I who must sing. In my girlish treble. Leave me, Nanny, my sweet dear old Nanny, I must sing."

This is a letter that breaks the bad news. I don't know how to begin. It didn't seem as bad when it first started. We were quite hopeful. The situation got worse only toward the end. I hope you will accept this as best you can. I hate to be the bearer of, etc.

Why people don't write letters anymore. (Much to be said about this, without ever mentioning the telephone.) People just don't want to take the time, what proves to be a great deal of time, because they lack confidence. Pen poised over the sheet of blank paper, they hesitate. The initial moment of exuberance refuses to translate fluently, rapidly into a voice that meets the standards of . . . what standards? More hesitations. They make a draft.

And then letters seem so—well, one-sided. Or lacking in velocity. One is too impatient for the answer.

The bad news is worse now. This is real bad news, the kind that invites ceremoniousness. He wrote to console me in a florid formal diction that I found heartrending.

Unlike lovers, unlike best friends, children and parents cannot revel in or despair at the thought that they did not have to have met. And they don't necessarily have to part, except when they do. Eugene is getting closer to what he wants to say. 'You have been generous, Father, and clearly think of yourself as having the best intentions toward me. Do not think me ungrateful for the monthly stipend you have provided since I graduated from Cadet School. But as you have acted according to your own principles, I must henceforth act in accord with mine." A frigid letter—the tone he is seeking is a kind of opaque sincerity—that will turn into a passionate, violent one.

The Hong Kong Letters, as the widower dubbed them, disclosed a relationship lasting nearly a decade whose inventive lechery he would never have dreamed his wife capable of. Their sexual transports are graphically recalled, as is her facility at giving herself full pleasure when they are apart at any moment, even fully clothed, in public (chatting at a cocktail party, giving a reading), if she had something to press herself against discreetly, with the merest thought of the rough pleasure they gave each other. And "he"—he is always "he," strewn respectfully throughout the letters: "he" and his endearingly limited needs, his protective asexual presence, outside whose lull she feared she could not write. Christ! Was that what his uxorious ardor was, for her? The conjugal drone? He would show his fangs now—it is never too late for a crime of passion. He purchases a plane ticket for Hong Kong.

And the forty-three-year-old salaryman from Osaka on the crippled jumbo jet now circling wildly as it loses altitude, plunging toward the mountain, who is able to master the white-hot blast of animal terror and pull a sheet of paper from the pad inside his briefcase, he too, like Dumane, is writing a farewell letter to his wife and children. But he will have three minutes only. Other passengers are screaming or moaning; some have dropped to their knees to pray as the overhead bins rain parcels and luggage and pillows and coats on their heads. His legs braced against the seat in front of him to keep from being pitched into the aisle, with his left arm cradling the briefcase on which he writes, rapidly but legibly, he enjoins his children to be obedient to their mother. To his wife he declares that he regrets nothing—"we've had a full life," he writes—and requests that she accept his death. He is signing as the plane turns upside down, he is stuffing the letter in his jacket pocket when he is hurled past his seat-mate against the window, head first, and smashed into the mercy of unconsciousness. When his broken body is recovered on the cedared slopes among the more than five hundred others, the letter is found, delivered by a red-eyed J.A.L. official to his wife, published on the first page of the newspapers. As one, all of Japan dissolves in tears.

Why people now write more many more letters than before. (Of course, written on a computer, they don't look as letters used to look.) People don't feel they're really letters, they're just something you type, without worrying about spelling mistakes or slips of the fingers on the keyboard. You can be curt. Answers pile up. All the velocity you want. Ping pong. Whizzing back and forth. For others, or all to see. Watch out. A tap on a key, that's all it takes. Your letter may be forwarded. Your indiscretion. Your letter may be forwarded and you might not ever know, so don't show any feeling you don't want shown to others. But most likely you will. Irresistible impulses to joke, especially when you're supposed to announce the subject of your letter at the top. It's part of the sending-the-letter form. More letters, more fragments, more information, more jokes. The letter-answer-letter-answer stack. When to summon a new page. Try it. You can be curt. Ping. Pong.

Her letters were so cozily aligned with loneliness. Separation became a value, the occasion and justification for writing letters.

This, from one of her letters to me:

"Soon after that I stayed a month on a lavender-scented island off the Dalmatian coast. I found a room to rent in a fisherman's house and fellow-tourists I liked, with whom I spent much of my time: scuba diving from a hired boat with a four-horsepower outboard engine, picnicking on broiled silver mackerel and freshly baked flat loaves of bread called *lepinja* on the pine-shaded rocks of a peninsula, recounting the lives we led elsewhere during long evenings in the café at the port. It was I who left first, before they scattered to Houston, London, Munich; and as the steamer pulled away from the jetty I waved more energetically. 'Write!' I shouted. 'Write!'

"The first one I met again was the lawyer from Texas, whom I saw the following spring in Geneva; we had exchanged many letters.

'You shouted "write,"' he teased me, 'as though you thought we were abandoning you. But it was you who decided to leave us, to move on.' My pride was stung. I have not written him since."

Again to me (a fragment): ". . . not to be taken as lack of trust or withdrawal. Or as rejection. One lives so badly when one is afraid to live alone."

To another, not me, she permits herself the lyrical tremolo.

"With his four dromedaries Don Pedro d'Alfaroubeira traversed the world and admired it. He did what I would like to do. If I had three dromedaries! Or two! I am writing this astride the steed at hand. I am seeing the world, the marvels therein. It is what I've always wanted to do, in my one and only life. But, meanwhile, I want to keep in touch."

Do want to keep. In touch.

With you. And you.

"You will be glad to hear, Father," Eugene adds, "that I have paid off my gambling debts." He means to be sarcastic, but perhaps he is trying to placate the old man. What does he care, what does he care, is he still seeking his father's approval? This part, where the failed poet indicates how he has not misspent his life, should be treated *presto,* in the manner of a note challenging someone to a duel.

Actually, one other passenger is writing as the plane falls—a fourteen-year-old girl who, returning to Tokyo after being treated by her aunt in Osaka to a joyous weekend of Takarazuka performances and about to start the thank-you note to her aunt when the pilot makes his first hoarse announcement, lifts her pen, shudders, then plunges it down to the paper to write instead: I'm scared, I'm scared. Help. Help. Help.

The characters are illegible. Her letter is never found.

Here's a cache of old letters. Old leaves . . . I have been having a go at rereading them. They are from my ex-husband. We had been married for seven years, and since we were going to be married forever we had granted me a sabbatical, I'd won a fellowship to Oxford, we had separated for the academic year, and we wrote each other blue aerograms every day. One didn't think of using the transatlantic telephone merely to stay in touch in those days, so long ago. We were poor, he was stingy. I was drifting away, discovering life was actually possible without him. But I did write, every evening. During the day I'd be composing my letter to him in my head, I was always talking to him in my head. I was, you see, so *used* to him. I felt safe. I didn't feel like a separate person. Whatever I saw when I was apart from him for an hour made me think first of how I would describe it to him; and we never separated for more than a few hours, just the time he taught his classes and I took mine—we were insatiable. My bladder might be aching, but I didn't want to interrupt myself or him; talking, he would follow me into the bathroom. Returning at midnight from what academics in that staid era were pleased to call parties, more than once we sat in the car until dawn lightened the street, forgetting to go into our own apartment, so absorbed were we in our dissections of his exasperating colleagues. So many years of that, the delirious amity of non-stop talking—now more than three times those years ago! I wonder if he kept my letters. Or did he, the better to unite with his second wife, pitch them into the fireplace? For a year after the divorce I awoke most mornings with a foolish smile on my face, from the surprise, the relief, of no longer being married to him. I've never felt so safe with anyone since. It's not right to feel so safe. I don't, I can't reread his letters. But I need to think of them there, in the shoebox, in the bottom of my closet. They are part of my life, my dead life.

Act I, Scene 2. "Why did you visit us, but why? Lost in our back-woods habitation, I would not have known you. Therefore I would have been spared this laceration. In time—who knows?—the agitation of inexperience would have passed. I would have found a friend, an-other, and calmly grown into my part, of virtuous mother and faithful wife." Tatyana has her indisputable feeling. But how does a feeling in one breast ignite a feeling in another? What are the laws of combus-tion? She can speak only of her own feeling—indisputably hers, after migrating from the lachrymose novels about love she loves to read. Of uniqueness. "Another! Now there can be no thought of another. Never could another rule my heart. My feeling for you is decreed for-ever, by Heaven's will. For you I'm set apart. And my whole life, whether you will or not, is pledged to you."

Pledges, promises—doesn't the fervor with which we make them testify to the strength of the opposing force, that of forgetfulness? An indomitable power of forgetfulness is necessary to close the doors and windows of consciousness, to make room for something new. Tatyana leans back in her chair, quivering, perspiring, and passes a hand over her brow. Nothing in her fragrant childhood spent among the silver birches has prepared her for this dire contraction. She tries vainly to conjure up her dear sister, her plump, kindly parents. The whole world has shrunk to the image of Eugene's grim, restless face. Then away with the past, let it be dissolved by the pale moon, evaporate like the treble notes of a perfume. Without forgetfulness there could be no happiness, no cheerfulness, no hope, no pride, no *present*. Without forgetfulness there could be no despair, no anxiety, no abjection, no longing, no *future*.

The first time I saw you, you had a white scarf knotted at the throat, the sun lay in your hair, your blouse was striped, you were wearing linen pants and espadrilles. From the table on the café terrace overlooking the Piazza del Popolo I saw you approaching. I didn't think you were beautiful. Talking gaily of having spent the night in jail after seizing the ticket for speeding the policeman had just written out and tearing it up, you sat down and ordered a lemon sherbet, I saw you and thought, If I cannot say I love you I am lost. But I didn't. Instead I am going to write a letter. The weakest move.

Now that I see how beautiful you are, your face gets in the way. As on a lenticular screen, the eyes follow me. I do not want to tell you you are beautiful. I must think of something else. Custom and my unfair heart demand that I flatter you. To coax a feeling from you. I want to pronounce those blessed words: love, love, love.

I received a letter from a close friend, I did not open it for a week. It lay moldering on my night table. The envelope bearing the name of a mere acquaintance I tore open eagerly as I came up the stairs, confident that the letter inside would contain nothing that could disturb or hurt me.

More effort than you can imagine—that's what it means. In my lair, under a dirty-paned window that lets in the sour light, I sit at the kitchen table pondering what I might say to you. This causes me to twiddle my hair, finger my chin, pass a hand over my eyes, rub my nose, push the lock back from my forehead, as if my task lay in that and not in putting words on the sheet of paper that lies before me. Perhaps I will fail in my effort to set something down, but I rather count on succeeding. I have to tell you that I write in a very tiny script, so tiny it could be thought impossible to decipher; except that it is not. This script might seem to express my unwillingness to be known, my retreat from human contact; except that I want you to know me, I do; hence this letter. You see I am writing you. Now.

A black-bordered envelope arrives from Germany, the printed announcement of a dear acquaintance's death, which I learned about by telephone a week earlier. I would find it easier to open my mail if all the major messages were color-coded. Black for death. (Christoph died at forty-nine of his second heart attack.) Red for love, Blue for longing. Yellow for rage. And an envelope with a border the color once known as ashes of roses—could that announce kindness? For I'm prone to forget this kind of letter exists, too: the expression of sheer kindness.

Hello, hello, how are you, how are you, I'm well, I'm well, how are, how is . . .

And you, my dear?

Act I, Scene 2. Sighing, trembling, Tatyana continues writing her letter, riddled with mistakes in French. (She's feverish, as I've suggested.) She hears herself, her words. And the nightingale's cadence. (Have I mentioned there was a nightingale in the garden?) Dawn is close to breaking, but she still needs the taper's feeble light. She sings her love. Or, rather, it is the opera singer singing Tatyana. Though Tatyana is very young, the role is often sung by a mature diva whose voice can no longer perform as it should. It should float. But when there is a tendency to labored phrasing, the vocal line rarely floats or springs; it seems held back or driven forward. Happily, this is a good performance. The line soars. Tatyana writes. And sings.

I cannot bear not getting a letter from you, and no longer go out. Can it be that I was once carefree and giddy? Now I drag a long shadow behind me that withers the greenery as I pass.

I stay indoors, waiting for your reply. My self-imposed house arrest is turning out to be a longer sentence than I ever envisaged. Sometimes I go back to bed in the late morning or early afternoon, after the mail has been delivered; the daytime sleep that inmates of prisons call fast time. Your letter *will* come.

I write your name. Two syllables. Two vowels. Your name inflates you, is bigger than you. You repose in a corner, sleeping; your name awakes you. I write it. You could not be named otherwise. Your name is your juice, your taste, your savor. Called by another name, you vanish. I write it. Your name.

"Dear Friend! Dear Friend! You are all that remains, my only hope, my one friend. Only you can save me. I want to come where you are, be near you, next to you. I won't bother you, I won't come visiting, I won't interrupt your work, I only need to know you are there, that beyond the wall of my room there is a living human presence. You. I need your warmth. They have crushed me! I am beaten! I am worn out! After the nightmare of this year I must come to you—under your wing! Could you find me a room? Anything will do, all I need is a table, and a view, that is, a window to look out from, where I see something, not a wall, but if it does look out on a wall, then it doesn't matter, as long as I am close to you. You will save me, you will show me what I must do, how I must live. And could you lend me the money for the ticket? I need nothing, I will ask nothing from you. I will not bother you once I am there, you have my solemn promise. Who understands better than I your need for privacy? How I admire your independence, your strength! And your generous heart. With you as my guiding star, I will be as independent as you. I will cook my own meals if I have to, I'm used to taking care of myself, but if you could find someone in the village who can look after my few simple needs, that would make it easier for me to just stay in my room, looking out the window, serenely thinking of you, never daring to bother you. You are the only one I can turn to, but you are the only one I need. Do you remember our first meeting, and how the filaments of the copper lamps glowed above our heads? You understood then. You have always understood me. Please work a miracle. Arrange it! Hide me! Find me a room!"

And I found him a room, a room in the house next to mine, on a hill above the dunes. And I wrote him that from the windows he would see trees and the open spaces, and children flying kites by the sea. And that we would fly them, too.

"It's the handwriting of a lunatic," said a friend to whom I showed the letter, with its oversized script, after his death. No, not of a lunatic but of a child: they were the same large letters a child makes, writing not with the hand alone but with the arm, from the shoulder. Dear Mommy, I LOVE YOU WITH ALL MY HEART. I WILL ALWAYS LOVE YOU.

I found him a room. And he never came.

In actual size above, fig. 1 (illustration to come), and enlarged below, fig. 2 (ditto), is an example of a writing used by Richard Anton in the nineteen-twenties, apparently as a means of protecting his man-uscripts from unwelcome scrutiny. Prof. Joachim Greichen has es-tablished that most such texts are decipherable as scribbled drafts of prose texts which Anton completed and later published. Although by 1931 he had returned to his normal hand, shown opposite, fig. 3 (ditto), he was still wont to vary the size of his writing. For instance, in his most personal correspondence he often wrote in very large printed capitals.

I NEED, I WANT. I NEED, I WANT.

I love a tender climate. I loll by the swimming pool. My letters are my diary. I deposit my life with another. With you. A summer thun-derstorm is on its way. Shall I describe the weather (or landscape), using weather (or landscape) to portray the vexations of self? If I write, I feel safe. I am humming something. I am bristling with sex-ual trepidation.

Desire is rapid as the postal system is slow. These delays in the mail make my letters obsolete at their creation, make whatever I write wrong. For even as I write, taking up each of the points in your last letter, there already exists a subsequent letter from you, written in response to the last one received from me, saying something else. As I write, there is already a new letter from you *which I have not read.* The Letter God is sporting with us. Our letters cross, but our limbs do not.

Mused the diva:

"I adore having visitors, I detest going to see people. I adore receiving letters, even reading them. But I detest writing letters. I adore giving advice but I detest being its recipient, and I never follow at once any wise advice that is given me."

Sometimes the letters contain a photograph, which the diva is pleased to sign. Yours, she writes. My best wishes. Your friend. Warmly. Love. Yes, on photographs to perfect strangers, but they are fans—exactly, that's what I said, perfect strangers—she signs Love.

Letters are sometimes a way of keeping someone at a distance. But for this purpose one must write a great many letters—at least one, sometimes two, a day. If I write you, I don't have to see you. Touch you. Put my tongue on your skin.

At first he writes mainly about his astonishing and now legendary discovery, that of a "six-class" marriage system on nearby Mortimer Island. Of course, he wishes she could have accompanied him. But she can see how impossible that would have been, even if they were already married. It's hard enough for a white man to gain the confidence of these people, but they've seen white men before, they've not yet seen an Englishwoman, whom they would think, if she were dressed sensibly (pants, shirt, hat) for this atrocious climate (mosquitoes, leeches, red ants), was dressing like a man. The sexes look very different here, he explained. The women are, he didn't quite know how to say it, so he didn't, bare-breasted. And, so, he continued, it was awfully uncomfortable, though he was getting used to the food, but she must believe he missed her, dreamed of her, was more in love with her than ever, and two years is not such a long time, is it, darling. Darling. Indeed, he told her, when he sat alone in his tent each night, as soon as he started transcribing his notes, the very act of putting pen to paper made him think of the joy of writing another letter to her. She was still receiving his letters for a month after receiving the telegram regretfully informing her that he had died of malaria. She was still rereading them fifty years later, and when she died bequeathed them—and a photograph taken just before he went out, not yet twenty-four—to her only grandchild to show the girl, silly shallow girl, how she had once been loved. Silly shallow girl.

I couldn't tell him I wanted a divorce, not by letter. My letters had to be loving. I had to wait till I returned. He met me at the airport, breaking out of the waiting area onto the tarmac as I stepped off the plane. We embraced, collected my suitcase, reached the parking lot. Once in our car, before he put his key in the ignition, I told him. We sat in the car, talking; we wept.

Of course, it should be easier to say no—or never, or no longer—in a letter. Easier, far, than face to misery-darkened face. And to say yes? Yes.

❧

Act I, Scene 2. Tatyana rereads the three pages she has written, and signed. Words are crossed out, tears stain the paper—but no matter, this is not a school exercise. It will stand as written, sealed.

Sunrise. She pulls the bell rope to summon her befuddled Nanny, who supposes her high-strung darling has simply risen earlier than usual, and instructs the old woman to give the letter to her grandson, who must carry it quickly, quickly to their new neighbor. Who? Who? Tatyana points mutely to the beloved name on the envelope.

And Eugene? Tatyana's Eugene. The pale, slim scowler in the expensive foreign boots, who had barely talked to anyone the other night when he had come, everyone hoped, to visit. The lover always sees the beloved as solitary. But Eugene (Eugene's Eugene) is, actually, as solitary and miserable as Tatyana imagines him.

So is this Eugene (my Eugene), who has finished a haughty letter of six pages breaking off all relations with his father. He will allow no claims on his heart; henceforth he will be dead, he vows, to all claims of affection.

But then he learns that his father has died (did he, before dying, receive Eugene's letter?) and—here my story rejoins theirs—returns to Petersburg for the funeral and to settle the estate, is about to go abroad, hears that his father's elder brother is dying (how mortal are these fierce old men!), arrives dutifully at his uncle's high-ceilinged manor in the remote countryside to find his uncle in the yard, already laid out in a coffin, and decides to stay for as long as it pleases him (could rustic life revive his poetic gift?), stays much alone, but after a month of seclusion most disapproved of by the neighboring gentry allows himself reluctantly to be brought to a gathering in the house of a local family with two daughters, a simple family night really, with a few neighbors. And he does notice the pretty gravity of the figure in the window seat, and thinks, If I could fall in love, it might be with a girl like that. He finds her air of melancholy . . . well-bred.

And when he receives Tatyana's letter, he is moved, but more from pity at her artless innocence, for love has been banished from his imagination. He rereads her letter, sighs; he does not wish to hurt her. At the end of the day, the longest day of Tatyana's life, he will ride over to her house—he will find her in the garden—to explain with as much gallantry as he can muster that he is not meant for marriage and might feel for her no more than the sentiments of a brother. No letter for Tatyana. She does not obsess him. He will do it face to face.

In the same way that you find the courage to write me, I find the courage to read your letter. Do not imagine that I mull over every line, but I think I've understood why it is hard for you to write me. (See, you *have* allowed me to know you.) It's because with each letter it is as if you were writing me for the first time.

Eugene does not know that, after their conversation in the garden, Tatyana falls ill, that she almost dies. Of shame, of grief. But he does hear two years later, from an old classmate at the Cadet School, that she has married, married well—indeed, her husband, a general and a decent man, is a friend of Eugene's family—and now lives in Petersburg.

Has he forgotten when, some two years after that, he is invited to a reception at the Gremin mansion in Petersburg? Presented by General Gremin to his young wife, at first Eugene doesn't recognize in the stately, tiaraed, even more beautiful woman the vulnerable, dark-browed girl he dismissed in her parents' garden. Her eyes see but they don't look. They don't ask anything.

Torchères, chandeliers.

He finds himself returning often to the Gremin mansion, contriving to meet her at the opera, at other parties, but he and Tatyana never exchange anything more than calm civilities. Sometimes he manages to be the one who sets her fur cape on her shoulders. She nods gravely—meaning what? Sometimes she seems to be hiding her dear face in her muff. Bewildered, he slowly acknowledges that he loves her, loves her beyond saying. That it is a love decreed by heaven. He knows this because he wants to write her. Could this be the solution to the riddle of his arid heart? Now he's ridiculous—no matter. One night he stays up until dawn writing a four-page epistolary howl of love. He writes another letter the next day. A third.

And he waits and waits. For a reply.

What did he do with the letter she sent him four years earlier? He did not even accord it the dignity of burning; it was simply tossed away. If only he could have it now, secreted in his wallet, to fold and unfold, to wet with his tears.

Please write me, just one letter, he asks humbling, at their last meeting. He has discovered her weeping: Tatyana has no more secrets. Irrevocably married, she has never ceased to love him. He kneels at her feet.

There will be no letter.

She forgets nothing.

There is no future.

❦

Now I take a deeper breath. Readying myself, ready, faltering. My longing is pitched. It lies at hand, in words.

Turn up the halogen lamp. There's not enough light in this room.

Love, please go on writing. Your letters will always reach me. You can write me in your real, your littlest script. I will hold it to the light. I will magnify it with my love.

To Have Been

Claudio Magris

❦

To Luca Doninelli

And so Jerry is dead. Never mind, that's not the problem, not for him, not for anyone. Not even for me, though I loved him and still do love him, because love does not conjugate—O Lord, in that sense yes, that's all we need! But love has its grammar, even though it doesn't recognize tenses but only moods, and only one of those, actually: the present in-fin-it-ive. When you love it's forever and the rest doesn't matter. Any old love, no matter what kind. Because it's not true that you get over it—you don't get over anything, which is a bit of a drawback most times; rather, you bring it along with you, like life, which in itself is nothing to shout about, except that you get over love even less than you do life. It's there, like the starlight. Who cares if the stars are alive or dead? They shine and that's that, and even though you can't see them in the daytime you know they're there.

So we won't hear that guitar any more—well, that's OK too; you can learn to do without anything. My God, how he could play it!

And when his hand gave out, he pulled down the blind and said cheerio to the lot. Well, I've no objection to make to that. Sooner or later it happens, and it doesn't much matter how; anyway, it has to happen, and who knows how many of us here this evening, ladies and gentlemen, will be alive in a month's time. Not everybody, that's for sure. It's statistically impossible. Somebody now elbowing his neighbour or complaining about the person in front of him blocking his view of the stage has already gone to the barber's for the last time. So what; a year more or less doesn't matter much. I'm not sorry for those who kick the bucket, nor do I envy those who just carry on, and I'm not much interested to know which group I belong to.

Amen for Jerry, as for everybody and everything else. As I said, I'm not criticizing his decision. When somebody wants to get off the bus then let him get off, and if he prefers to jump off while it's moving, before it reaches the bus stop, that's his business. A guy can be fed up, tired, unable to take any more or God knows what. But when I saw how down he was because he couldn't play the guitar like he used to, and told him, so as to buck him up, that he had been a great guitarist, he replied that it wasn't enough for him to have been. He wanted to be—it didn't matter what, a musician, a lover, anything, but to be.

Ah, ladies and gentlemen, in that instant I understood how lucky it is to be born, like me, or to have an uncle or a grandfather or whatever, born in Bratislava or Leopoli or Kalocsa or any other dump in this shabby Mitteleuropa, which is a hell, a real cesspool. It's enough to smell that musty odour, that stink, which is the same in Vienna and Czernowitz; but at least it doesn't force you to be. Quite the contrary. If only Jerry had realised, when his hand gave out, his great good fortune in having been! The freedom, the holiday, the tremendous license of not having to be any more, of not having to play music any more, his free pass-out from the barracks of life!

But maybe he couldn't, because he wasn't born and didn't live in that stagnant air of Pannonia, thick as a blanket, in that smoke-filled tavern where you eat badly and drink worse but you feel good when it's raining outside and the wind is blowing—and outside, in life, it's always raining and the wind cuts like a knife. Sure, any grocer of Nitra or Varazdin could teach the whole of Fifth Avenue—except those who arrived there from perhaps Nitra or Varazdin or some other neck of those filthy woods—the happiness of having been.

Oh, the modesty, the lightness of having been, that uncertain and accommodating space where everything is as light as a feather, as opposed to the presumption, the weight, the squalor, the dismay of being! Don't misunderstand me, I'm not talking about any particular past and certainly not about nostalgia, which is stupid and hurts, as the word itself indicates: nostalgia, the pain of returning. The past is horrendous. We are barbaric and evil, but our grandparents and great-grandparents were a great deal worse, ferocious savages. I certainly wouldn't want to be, to live when they were alive. No, I'm not saying that I would like to always have already been, exempt from the military service of existing. A slight disability is sometimes a saving grace, it protects you from the obligation of taking part and losing your skin.

Being hurts, it doesn't let up, ever. Do this, do that, work, struggle, win, fall in love, be happy, you must be happy, living is this duty to be happy, if you aren't it's a disgrace. So, you do all you possibly can to obey, to be good and clever and happy like you're supposed to be, but how can you when things just collapse on top of you, love thumps you on the head like a cornice falling from the roof, a bad bruise or worse, you walk hugging the walls to avoid those lunatic cars, but the walls are falling to bits—sharp stones, pieces of glass cut your skin and make you bleed, you're in bed with someone and for a moment you understand what real life could and should be and it is unbearable affliction, to have to pick up your clothes off the floor, get dressed, go out and away, thank God there's a bar around the corner, what a relief to drink a cup of coffee or a beer.

Yes, that's right, drinking a beer, for example, is a way of having been. You're there, sitting down, you look at the foam evaporating, one little bubble every second, a heartbeat, one beat less, rest and the promise of rest for your tired heart, everything is behind you. I remember that my grandmother, when we went to see her in Subotica, used to cover the sharp edges of the furniture with clothes and took away an iron table, so we children wouldn't get hurt if we ran into something while racing around the house, and she would even cover over the electric sockets. To have been is this, to live in this space where there are no sharp edges, you don't scrape your knee, you can't turn on the lamp that hurts your eyes, all is still, out of the game, no traps.

So ladies and gentlemen, this is the heritage that Central Europe has left us. A safe-deposit box, empty but with a lock on it, to discourage bank-robbers who might want to put who knows what inside it. Empty, nothing that seizes your heart and bites into your soul, life is there, already been, safe, protected from all accidents, a non-circulating banknote for a hundred old crowns that you hang on the wall, under glass, and it will never fear inflation. Also in a novel, the best part, at least for the writer, is the epilogue. Everything has already happened, all has been written, solved, the characters live happily ever after or else they're dead, it's all the same, in any case nothing more can happen. The writer holds the epilogue in his hands, he re-reads it, maybe he changes a comma, but he runs no risks.

Every epilogue is happy, because it is an epilogue. You go out on the balcony, a bit of wind blows through the geraniums and the pansies, a drop of rain slides down your face, if it rains harder you like to listen to the drumming of the drops on the awning, when it stops you go out for a short walk, you chat a bit with the neighbour you meet on the stairs, it doesn't matter to either of you what you say but it's pleasant to exchange a few words and from the window of the landing you can see, down below, far off, a stretch of sea that the sun, now coming out of the clouds, lights up like a blade. Next week we're leaving for Florence, your neighbour says. Oh, yes, it's nice, I've been there. And thus you save yourself all the hassle of travelling, standing in queues, the heat, the crowds, looking for a restaurant. A short walk in the evening air, refreshed by the rain, then back home again. You mustn't get overtired, otherwise you get upset and you can't sleep. And insomnia, ladies and gentlemen, believe me, is a terrible thing, it crushes you it suffocates you it runs after you it follows on your heels it poisons you—yes, insomnia is the supreme form of being, being insomnia, that's why you have to sleep. Sleeping is the antechamber of true having already been, but in the meantime it's already something, a breath of relief . . .

translated by Gerald Parks

A Meeting, At Last

Hanif Kureishi

❧

M organ's lover's husband held out his hand.

'Hallo, at last,' he said. 'I enjoyed watching you standing across the road. I was delighted when, after some consideration, you made up your mind to speak with me. Will you sit down?'

'Morgan,' said Morgan.

'Eric.'

Morgan nodded, dropped his car keys on the table and sat down on the edge of a chair.

The two men looked at one another.

Eric said, 'Are you drinking?'

'In a while—maybe.'

Eric called for another bottle. There were two already on the table.

'You don't mind if I do?'

'Feel free.'

'I do now.'

Eric finished his bottle and replaced it on the table with his fingers around the neck. Morgan saw Eric's thin gold wedding ring. Caroline would always drop hers in a dish on the table in Morgan's hall, and replace it when she left.

Eric had said on the phone, 'Is that Morgan?'

'Yes,' Morgan replied. 'Who—'

The voice went on, 'Are you Caroline's boyfriend?'

'But who is this asking?' said Morgan. 'Who are you?'

'The man she lives with. Eric. Her husband. Okay?'

'Right. I see.'

'Good. You see.'

Eric had said 'please' on the phone. 'Please meet me. Please.'

'Why?' Morgan had said. 'Why should I?'

'There are some things I need to know.'

Eric named a café and the time. It was later that day. He would be there. He would wait.

Morgan rang Caroline. She was in meetings, as Eric must have known. Morgan deliberated all day but it wasn't until the last moment, pacing up and down his front room when he was already late, that he walked out of the house, got in his car and stood across the road from the café.

Although Caroline had described Eric's parents, his inarticulate furies, the way his head hung when he felt low and even, as Morgan laughed, the way he scratched his backside, Eric had been a shadow man, an unfocused dark figure that had lain across their life since they had met. And while Morgan knew things about him that he didn't need to know, he had little idea of what Eric knew of him. He had yet to find out what Caroline might have recently told him. The last few days had been the craziest of Morgan's life.

The waitress brought Eric a beer. Morgan was about to order one for himself but changed his mind and asked for water.

Eric smiled grimly.

'So,' he said. 'How are you?'

Morgan knew that Eric worked long hours. He came home late and got up after the children had gone to school. Looking at him, Morgan tried to visualise something Caroline had said. As she prepared for work in the morning, he lay in bed in his pyjamas for an hour, saying nothing, but thinking intently with his hands over his eyes, as if he were in pain, and had to work something out.

Caroline left for work as early as she could in order to phone Morgan from the office.

After a couple of months, Morgan requested her not to speak about Eric, and particularly not about their attempts at love-making. But as Morgan's meetings with Caroline were arranged around Eric's absences, he was, inevitably, mentioned.

Morgan said, 'What can I do for you?'

'There are things I want to know. I am entitled.'

'Are you?'

'Don't I have any rights?'

Morgan knew that seeing this man was not going to be easy. In the car he had tried to prepare, but it was like revising for an exam without having been told the subject.

'All right,' Morgan said, to calm him down. 'I understand you.'

'After all, you have taken my life.'

'Sorry?'

'I mean my wife. My wife.'

Eric swigged at his bottle. Then he took out a small pot of pills and shook it. It was empty.

'You haven't got any painkillers, have you?'

'No.'

Eric wiped his face with a napkin.

He said, 'I'm having to take these.'

He was upset, no doubt. He would be in shock. Morgan was; Caroline too, of course.

Morgan was aware that she had started with him to cheer herself up. She had two children and a good, if dull, job. Then her best friend took a lover. Caroline met Morgan through work and decided immediately that he had the right credentials. Love and romance suited her. Why hadn't she been dipped in such delight every day? She thought everything else could remain the same, apart from her 'treat'. But as Morgan liked to say, there were 'consequences'. In bed, she would call him 'Mr Consequences'.

'I'm not moving out of my house,' Eric said. 'It's my home. You're not intending to take that from me, as well as my wife?'

'Your wife . . . Caroline,' Morgan said, restoring her as her own person. 'I didn't steal her. I didn't have to persuade her. She gave herself to me.'

'She gave herself?' Eric said. 'She wanted you? You?'

'That's the truth.'

'Do women do that to you?'

Morgan tried to laugh.

'Do they?' Eric said.

'Only her—recently.'

Eric stared, waiting for him to continue. But Morgan said nothing, reminding himself that he could walk out at any time, that he didn't have to take anything from this man.

Eric said, 'Do you want her?'

'I think so, yes.'

'You're not sure? After doing all this, you're not sure?'

'I didn't say that.'

'What do you mean then?'

'Nothing.'

But perhaps he wasn't sure. He had become used to their arrange-
ment. There were too many hurried phone calls, misunderstood letters, snatched meetings and painful partings. But they had lived
within it. They even had a routine. He had received more from Eric's
wife—seeing her twice a week—than he had from any other woman.
Otherwise, when he wasn't working, he visited art galleries with his
daughter; he packed his shoulder bag, took his guide book and
walked about parts of the city he'd never seen; he sat by the river and
wrote notes about the past. What had he learned through her? A reverence for the world; the ability to see feeling, certain created objects,
and other people as important—indeed, invaluable. She had intro-
duced him to the pleasures of carelessness.

Eric said, 'I met Caroline when she was twenty-one. She didn't
have a line on her face. Her cheeks were rosy. She was acting in a
play at university.'

'Was she a good actress? She's good at a lot of things, isn't she?
She likes doing things well.'

Eric said, 'It wasn't long before we developed bad habits.'

Morgan asked, 'What sort of thing?'

'In our . . . relationship. That's the word everyone uses.' Eric
said, 'We didn't have the skill, the talent, the ability to get out of
them. How long have you known her?'

'Two years.'

'Two years!'

Morgan was confused. 'What did she tell you? Haven't you been
discussing it?'

Eric said, 'How long do you think will it take me to digest all this?'

Morgan said, 'What are you doing?'

He had been watching Eric's hands, wondering whether he

would grasp the neck of the bottle. But Eric was hunting through the briefcase he had pulled out from under the table.

'What date? Surely you remember that! Don't you two have anniversaries?' Eric dragged out a large red book. 'My journal. Perhaps I made a note that day! The past two years have to be rethought! When you are deceived, every day has another complexion!'

Morgan looked round at the other people in the café.

'I don't like being shouted at,' he said. 'I'm too tired for that.'

'No, no. Sorry.'

Eric flipped through the pages of the book. When he saw Morgan watching, he shut the journal.

Eric said in a low voice, 'Have you ever been deceived? Has that ever happened to you?'

'I would imagine so,' said Morgan.

'How pompous! And do you think that deceiving someone is all right?'

'One might say that there are circumstances which make it inevitable.'

Eric said, 'It falsifies everything.' He went on, 'Your demeanour suggests that it doesn't matter, either. Are you that cynical? This is important. Look at the century!'

'Sorry?'

'I work in television news. I know what goes on. Your cruelty is the same thing. Think of the Jews—'

'Come on—'

'That other people don't have feelings! That they don't matter! That you can trample over them!'

'I haven't killed you, Eric.'

'I could die of this. I could die.'

Morgan nodded. 'I understand that.'

He remembered one night, when she had to get home, to slip into bed with Eric, Caroline had said, 'If only Eric would die . . . just die . . .'

'Peacefully?'

'Quite peacefully.'

Eric leaned across the table. 'Have you felt rough, then?'

'Yes.'

'Over this?'

'Over this.' Morgan laughed. 'Over everything. But definitely over this.'

'Good. Good.' Eric said, 'Middle age is a lonely time.'

'Without a doubt,' said Morgan.

'That's interesting. More lonely than any other time, do you think?'

'Yes,' said Morgan. 'All you lack seems irrevocable.'

Eric said, 'Between the age of twelve and thirteen my elder brother, whom I adored, committed suicide, my father died of grief, and my grandfather just died. Do you think I still miss them?'

'How could you not?'

Eric drank his beer and thought about this.

'You're right, there's a hole in me.' He said, 'I wish there were a hole in you.'

Morgan said, 'She has listened to me. And me to her.'

Eric said, 'You really pay attention to one another, do you?'

'There's something about being attended to that makes you feel better. I'm never lonely when I'm with her.'

'Good.'

'I've been determined, this time, not to shut myself off.'

'But she's my wife.'

There was a pause.

Eric said, 'What is it people say these days? It's your problem! It's my problem! Do you believe that? What do you think?'

Morgan had been drinking a lot of whisky and smoking grass, for the first time. He had been at university in the late sixties but had identified with the puritanical left, not the hippies. These days, when he needed to switch off his brain, he noticed how tenacious consciousness was. Perhaps he wanted to shut off his mind because in the past few days he had been considering forgetting Caroline. Forgetting about them all, Caroline, Eric and their kids. Maybe he would, now. Perhaps the secrecy, and her inaccessibility, had kept them all at the right distance.

'Yes.'

Morgan realised he had been thinking for some time. He turned to Eric again, who was tapping the bottle with his nail.

'I do like your house,' said Eric. 'But it's big, for one person.'

'My house, did you say? Have you seen it?'

'Yes.'

Morgan looked at Eric's eyes. He seemed rather spirited. Morgan almost envied him. Hatred could give you great energy.

Eric said, 'You look good in your white shorts and white socks, when you go out running. It always makes me laugh.'

'Haven't you got anything better to do than stand outside my house?'

'Haven't you got anything better to do than steal my wife?' Eric pointed his finger at him. 'One day, Morgan, perhaps you will wake up and find in the morning that things aren't the way they were last night. That everything you have has been sullied and corrupted in some way. Can you imagine that?'

'All right,' said Morgan. 'All right, all right.'

Eric had knocked his bottle over. He put his napkin on the spilled beer and popped his bottle on top of that.

He said, 'Are you intending to take my children away?'

'What? Why should I?'

'I can tell you now, I have had that house altered to my specifications, you know. I have a pergola. I'm not moving out, and I'm not selling it. Actually, to tell the truth'—Eric had a sort of half-grin, half-grimace on his face—'I might be better off without my wife and kids.'

'What?' said Morgan. 'What did you say?'

Eric raised his eyebrows at him.

'You know what I mean,' Eric said.

Morgan's children were with their mother, the girl away at university, the boy at private school. Both of them were doing well. Morgan had met Eric's kids only briefly. He had offered to take them in if Caroline was prepared to be with him. He was ready for that, he thought. He didn't want to shirk the large tasks. But in time one of the kids could, say, become a junkie; the other a teenage prostitute. And Morgan, having fallen for their mother, might find himself burdened. He knew people it had happened to.

Eric said, 'My children are going to be pretty angry with you when they find out what you've done to us.'

'Yes,' said Morgan. 'Who could blame them?'

'They're big and expensive. They eat like horses.'

'Christ.'

Eric said, 'Do you know about my job?'

'Not as much as you know about mine, I shouldn't think.'

Eric didn't respond, but said, 'Funny to think of you two talking about me. I bet you'd lie there wishing I'd have a car crash.'

Morgan blinked.

'It's prestigious,' Eric said. 'In the newsroom, you know. Well paid. Plenty of action, continuous turnover of stories. But it's bland, worthless. I can see that now. And the people burn out. They're exhausted, and on an adrenalin rush at the same time. I've always wanted to take up walking . . . hill-walking, you know, boots and rucksacks. I want to write a novel. And travel, and have adventures. This could be an opportunity.'

Morgan wondered at this. Caroline had said that Eric took little interest in the outside world, except through the medium of journalism. The way things looked, smelled, tasted, held no fascination for him; nor did the inner motives of living people. Whereas Morgan and Caroline, dawdling in a bar with their hands playing on one another, loved to discuss the relationships of mutual acquaintances, as if together they might distil the spirit of a working love.

Morgan picked up his car keys. He said, 'Sounds good. You'll be fine then, Eric. Best of luck.'

'Thanks a bunch.'

Eric showed no sign of moving.

He said, 'What do you like about her?'

Morgan wanted to shout at him, he wanted to pound on the table in front of him, saying, I love the way she pulls down her clothes, lies on her side and lets me lick and kiss her soft parts, as if I have lifted the dish of life up to my face and burst through it into the wonderland of love for ever!

Eric was tensing up. 'What is it?'

'What?'

'You like about her! If you don't know, maybe you would be good enough to leave us alone!'

'Look, Eric,' Morgan said, 'if you calm yourself a minute, I'll say this. More than a year ago, she said she wanted to be with me. I've been waiting for her.' He pointed at Eric. 'You've had your time with her. You've had plenty, I would say you've had enough. Now it's my turn.'

He got up and walked to the door. It was simple. Then it felt good to be outside. He didn't look back.

Morgan sat in the car and sighed. He started off and stopped at the lights on the corner. He was thinking he would go to the super-market. Caroline could come round after work and he would cook. He would mix her favourite drink, a whisky mac. She would appre-ciate being looked after. They could lie down together on the bed.

Eric pulled open the door, got in, and shut the door. Morgan stared at him. The driver behind beeped his horn repeatedly. Morgan drove across the road.

'Do you want me to drop you somewhere?'

'I haven't finished with you,' said Eric.

Morgan looked alternately at the road and at Eric. Eric was sitting in his car, in his seat, with his feet on his rubber mat.

Morgan was swearing under his breath.

Eric said, 'What are you going to do? Have you decided?'

Morgan drove on. He saw that Eric had picked up a piece of pa-per from the dashboard. Morgan remembered it was a shopping list that Caroline had made out for him. Eric put it back.

Morgan turned the car round and accelerated.

'We'll go to her office now and discuss it with her. Is that what you want? I'm sure she'll tell you everything you want to know. Otherwise—let me know when you want to get out,' said Morgan. 'Say when.'

Eric just stared ahead.

Morgan thought he had been afraid of happiness, and kept it

away; he had been afraid of other people, and had kept them away. He was still afraid, but it was too late for that.

Suddenly he banged the steering wheel and said, 'Okay.'

'What?' said Eric.

'I've decided,' said Morgan. 'The answer is yes. Yes to everything! Now you must get out.' He stopped the car. 'Out, I said!'

Driving away, he watched Eric in the mirror getting smaller and smaller.

Associations in Blue

Christa Wolf

❧

> *Who was it shouted with joy*
> *when blue was born?*
> —Pablo Neruda

You ask odd questions, Pablo. Blue? Born? But didn't it always exist? As the sky-blue over the landscape of childhood? As the Most Everlasting Blue there is? Outside is the loveliest blue sky, and here you are inside, huddling over your book! You're going to turn into a bluestocking after all, then you won't get a husband later on.

Blue wrote stories.

Annemarie's boyfriend said he wants to bring her down the blue from out of the sky. I'm going to bring you the blue down from heaven. Lordy, that's just the sort of thing guys like him say, talking a blue streak. But she claims he's true to her. A likely story. She's blond, so she should wear blue, her boyfriend says. Blue, blue, all my clothes are blue. Blue is the color of faithfulness. But lately she has red shoes, he actually gave them to her. Red and blue are finery to the sow, and for the wife of the clown they make a fine gown. Her boyfriend likes to paint the town blue now and then. Blue today, blue tomorrow, and blue again the day after that. Blue Monday. See what I mean? Blue idle on Monday, hungry on Tuesday, we all know that saying. And right now, unfortunately, he is outside, staggering across the square, singing "Cornflower blue is the sky beside the mighty Rhine." Totally blue the man is, that is, dead drunk. He's past help from a Blue Cross nurse. Cornflower blue are women's eyes by the mighty wine. Boy are they ever. Recently he beat her black and blue, see? And then her brother said, Now that guy is in for a big blue surprise, and gave him a good beating. Once again he got off lightly, with a black-and-blue eye. That's fine. But now let's hope Annemarie will stop pulling blue wool over her eyes about him. Even she can't be that blue-eyed.

"From the blue mountains we're coming, my dear,/ O my darling you are so far from here." We used to sing it, "The teacher's as dumb as we are, I fear." The sky is blue, the weather is fine, dear Teacher, we want to go out for a walk. I suppose you kids want a blue-ink report to your parents? Instead why don't you memorize the colors of the rainbow: red orange yellow green blue indigo violet. ROYGBIV. Or are you just interested in hearing something about the war again, when the bluebottles were flying around our guys' ears? Forward march! A song. "The blue-coated dragoons are riding with trumpets and drums through the gates."

Can't you all sing something nice for once? The beautiful blue Danube. That was the first waltz I danced with Hans. Yup, it's the same old story. Things ended badly with her bluejacket sailor. Grete can't get over it. "A bluejacket lad, he sails the sea,/ he loved a girl but he hadn't a penny./ The maiden's disgraced, and who's to blame?/ The amorous sailor with no penny to his name." That sort of tale can end badly. Madame X has just had to be carted off by the police with their blue lights flashing. Blue cyanide is my guess. Her lips already looked quite blue. In a case like that, help always arrives too late.

The sleek dude who left her in the lurch supposedly has blue blood, at least that's what he told her. We all know about King Bluebeard. "The strange knight had a beard that was all blue, and she had a dread of it and felt uneasy every time she looked at him." If only people had paid attention to her feelings. But he gave her a blue arctic fox as a gift, and she thought, a man like that cannot lie, and went weak at the knees.

This is going to cost you a pretty blue penny or two, you'll have to earn them first. I'll do it even so. We always use blue ink to sign the clean copy. But first draw me up a blueprint, please: after all, with a scheme like this you don't want to just take off into the wild blue yonder. But some people aim at the wild blue yonder and hit the black bull's-eye.

We used to fill up the milk can with blueberries in two hours. And by the afternoon the cake was baked. Carp poached blue at New Year's? Never. Carp should be served in a beer sauce. And poached trout is a dish for posh people. Blue simply isn't a color for stuff to eat. Better suited to flowers. Violets, for instance. "A violet in the meadow stood, bent over and unknown, it was a lovely violet." Blue cabbage, that is, bluish-red cabbage down south, well that's okay with me. And there's blue liqueur, curaçao I think it's called.

And there's Blue Master cheese with blue mold in it, not something I like. I will never understand how people can grow blue potatoes and name them "blue mice." It's so unnatural.

Goethe's Theory of Color. "This color creates a peculiar and almost inexpressible effect on the eye. As a color, it represents an energy . . ."

Blue, Pablo, is the color of longing. Is that what you meant? "Spring lets its blue ribbon flutter through the air again." The blue hills in the blue distance. "On horizons of too blue," "Blue flags to Berlin." Prussian blue, Berlin blue, an important blue pigment made of ferrous sulphate and potassium ferrocyanide. A delicate stroke on china. The deep cobalt blue of glass vases, bowls and ashtrays, my favorite color. Tablecloths printed with indigo in classic patterns. A craft that is dying out.

Once in my life to be by the blue Adriatic. O heaven, radiant azure. The blue butterfly fluttering ahead of us. The blue bird on the curtain that the artist Liessner-Blomberg used at the cabaret of Russian emigrants in 1920s Berlin. Kandinsky's Blue Rider school of painters. Franz Marc's painting, The Tower of Blue Horses. Picasso's blue period. The unforgettable blue of Yves Klein at the museum in Nice. "Just as we feel inclined to pursue an attractive object that is fleeing from us, so we like to look at blue not because it pushes toward us but because it draws us after it." Goethe's Theory of Color.

The blue hour between daylight and dreaming. Night-blue. Dove-gray-blue. The blue light from the fountain in the Grimm's fairy tale which, when the trusty and unjustly treated soldier lights his pipe in it, not only gives him reparation but a whole kingdom and the king's daughter to boot. That's the only way to go.

General Franco's ghastly Blue Division in the Spanish Civil War. The blue flag of the European Union. And the care packages of food that the Americans are dropping in Afghanistan are now blue and no longer yellow, so people can tell them apart from the yellow cluster bombs that they are dropping at the same time.

On the other hand you have the Blue Flower, Pablo, the symbol of German Romanticism, a creation of Count Friedrich von Hardenberg, known as Novalis. The protagonist of whose novel, Heinrich von Ofterdingen, sees it in a dream, "a tall, pale blue flower that stood by the spring and touched him with its wide, shining petals . . . He saw nothing but the flower and contemplated it for a long time with inexpressible tenderness." He pursues this image of longing, seeing in it "a bulwark against the uniformity and habitualness of life," a magic charm against the monotony of the earthly.

But who was it shouted with joy when blue was born? What were you thinking, Pablo? We don't know. But I think: It was the extraterrestrials who shouted with joy at the birth of the earth, the blue planet.

translated by Jan van Heurck

The Rejection

Woody Allen

❧

When Boris Ivanovich opened the letter and read its contents he
and his wife Anna turned pale. It was a rejection of their three-
year-old son Mischa by the very best nursery school in Manhattan.

"This can't be," Boris Ivanovich said, stricken.

"No, no—there must be some mistake," his wife concurred. "After all, he's a bright boy, pleasant and outgoing, with good verbal
skills and facile with crayons and Mr. Potato Head."

Boris Ivanovich had tuned out and was lost in his own reveries.
How could he face his co-workers at Bear Stearns when little Mischa
had failed to get into a preschool of reputation? He could hear Siminov's mocking voice: "You don't understand these matters. Connec-
tions are important. Money must change hands. You're such a
bumpkin, Boris Ivanovich."

"No, no—it isn't that," Boris Ivanovich heard himself protest. "I
greased everybody, from the teachers to the window washers, and
still the kid couldn't hack it."

"Did he do well at his interview?" Siminov would ask.

"Yes," Boris would reply, "although he had some difficulty stacking blocks—"

"Tentative with blocks," Siminov whined in his contemptuous fashion. "That speaks for serious emotional difficulties. Who'd want an oaf that can't make a castle?"

But why should I even discuss all that with Siminov, Boris Ivanovich thought. Perhaps he won't have heard about it.

The following Monday, however, when Boris Ivanovich went into his office it was clear that everyone knew. There was a dead hare lying on his desk. Siminov came in, his face like a thundercloud. "You understand," Siminov said, "the lad will never be accepted at any decent college. Certainly not in the Ivy League."

"Just because of this, Dmitri Siminov? Nursery school will impact on his higher education?"

"I don't like to mention names," Siminov said, "but many years ago a renowned investment banker failed to get his son into a kindergarten of ample distinction. Apparently there was some scandal about the boy's ability to finger-paint. At any rate, the lad, having been rejected by the school of his parents' choice, was forced to—to—"

"What? Tell me, Dmitri Siminov."

"Let's just say that when he turned five he was forced to attend— a public school."

"Then there is no God," Boris Ivanovich said.

"At eighteen his onetime companions all entered Yale or Stanford," Siminov continued, "but this poor wretch, never having acquired the proper credentials at a preschool of—shall I say— appropriate status, was accepted only at barber college."

"Forced to trim whiskers," Boris Ivanovich cried, picturing poor Mischa in a white uniform, shaving the wealthy.

"Having no substantial background in such matters as decorating cupcakes or the sandbox, the boy was totally unprepared for the cruelties life held," Siminov went on. "In the end, he worked at some menial jobs, finally pilfering from his employer to keep up an alcohol habit. By then he was a hopeless drunkard. Of course, pilfering led to thievery and ended up with the slaughter of his landlady and her dismemberment. At the hanging, the boy attributed it all to failing to get into the correct nursery school."

That night, Boris Ivanovich could not sleep. He envisioned the unattainable Upper East Side preschool, with its cheerful, bright classrooms. He pictured three-year-olds in Bonpoint outfits cutting and pasting and then having some comforting snack—a cup of juice and perhaps a Goldfish or a Chocolate Graham. If Mischa could be denied this, there was no meaning in life or in all of existence. He imagined his son, a man now, standing before the C.E.O. of a prestigious firm, who was quizzing Mischa on his knowledge of animals and shapes, things he would be expected to have a deep understanding of.

"Why—er," Mischa said, trembling, "that's a triangle—no, no, an octagon. And that's a bunny—I'm sorry, a kangaroo."

"And the words to 'Do You Know the Muffin Man?'" the C.E.O. demanded. "All the vice-presidents here at Smith Barney can sing them."

"To be honest, sir, I never learned the song properly," the young man admitted, while his job application fluttered into the wastebasket.

❧

In the days following the rejection, Anna Ivanovich became listless. She quarrelled with the nanny and accused her of brushing Mischa's teeth sideways rather than up and down. She stopped eating regularly, and wept to her shrink. "I must have transgressed against God's will to bring this on," she wailed. "I must have sinned beyond measure—too many shoes from Prada." She imagined that the Hampton Jitney tried to run her over, and when Armani cancelled her charge account for no apparent reason she took to her bedroom and began having an affair. This was hard to conceal from Boris Ivanovich, since he shared the same bedroom and asked repeatedly who the man next to them was.

When all seemed blackest, a lawyer friend, Shamsky, called Boris Ivanovich and said there was a ray of hope. He suggested they meet at Le Cirque for lunch. Boris Ivanovich arrived in disguise, since the restaurant had refused him admittance when the nursery-school decision came out.

"There is a man, a certain Fyodorovich," Shamsky said, spooning up his portion of crème brûlée. "He can secure a second interview for your offspring and in return all you have to do is keep him secretly informed of any confidential information about certain companies that might cause their stocks to suddenly rise or fall dramatically."

"But that's insider trading," Boris Ivanovich said.

"Only if you're a stickler for federal law," Shamsky pointed out. "My God, we're talking about admission to an exclusive nursery school. Of course, a donation will help as well. Nothing showy. I know they're looking for someone to pick up the tab for a new annex."

At that moment, one of the waiters recognized Boris Ivanovich behind his false nose and his wig. The staff fell upon him in a fury and dragged him out the door. "So!" the headwaiter said. "Thought you'd fool us. Out! Oh, and as for your son's future, we're always looking for busboys. Au revoir, beanbag."

At home that night, Boris Ivanovich told his wife they would have to sell their home in Amagansett to raise money for a bribe.

"What? Our dear country house?" Anna cried. "My sisters and I grew up in that house. We had an easement that cut through a neighbor's property to the sea. The easement ran right across the neighbor's kitchen table. I remember walking with my family through bowls of Cheerios to go swimming and play in the ocean."

As fate would have it, on the morning of Mischa's second interview his guppy passed away suddenly. There had been no warning—no previous illness. In fact, the guppy had just had a complete physical and was pronounced in A-1 health. Naturally, the boy was disconsolate. At his interview he would not touch the Lego or the Lite Brite. When the teacher asked him how old he was, he said sharply, "Who wants to know, lard bucket?" He was passed over once again.

Boris Ivanovich and Anna, now destitute, went to live in a shelter for the homeless. There they met many other families whose children had been turned down by élite schools. They sometimes shared food with these people and traded nostalgic stories of private planes and winters at Mar-a-Lago. Boris Ivanovich discovered souls even less fortunate than himself, simple folk who had been turned down by co-op boards for not having sufficient net worth. These people all had a great religious beauty behind their suffering faces.

"I now believe in something," he told his wife one day. "I believe there is meaning in life and that all people, rich and poor, will eventually dwell in the City of God, because Manhattan is definitely getting unlivable."

The Ultimate Safari

Nadine Gordimer

❧

The African Adventure Lives On . . . You can do it!
The ultimate safari or expedition
With leaders who know *Africa.*
—Travel Adverstisement,
Observer, London, 27/11/88

That night our mother went to the shop and she didn't come back. Ever. What happened? I don't know. My father also had gone away one day and never came back; but he was fighting in the war. We were in the war, too, but we were children, we were like our grandmother and grandfather, we didn't have guns. The people my father was fighting—the bandits, they are called by our government—ran all over the place and we ran away from them like chickens chased by dogs. We didn't know where to go. Our mother went to the shop because someone said you could get some oil for cooking. We were happy because we hadn't tasted oil for a long time; perhaps she got the oil and someone knocked her down in the dark and took that oil from her. Perhaps she met the bandits. If you meet them, they will kill you. Twice they came to our village and we ran and hid in the bush and when they'd gone we came back and found they had taken everything; but the third time they came back there was nothing to take, no oil, no food, so they burned the thatch and the roofs of our houses fell in. My mother found some pieces of tin and we put those up over part of the house. We were waiting there for her that night she never came back.

We were frightened to go out, even to do our business, because the bandits did come. Not into our house—without a roof it must have looked as if there was no one in it, everything gone—but all through the village. We heard people screaming and running. We were afraid even to run, without our mother to tell us where. I am the middle one, the girl, and my little brother clung against my stomach with his arms round my neck and his legs round my waist like a baby monkey to its mother. All night my first-born brother kept in his hand a broken piece of wood from one of our burnt house-poles. It was to save himself if the bandits found him.

We stayed there all day. Waiting for her. I don't know what day it was; there was no school, no church any more in our village, so you didn't know whether it was a Sunday or a Monday.

When the sun was going down, our grandmother and grandfather came. Someone from our village had told them we children were alone, our mother had not come back. I say 'grandmother' before 'grandfather' because it's like that: our grandmother is big and strong, not yet old, and our grandfather is small, you don't know where he is, in his loose trousers, he smiles but he hasn't heard what you're saying, and his hair looks as if he's left it full of soap suds. Our grandmother took us—me, the baby, my first-born brother, our grandfather—back to her house and we were all afraid (except the baby, asleep on our grandmother's back) of meeting the bandits on the way. We waited a long time at our grandmother's place. Perhaps it was a month. We were hungry. Our mother never came. While we were waiting for her to fetch us our grandmother had no food for us, no food for our grandfather and herself. A woman with milk in her breasts gave us some for my little brother, although at our house he used to eat porridge, same as we did. Our grandmother took us to look for wild spinach but everyone else in her village did the same and there wasn't a leaf left.

Our grandfather, walking a little behind some young men, went to look for our mother but didn't find her. Our grandmother cried with other women and I sang the hymns with them. They brought a little food—some beans—but after two days there was nothing again. Our grandfather used to have three sheep and a cow and a vegetable garden but the bandits had long ago taken the sheep and the cow, because they were hungry, too; and when planting time came our grandfather had no seed to plant.

So they decided—our grandmother did; our grandfather made little noises and rocked from side to side, but she took no notice—we would go away. We children were pleased. We wanted to go away from where our mother wasn't and where we were hungry. We wanted to go where there were no bandits and there was food. We were glad to think there must be such a place; away.

Our grandmother gave her church clothes to someone in exchange for some dried mealies and she boiled them and tied them in a rag. We took them with us when we went and she thought we would get water from the rivers but we didn't come to any river and we got so thirsty we had to turn back. Not all the way to our grandparents' place but to a village where there was a pump. She opened the basket where she carried some clothes and the mealies and she sold her shoes to buy a big plastic container for water. I said, *Gogo,* how will you go to church now even without shoes, but she said we had a long journey and too much to carry. At that village we met other people who were also going away. We joined them because they seemed to know where that was better than we did.

To get there we had to go through the Kruger Park. We knew about the Kruger Park. A kind of whole country of animals—elephants, lions, jackals, hyenas, hippos, crocodiles, all kinds of animals. We had some of them in our own country, before the war (our grandfather remembers; we children weren't born yet) but the bandits kill the elephants and sell their tusks, and the bandits and our soldiers have eaten all the buck. There was a man in our village without legs—a crocodile took them off, in our river; but all the same our country is a country of people, not animals. We knew about the Kruger Park because some of our men used to leave home to work there in the places where white people come to stay and look at the animals.

So we started to go away again. There were women and other children like me who had to carry the small ones on their backs when the women got tired. A man led us into the Kruger Park; are we there yet, are we there yet, I kept asking our grandmother. Not yet, the man said, when she asked him for me. He told us we had to take a long way to get round the fence, which he explained would kill you, roast off your skin the moment you touched it, like the wires high up on poles that give electric light in our towns. I've seen that sign of a head without eyes or skin or hair on an iron box at the mission hospital we used to have before it was blown up.

When I asked the next time, they said we'd been walking in the Kruger Park for an hour. But it looked just like the bush we'd been walking through all day, and we hadn't seen any animals except the monkeys and birds which live around us at home, and a tortoise that, of course, couldn't get away from us. My first-born brother and the other boys brought it to the man so it could be killed and we could cook and eat it. He let it go because he told us we could not make a fire; all the time we were in the Park we must not make a fire because the smoke would show we were there. Police, wardens, would come and send us back where we came from. He said we must move like animals among the animals, away from the roads, away from the white people's camps. And at that moment I heard—I'm sure I was the first to hear—cracking branches and the sound of something parting grasses and I almost squealed because I thought it was the police, wardens—the people he was telling us to look out for—who had found us already. And it was an elephant, and another elephant, and more elephants, big blots of dark moved wherever you looked between the trees. They were curling their trunks round the red leaves of the Mopane trees and stuffing them into their mouths. The babies leant against their mothers. The almost grown-up ones wrestled like my first-born brother with his friends—only they used trunks instead of arms. I was so interested I forgot to be afraid. The man said we should just stand still and be quiet while the elephants passed. They passed very slowly because elephants are too big to need to run from anyone.

The buck ran from us. They jumped so high they seemed to fly. The warthogs stopped dead, when they heard us, and swerved off the way a boy in our village used to zigzag on the bicycle his father had brought back from the mines. We followed the animals to where they drank. When they had gone, we went to their water-holes. We were never thirsty without finding water, but the animals ate, ate all the time. Whenever you saw them they were eating, grass, trees, roots. And there was nothing for us. The mealies were finished. The only food we could eat was what the baboons ate, dry little figs full of ants that grow along the branches of the trees at the rivers. It was hard to be like the animals.

When it was very hot during the day we would find lions lying asleep. They were the colour of the grass and we didn't see them at first but the man did, and he led us back and a long way round where they slept. I wanted to lie down like the lions. My little brother was getting thin but he was very heavy. When our grandmother looked for me, to put him on my back, I tried not to see. My first-born brother stopped talking; and when we rested he had to be shaken to get up again, as if he was just like our grandfather, he couldn't hear. I saw flies crawling on our grandmother's face and she didn't brush them off; I was frightened. I picked a palm leaf and chased them.

We walked at night as well as by day. We could see the fires where the white people were cooking in the camps and we could smell the smoke and the meat. We watched the hyenas with their backs that slope as if they're ashamed, slipping through the bush after the smell. If one turned its head, you saw it had big brown shining eyes like our own, when we looked at each other in the dark. The wind brought voices in our own language from the compounds where the people who work in the camps live. A woman among us wanted to go to them at night and ask them to help us. They can give us the food from the dustbins, she said, she started wailing and our grandmother had to grab her and put a hand over her mouth. The man who led us had told us that we must keep out of the way of our people who worked at the Kruger Park; if they helped us they would lose their work. If they saw us, all they could do was pretend we were not there; they had seen only animals.

Sometimes we stopped to sleep for a little while at night. We slept close together. I don't know which night it was—because we were walking, walking, any time, all the time—we heard the lions very near. Not groaning loudly the way they did far off. Panting, like we do when we run, but it's a different kind of panting: you can hear they're not running, they're waiting, somewhere near. We all rolled closer together, on top of each other, the ones on the edge fighting to get into the middle. I was squashed against a woman who smelled bad because she was afraid but I was glad to hold tight on to her. I prayed to God to make the lions take someone on the edge and go. I shut my eyes not to see the tree from which a lion might jump right into the middle of us, where I was. The man who led us jumped up instead, and beat on the tree with a dead branch. He had taught us never to make a sound but he shouted. He shouted at the lions like a drunk man shouting at nobody, in our village. The lions went away. We heard them groaning, shouting back at him from far off.

We were tired, so tired. My first-born brother and the man had to lift our grandfather from stone to stone where we found places to cross the rivers. Our grandmother is strong but her feet were bleeding. We could not carry the basket on our heads any longer, we couldn't carry anything except my little brother. We left our things under a bush. As long as our bodies get there, our grandmother said. Then we ate some wild fruit we didn't know from home and our stomachs ran. We were in the grass called elephant grass because it is nearly as tall as an elephant, that day we had those pains, and our grandfather couldn't just get down in front of people like my little brother, he went off into the grass to be on his own. We had to keep up, the man who led us always kept telling us, we must catch up, but we asked him to wait for our grandfather.

So everyone waited for our grandfather to catch up. But he didn't. It was the middle of the day; insects were singing in our ears and we couldn't hear him moving through the grass. We couldn't see him because the grass was so high and he was so small. But he must have been somewhere there inside his loose trousers and his shirt that was torn and our grandmother couldn't sew because she had no cotton. We knew he couldn't have gone far because he was weak and slow. We all went to look for him, but in groups, so we too wouldn't be hidden from each other in that grass. It got into our eyes and noses; we called him softly but the noise of the insects must have filled the little space left for hearing in his ears. We looked and looked but we couldn't find him. We stayed in that long grass all night. In my sleep I found him curled round in a place he had tramped down for himself, like the places we'd seen where the buck hide their babies.

When I woke up he still wasn't anywhere. So we looked again, and by now there were paths we'd made by going through the grass many times, it would be easy for him to find us if we couldn't find him. All that day we just sat and waited. Everything is very quiet when the sun is on your head, inside your head, even if you lie, like the animals, under the trees. I lay on my back and saw those ugly birds with hooked beaks and plucked necks flying round and round above us. We had passed them often where they were feeding on the bones of dead animals, nothing was ever left there for us to eat. Round and round, high up and then lower down and then high again. I saw their necks poking to this side and that. Flying round and round. I saw our grandmother, who sat up all the time with my little brother on her lap, was seeing them, too.

In the afternoon the man who led us came to our grandmother and told her the other people must move on. He said, If their children don't eat soon they will die.

Our grandmother said nothing.

I'll bring you water before we go, he told her.

Our grandmother looked at us, me, my first-born brother, and
my little brother on her lap. We watched the other people getting up
to leave. I didn't believe the grass would be empty, all around us,
where they had been. That we would be alone in this place, the
Kruger Park, the police or the animals would find us. Tears came
out of my eyes and nose onto my hands but our grandmother took
no notice. She got up, with her feet apart the way she puts them
when she is going to lift firewood, at home in our village, she swung
my little brother onto her back, tied him in her cloth—the top of her
dress was torn and her big breasts were showing but there was nothing in them for him. She said, Come.

So we left the place with the long grass. Left behind. We went
with the others and the man who led us. We started to go away, again.

There's a very big tent, bigger than a church or a school, tied down
to the ground. I didn't understand that was what it would be, when
we got there, away. I saw a thing like that the time our mother took us
to the town because she heard our soldiers were there and she
wanted to ask them if they knew where our father was. In that tent,
people were praying and singing. This one is blue and white like
that one but it's not for praying and singing, we live in it with other
people who've come from our country. Sister from the clinic says
we're two hundred without counting the babies, and we have new
babies, some were born on the way through the Kruger Park.

Inside, even when the sun is bright it's dark and there's a kind of
whole village in there. Instead of houses each family has a little place
closed off with sacks or cardboard from boxes—whatever we can
find—to show the other families it's yours and they shouldn't come
in even though there's no door and no windows and no thatch, so

that if you're standing up and you're not a small child you can see into everybody's house. Some people have even made paint from ground rocks and drawn designs on the sacks.

Of course, there really is a roof—the tent is the roof, far, high up. It's like a sky. It's like a mountain and we're inside it; through the cracks paths of dust lead down, so thick you think you could climb them. The tent keeps off the rain overhead but the water comes in at the sides and in the little streets between our places—you can only move along them one person at a time—the small kids like my little brother play in the mud. You have to step over them. My little brother doesn't play. Our grandmother takes him to the clinic when the doctor comes on Mondays. Sister says there's something wrong with his head, she thinks it's because we didn't have enough food at home. Because of the war. Because our father wasn't there. And then because he was so hungry in the Kruger Park. He likes just to lie about on our grandmother all day, on her lap or against her somewhere, and he looks at us and looks at us. He wants to ask something but you can see he can't. If I tickle him he may just smile. The clinic gives us special powder to make into porridge for him and perhaps one day he'll be all right.

When we arrived we were like him—my first-born brother and I. I can hardly remember. The people who live in the village near the tent took us to the clinic, it's where you have to sign that you've come—away, through the Kruger Park. We sat on the grass and everything was muddled. One Sister was pretty with her hair straightened and beautiful high-heeled shoes and she brought us the special powder. She said we must mix it with water and drink it slowly. We tore the packets open with our teeth and licked it all up, it stuck round my mouth and I sucked it from my lips and fingers. Some other children who had walked with us vomited. But I only felt everything in my belly moving, the stuff going down and around like a snake, and hiccups hurt me. Another Sister called us to stand in line on the verandah of the clinic but we couldn't. We sat all over the place there, falling against each other; the Sisters helped each of us up by the arm and then stuck a needle in it. Other needles drew our blood into tiny bottles. This was against sickness, but I didn't understand, every time my eyes dropped closed I thought I was walking, the grass was long, I saw the elephants, I didn't know we were away.

But our grandmother was still strong, she could still stand up, she knows how to write and she signed for us. Our grandmother got us this place in the tent against one of the sides, it's the best kind of place there because although the rain comes in, we can lift the flap when the weather is good and then the sun shines on us, the smells in the tent go out. Our grandmother knows a woman here who showed her where there is good grass for sleeping mats, and our grandmother made some for us. Once every month the food truck comes to the clinic. Our grandmother takes along one of the cards she signed and when it has been punched we get a sack of mealie meal. There are wheelbarrows to take it back to the tent; my first-born brother does this for her and then he and the other boys have races, steering the empty wheelbarrows back to the clinic. Some-times he's lucky and a man who's bought beer in the village gives him money to deliver it—though that's not allowed, you're supposed to take that wheelbarrow straight back to the Sisters. He buys a cold drink and shares it with me if I catch him. On another day, every month, the church leaves a pile of old clothes in the clinic yard. Our grandmother has another card to get punched, and then we can choose something: I have two dresses, two pants and a jersey, so I can go to school.

The people in the village have let us join their school. I was surprised to find they speak our language; our grandmother told me, That's why they allow us to stay on their land. Long ago, in the time of our fathers, there was no fence that kills you, there was no Kruger Park between them and us, we were the same people under our own king, right from our village we left to this place we've come to.

Now that we've been in the tent so long—I have turned eleven and my little brother is nearly three although he is so small, only his head is big, he's not come right in it yet—some people have dug up the bare ground around the tent and planted beans and mealies and cabbage. The old men weave branches to put up fences round their gardens. No one is allowed to look for work in the towns but some of the women have found work in the village and can buy things. Our grandmother, because she's still strong, finds work where people are building houses—in this village the people build nice houses with bricks and cement, not mud like we used to have at our home. Our grandmother carries bricks for these people and fetches baskets of stones on her head. And so she has money to buy sugar and tea and milk and soap. The store gave her a calendar she has hung up on our flap of the tent. I am clever at school and she collected advertising paper people throw away outside the store and covered my schoolbooks with it. She makes my first-born brother and me do our homework every afternoon before it gets dark because there is no room except to lie down, close together, just as we did in the Kruger Park, in our place in the tent, and candles are expensive. Our grandmother hasn't been able to buy herself a pair of shoes for church yet, but she has bought black school shoes and polish to clean them with for my first-born brother and me. Every morning, when people are getting up in the tent, the babies are crying, people are pushing each other at the taps outside and some children are already pulling the crusts of porridge off the pots we ate from last night, my first-born brother and I clean our shoes. Our grandmother makes us sit on our mats with our legs straight out so she can look carefully at our shoes to make sure we have done it properly. No other children in the tent have real school shoes. When we three look at them it's as if we are in a real house again, with no war, no away.

Some white people came to take photographs of our people living in the tent—they said they were making a film, I've never seen what that is though I know about it. A white woman squeezed into our space and asked our grandmother questions which were told to us in our language by someone who understands the white woman's.

How long have you been living like this?

She means here? our grandmother said. In this tent, two years and one month.

And what do you hope for the future?

Nothing. I'm here.

But for your children?

I want them to learn so that they can get good jobs and money.

Do you hope to go back to Mozambique—to your own country?

I will not go back.

But when the war is over—you won't be allowed to stay here? Don't you want to go home?

I didn't think our grandmother wanted to speak again. I didn't think she was going to answer the white woman. The white woman put her head on one side and smiled at us.

Our grandmother looked away from her and spoke—There is nothing. No home.

Why does our grandmother say that? Why? I'll go back. I'll go back through that Kruger Park. After the war, if there are no bandits any more, our mother may be waiting for us. And maybe when we left our grandfather, he was only left behind, he found his way somehow, slowly, through the Kruger Park, and he'll be there. They'll be home, and I'll remember them.

Abandoned Children of This Planet

Kenzaburo Oe

❧

The funeral ceremony commenced at three o'clock, although it's customary in the village to have them much earlier in the day. Apparently, they had arranged for it to start later, to accommodate the time of our incoming flight. The procession started in front of Father's home and followed a path downstream to Bodhi Temple. Eeyore and I saw the mourners off, flanking Grandma, who held a walking stick in her left hand. At the head of the procession was Great-uncle's picture, then his mortuary tablet, and following this, in single file, were bamboo poles with baskets hanging from them, and tall floral wreaths, which were trailed by a long line of strangely shaped paper banners. On went the procession, between the villagers, some dressed in black, some in their everyday attire, who were standing under the eaves of the houses along both sides of the road to pay their last respects to the deceased. A bright late-autumn shower crossed over from the mountainside facing the river to the south-facing side, which was dark with the colors of evergreens.

Against this backdrop, the whole panorama of the procession presented a strange sight. The way paper flowers were poured from the baskets on the bamboo poles, each time the mourners crowding in on the weighty coffin circled around it, resembled funerals among indigenous peoples in remote areas of Polynesia. It also impressed me as being gentle and nostalgic. Each time small red, blue, and yellow paper flowers flew from the baskets on the bamboo poles, Grandma raised her head on her emaciated neck, and seemed to strain her eyes to see beneath her triangular eyelids.

When the tail end of the procession started off, Grandma, Eeyore, and I retired to the cottage, where we rested for a while, and then headed for the temple, again in Shu-chan's car. Because Grandma can't walk far, Shu-chan took a side road, and we got off at a fork where the precincts of Bodhi Temple and its graveyard meet a woodland trail that climbs into the forest. We entered the temple from its backyard path and found that the funeral services were just about to commence. The monk conducting the funeral and the other monks in attendance were making their entrance into the main sanctuary, while a corpulent undertaker from the basin town, the distribution base, shouted from the housetops to the attending mourners, as though he were giving orders, military fashion—like in an old movie—to sit up straight and correct. Grandma, who sat between me and Eeyore in the middle of the section allocated for surviving members of the family and relatives, stretched her back and began waving for the chief monk to come over. Apparently she had something to say to him. The monk halted in the midst of his procession and sent a young monk to see what she wanted.

The import of what Grandma conveyed was: "Could you please ask that man who's trying to preside over the funeral service to leave?" The chief monk nodded when his disciple returned and repeated

Grandma's message, which he in turn relayed to the undertaker. There were no more shouted commands after this, and the ceremony progressed in a natural manner. After the service, as I left the sanctuary and stepped down into the garden, I noticed, in the corner of the wet veranda, the undertaker in his black mourning suit, vest, and bow tie, sitting there hugging his knees, looking at the clintonia leaves on which the rain was spattering.

Great-uncle's eldest son made a brief speech of thanks to the mourners who stood in the garden before the sanctuary. Grandma deemed this to be the end of it all. While we waited for Great-uncle's body to be placed in the hearse and then taken to the crematory upstream, Grandma returned to the antechamber of the sanctuary and talked with the chief monk, who seemed to be an old friend of hers. Watching this, Aunt Fusa remarked, "She's evading her responsibilities. She doesn't like to be greeted by her acquaintances from far away." Soon afterwards, Shu-chan, who looked like the lumpy figure in those Michelin ads, in that his mourning suit was much too small for him, came to tell us that Grandma had left from the rear entrance and was waiting for us at the place where he had dropped us off earlier.

So we went back up the pretty little path lined with small shrubs of various kinds sparkling in their colorful leaves of autumn, and found Grandma seated in the back of the car, pushing the passenger seat forward to help Eeyore get in and sit beside her. On the way to the temple Grandma, Aunt Fusa, and I had shared the backseat, and though we're all thin, and on the small side, we did feel cramped. But on the way back, Grandma seemed bent on monopolizing the backseat with Eeyore, for as soon as he entered, she pulled the front seat back again.

"I guess you want Eeyore to see the forest, is that it, Grandma?"

Aunt Fusa asked, sprinkling the postfuneral purifying salt on the
two in the car, and on the three of us, including herself, outside. "If
what you've got in mind is a forced march all the way up to the
higher places, then three in the rear would indeed be backbreaking.
Ma-chan, why don't you sit up front, and I'll do the driving. Shu,
you run home on those legs of yours you're so proud of, and help
put things back in order there."

We drove down the woodland path, crossed the bridge over the
village river, and headed for the road that wound around the mountain beyond. I looked back as we turned the sharp corner at the end
of the bridge, and caught sight of Shu-chan, looking exactly like the
Michelin man, running firmly and "soberly" down the path along
the cliff, rock-bare now that the trees had shed their leaves.

The ever-ascending drive to the top of the mountainside we were
headed for was beguilingly tortuous. It's a family joke that the very
first time Father took us to his village, I asked O-chan, my intellectual mentor ever since I was small. "Did mammoths still roam this
place when Papa was a child?" I don't remember asking this question, but the long stretch of the road up to and down from Father's
home before the tunnel was built is vividly etched in my memory.
Still, I actually felt that the climb from the road along the river up to
the hamlet of the "country"—to put it in the language of the village
map—was an even longer journey.

The scenery we glided through was breathtaking beyond measure. After passing through the basin town, I became aware that, on
the slopes of the hills on both sides of the road leading to Father's
village in the hollow, there were parcels of land where autumn's orange foliage was tinctured with sparkling red. As we climbed farther
up into the higher regions of the "country," I realized that the colors
were from persimmon patches. Patches, not orchards, is the word.

Originally they were farmland, cleared during the postwar years for growing wheat, in the days of food shortages. Grandma, who had once been the proprietor of a "mountain-produce wholesale store," explained to me that after the wheat came chestnut trees, and then the switch to persimmons.

After a while, the road we were driving on was enveloped by a bright crimson-orange: sparkling red-ocher over us, below us, to our right, and to our left. And we got into more of this as we navigated upward. Whenever we came to relatively level topography, we saw stately houses standing on top of firm, solid stone masonry, roofed in part with thatch, in part with tile, unlike the roofing of the houses in the hollow. Such decorous houses lined the road, at intervals, and they continued to appear with a certain consistency of style. Eventually, Aunt Fusa stopped the car on a spur from which unrolled a panoramic view. On one side lay a wide, deep-cut valley that sloped down like an enormous earthenware mortar. Beyond the valley, at eye level, across the deep, wide gully, stretched an overlapping range of quiet, somber blue mountains.

"Over there is the Shikoku Range," Aunt Fusa said. "I understand our ancestors finally found refuge from their pursuers in the depths of this forest after trudging over the many trails that meander between those ridges. It's a wonder how, despite all the difficulties, they still dreamed of establishing a new settlement. It's pitiful," she sighed, her eyes traveling over the scenery. Eeyore was helping Grandma out of the car.

"I thought the same thing," Grandma rejoined, "while standing on this high ground, when they wheeled me here on our cart for me to buy chestnuts for the store. But many years have passed since then, and looking at the village in the hollow now, I can see this place is spacious enough—big as it already is—to sustain a sizable community. In any case, just look at those slopes. There're so many of them I don't think human feet could ever walk their every nook and cranny. The place is truly vast! And it's because the place is so vast that a legend such as 'The Marvels of the Forest' has remained in the hearts of the people for so long. But Eeyore-san, you're the only one who's composed music about the legend. . . . I listened to the cassette tape you sent me, right here on this spur. Your music really made me think of 'The Marvels of the Forest.' By the way, Eeyore-san, what's your most recent composition?"

" 'Sutego' is its title," Eeyore emphatically replied.

I wasn't the only one startled. Grandma and Aunt Fusa stood there in fearful silence with their bodies and faces petrified in the direction they were looking. Seeing them in that state, I wondered to myself why two women whose ages were so different—granted they were mother and daughter—could react in so much the same way. Then endearing thoughts of Mother far away in California struck my heart. So strong was the emotion that I wanted to cry out, "Help me, too, Mother! Help me with my 'pinch.' " But Eeyore, the source of the ripples in my heart, had nonchalantly walked over to the side of the road, beyond which, a step lower, lay a patch of common persimmon trees pruned short for picking. Holding his face close to a red-and-yellow-studded leaf, he was smelling the sparkling beads the passing rain had caused to form on it. . . .

"If you go so close to the persimmons, Eeyore, they might think you'll pick and eat a few," I exclaimed. The words my mouth uttered were different from those that had welled up from the depths of my heart.

"Nobody's going to think that," Grandma said, recovering her smile. "If this were ten, fifteen years ago, the farmers would have built wire fences around these fields. But everything has changed now. You saw those piles of ripe persimmons in front of every farmer's house, didn't you? They're the ones that were culled as too ripe to ship. With all these persimmons, the children are indifferent toward even those that are just waiting to be picked and eaten. . . . The things children do change at a frightening pace, don't they, Ma-chan? When we were children, we wore straw sandals, had one un-lined kimono to wear, and one red, stringy band of cloth for an obi. We used to build a fire on the bare ground with dried branches to bake sweet potatoes, strip down to the waist and catch fish in the river, and scoop them out with a small bamboo basket. You've seen books, haven't you . . . like *Premodern Children's Customs and Chil-dren's Festivals?* The illustrations in them show exactly the things we used to do."

"You're premodern, Grandma," Aunt Fusa said. "We've already leapt the premodern and are modern. Eeyore and the others are stepping into the future."

"Well, then," Grandma observed, "shall the premodern and fu-ture have a relaxed conversation? Eeyore-san, will you tell me about your music composition?"

"Very well," Eeyore replied. Immediately showing interest, he raised his body, which was stooped over the foliage, and returned to where Grandma was.

"Then let us, the contemporary pair, go and talk a little farther up," Aunt Fusa said. "There could very well be an unexpected con-currence of minds if the modern age and the future converse."

As I had suspected, what Aunt Fusa wanted to personally ask me about—as two contemporaries—was "Sutego." She discussed this in the practical manner that was so typical of her. She matter-of-factly told me that if my parents' long-term stay at an American university was making Eeyore feel abandoned, I should call and ask them to come back immediately. What need was there for K-chan, who wrote in Japanese, to be a writer-in-residence in America, and put a burden on that country at a time when the value of the dollar was so low? He claimed that communication with his fellow professors was important, but how much could he accomplish in an English that he confuses with French? K-chan himself, she said, quite honestly admitted this when she last talked to him on the phone.

I didn't think I could tell her about Father's "pinch." I only told her that, although Eeyore did in fact compose a piece he had titled "Sutego," he didn't appear to be suffering the emotions of an abandoned child while working on it. And when it was completed, he was eager about the chords in the final part, and seemed more concerned about the technical results than about its theme.

Because Aunt Fusa had parked the car on one of the topographical overlooks of the delicately undulating mountainside, we could see, after climbing a little farther up, the whole valley below our eyes like the bottom of an earthenware mortar. Upstream the river was as tortuous as the road, and its water sparkled brightly at every short bend. Upriver some distance was a thickly wooded hill of tall, straight cypress trees that protruded like an appendage of the forest, and there a thick congregation of age-old cedars rose fiercely high above the cypresses. Among those trees, quite out of character with the forest, stood a boxlike, concrete structure with a tall chimney. Plumes of white smoke suddenly rose from the chimney with force. Aunt Fusa gazed down on this smoke with a stern expression, and appeared to be immersed in thought.

Alone, I kept looking up at the sky, blue as ever without a trace of the late-autumn shower it had just rained down on us. Confronting the sun, I sneezed: a blessing in disguise, for it unfettered Aunt Fusa from the thoughts that bound her, of Eeyore's "Sutego" or of Great-uncle being burned at the crematory, though most likely a mixture of the two.

"So the sun makes you sneeze, too, Ma-chan!" she said, vigorously raising her head and turning it toward me. "When K-chan was in middle school, he once read a magazine article about that. So he thought of an experiment to see if there was actually any relationship between the sun and sneezing. With only a limited number of subjects, he had me look at the sun every morning, which was no easy task for me. In those days, K-chan was a science nut, just like O-chan."

Aunt Fusa squinted her eyes and gazed at the sun in the western sky, and then sneezed a cute sneeze. We continued to laugh for a while, I then decided to ask her something.

"I guess this happened when Father was even younger." I began, "I heard that after he read about St. Francis, at the water mill where he took some wheat to have it ground, he seriously worried about whether he should immediately begin doing something concerning *matters of the soul.*"

"That's right. It's a true story," Aunt Fusa said. "You see down there where the river forks out into two streams, one shining, the other shaded? The water mill is quite a distance up that narrow, darker one, and K-chan came back tightly clutching the bag of flour to his chest, and his face was all white. Fearing that a neighborhood St. Francis of Assisi might appear out of the shade of a nearby tree and lure him to engage in matters of the soul, he began to shed tears, and his eyes looked like those of a raccoon dog . . ."

"From what Father said in the lecture, I understand that you told him he looked like a white monkey. . . ."

"He's embellished his memory a bit because this concerns him personally. A raw-boned raccoon dog, a runty raccoon dog: that's what he looked like. . . . But I expect he's lived his life ever since in fear of the day he would have to abandon everything in order to dedicate himself to *matters of the soul.* At least that's the kind of person he was while he lived with us, until he graduated from high school. He used to get so depressed when his friends invited him to go with them to study the Bible in English. . ."

"Big Brother was also very much concerned about this. He worried whether K-chan would join some religious organization in Tokyo, though he didn't mind political parties. And once he lamented that if this ever happened it would spell the end of K-chan's future, in a social sense. Come to think of it, though, both Big Brother and K-chan were pitiful young men who were constantly hounded by *matters of the soul.* But one of them has already turned into white smoke, without doing anything about *matters of the soul.* . ."

"In connection with this, 'The Marvels of the Forest,' the legend Grandma spoke of when she was talking about Eeyore's composition, is a story Grandma's mother once related to K-chan. Or perhaps I should say that K-chan unearthed the strange legend with his power. The science-minded child that he was in those days, he tried interpreting it all sorts of ways. He once even said that 'The Marvels of the Forest' may have been delivered to Earth by a rocket from either the solar system or from the universe beyond it. Anyway, he said that civilization may have started on this planet with this as its genesis. I've always been a simple-minded girl, and so I imagined a shoal of children from some faraway star, packed like sardines in the 'Marvels of the Forest' rocket, being abandoned here on Earth. And I used to get so lonely. . ."

"When you think of it, though, don't you feel that Eeyore and I share a similar vocabulary of imagination somewhere? And K-chan's probably behind it all. I felt really lonely, thinking about the 'Marvels of the Forest' rocket, probably because he had said something to the effect that we were interplanetary abandoned children. I wouldn't be surprised if he's directed remarks of a similar vein at Eeyore. And then having done something so careless, he himself leaves for California with Oyu-san! It may surprise some people, but that's the kind of person he is."

Grandma and Eeyore had been gently leaning their backs against the stone wall that retained the persimmon patch above them on the upper side of the road. Then Grandma briskly pulled her small shoulders away from the wall. She raised her right hand, in which she again held her cane, and waved at us. Until then, I had thought that both Grandma and Eeyore had been looking in silence at the forest, the sunlight and its reflections on the red-orange foliage of the persimmon trees. But evidently Grandma had, all the while, been very patiently conversing with Eeyore. Half tripping, we ran to her, and heard her voice emphatically ring out.

"The title of 'Sutego' in full," she called out, "is 'Rescuing a Sutego.' Eeyore-san and his co-workers at the welfare workshop clean the park every Tuesday, don't they? He's told me that some of his co-workers once found an abandoned baby there and saved it. Eeyore-san has set his heart on saving such a baby if ever he finds one while he's on duty. That's what he had on his mind while composing his music, and that's why the piece was titled 'Rescuing a Sutego.'"

"Ah, so that's what it was, Eeyore!" I exclaimed. "Yes, I remember that occasion, when they saved a baby while park cleaning. I should have remembered it as soon as I heard the title . . . but it was so long ago. So that's what it was all about, Eeyore. So it's all right for the melody to be sad. After all it's about rescuing a *sutego*!" I said, savoring a sensation of quiet happiness.

Kenzaburo Oe

"Oh, so that's what it was!" Aunt Fusa repeated. Her way of understanding the situation was the same as mine, but in her own characteristic manner, she crowned this understanding with a conclusion. "If we think of all the people on this planet as being abandoned children, then Eeyore's composition expresses something very grand in scale!"

translated by Kunioki Yanagishita
and William Wetherall

The Contributors

❧

Chinua Achebe, born in Nigeria and raised by Christian parents in Ogidi, Eastern region. A graduate of University College, Ibadan, he left his first career in broadcasting during the violent upheavals that unleashed the Biafran war. He has published fiction, including *Things Fall Apart,* a landmark in African literature; poetry, essays and children's books. His works are published in some fifty languages. His collected poems will be published in 2004.

Woody Allen is a writer, director and actor for stage and screen.

Margaret Atwood is the author of more than thirty-five books of fiction, poetry and critical essays. Her novels *Oryx & Crake, The Handmaiden's Tale, Cat's Eye* and *Alias Grace* (winner of the Giller Prize and the Premio Mondello) were nominated for the Booker Prize, which she won for *The Blind Assassin* in 2000. She lives in Toronto with writer Graeme Gibson.

Gabriel García Márquez, born in 1927 in Columbia, describes himself as journalist and writer. Among his works translated into many languages is the novel *One Hundred Years of Solitude.* He was awarded the Nobel Prize in

Literature, 1982. He lives in Mexico, and is married to Mercedes Barcha, has two children and five grandchildren.

Nadine Gordimer is the author of thirteen novels, ten short story collections and several nonfiction collections, all translated into many languages. She was awarded the Nobel Prize in Literature, 1991. She lives in Johannesburg.

Günter Grass was born in Danzig, Germany, 1927. He is a novelist, poet, playwright, essayist, graphic artist and creator of works that defy any description of conventional genre. He was awarded the Nobel Prize in Literature, 2000. His most recent novel is *Crabwalk*.

Hanif Kureishi was born and grew up in England. His novels are *The Buddha of Suburbia, The Black Album, Intimacy* and *The Body*. He has written numerous screen plays, including *My Beautiful Laundrette* and *The Mother*. He lives in London.

Claudio Magris, born in Trieste, 1939, is professor of modern German literature at the University of Trieste. His books, including his latest work *La Mostra,* have been translated into numerous languages and among his awards are Prix du Meilleur Livre Etranger, Premio Strega, Leipziger Buchpreis zur Europäischen Verständigung, Praemium Erasmianum.

Arthur Miller's most recent works, apart from four short stories, are two new plays, *Resurrection Blues* and *Finishing the Picture,* both in production for the season of 2004. He has won the Pulitzer Prize, the Prix Molière of the French Theatre, three Tony Awards for his plays and a Lifetime Achievement Award. He has honorary degrees from Oxford University and Harvard University. He lives in the United States of America.

Es'kia Mphahlele, born in Marabastad, Pretoria, 1919, went into exile 1957–1977, in West and East Africa, France, and the United States of America. He changed his name from Ezekiel to its Sesotho equivalent after his return to South Africa. He published his best-known book *Down Second Avenue* in 1959, followed by volumes of short stories, novellas, novels, poetry and essays, the latter while teaching. He obtained his Ph.d. in the United States of America and has been honoured with DLitt., by universities at home and abroad.

Njabulo S. Ndebele is currently vice-chancellor of the University of Capetown. His most recent novel is *The Cry of Winnie Mandela*. Other publications include award-winning *Fools,* a story collection, and an acclaimed collection of critical essays *Rediscovery of the Ordinary*. He was president of the Congress of South African Writers for many years.

Kenzaburo Oe, born in rural Japan in 1935, began to publish his writings while still an undergraduate. In 1963 his son was born brain-damaged and this led him to research the problems of A-bomb survivors. Among his novels and stories is *A Personal Matter,* a novel about coming to terms with living with and loving a severely handicapped child. The theme is linked to his other fiction and essays focused on Hiroshima and its consequences. He was awarded the Nobel Prize in Literature, 1994.

Amos Oz was born in Jerusalem in 1939. He lived for thirty years on Kibbutz Hulda, working the land, writing and teaching. He is the author of eleven novels, many collections of short stories, essays, and is published in more than thirty languages. His work has been awarded numerous international prizes. For thirty-five years he has been a prominent figure in the Israeli Peace Movement, advocating Israeli-Palestinian peace based on historic compromises and a two-state solution.

Salman Rushdie is the author of eight novels, *Fury, The Ground Beneath Her Feet, The Moor's Last Sigh, Midnight's Children* (which won both the Booker Prize and the Booker of Bookers), *Shame, The Satanic Verses, Grimus, Haroun & The Sea of Stories* and a story collection *East, West*. He has published a book of reportage *The Jaguar Smile* and two essay collections, *Step Across This Line: Collected Nonfiction 1992–2002* and *Imaginary Homelands*. He lives in New York and London.

José Saramago was born in Portugal in 1922. He has been a mechanic, a draughtsman, a publisher's reader, an editor and translator. He has written volumes of plays, essays, short stories, ten novels and has received numerous honours. He was awarded the Nobel Prize in Literature, 1998. He lives in Lanzerote, Canary Islands, Spain.

Ingo Schulze was born in Dresden in 1962. After receiving an Arts Degree at the University of Jena he was dramatic arts advisor at the State Theatre Altenburg in the former GDR, for two years, founded an advertising paper and spent six months in St. Petersburg, where his experiences inspired him to write *33 Moments of Happiness,* his debut story collection in 1995. His stories and novels have been awarded a number of prizes and are translated into twenty languages.

Susan Sontag is the author of four novels, *The Benefactor, Death Kit, The Volcano Lover,* and *In America;* a collection of stories *I, etcetera,* several plays including *Alice In Bed* and *Lady From The Sea,* and seven works of nonfiction, among them *On Photography, Illness as Metaphor* and *Regarding the Pain of Others.* Her books are translated into thirty-two languages. She lives in New York.

Paul Theroux, a teacher and traveller in Africa, lived in Britain for seventeen years. He returned to the United States of America in 1990 and now lives in Hawaii. He has published four story collections and his novels include *The Mosquito Coast* and *My Secret History.* His most recent travel book is *Dark Star Safari,* an account of his 2001 overland trip from Cairo to Cape Town.

Michel Tournier, born in Paris in 1924, began his study of philosophy at school and pursued this at the University of Tübingen, Germany. He has had a career in the press, publicity and in publishing. He directed the services at Editions Plon, Paris. His first novel *Vendredi ou les Limbes du Pacique* received the Grand Prix du Roman de l'Academie Francaise, followed by *Le Roi des Aulnes* awarded the Prix Goncourt, *Les Meteores, Gaspard, Melchior et Balthazar,* five nonfiction works and three books for children. Volker Schlöndorff filmed *Le Roi des Aulnes* in 1996. Michel Tournier is a member of the Academie Goncourt and lives in the ancient presbytery of a village in France.

John Updike, born in Shillington, Pennsylvania, 1932, attended local schools and Harvard College. From 1955 to 1957 he was a member of the staff of *The New Yorker,* and since then he has lived in Massachusetts. He is the father of four children and the author of more than fifty books, including twenty-one novels and collections of poetry, short stories and criticism.

Christa Wolf is an editor, critic, author of essays, film scripts, novels and short stories. Her latest work is *One Day In The Year*. She has received the National Prize of the GDR, the Georg Büchner Prize, The Austrian State Prize for European Literature and the Geschwister-Scholl-Preis. She lives in Berlin.

Karel Nel, artist, curator, academic and writer on African art, is an associate professor in the Witwatersrand University School of the Arts. He is particularly interested in the links between art and science. He exhibits in London, New York, Los Angeles, and his work is represented in the South African National Gallery, The Smithsonian Institute in Washington, and the Metropolitan Museum, New York.

Kevin Shenton graduated in Typography & Graphic Communication at Reading University, England. He worked for various London publishing houses and advertising agencies before moving to South Africa. He lives in Johannesburg where he practices as a specialist book designer and communications consultant.

These CVs for the authors and jacket artists vary in length and detail because I thought it best if the writers and artists themselves decided how they wanted to be presented.   Nadine Gordimer

Source Notes

ABOUT TAC

The Treatment Action Campaign, known as TAC, is an independent non-profit organization whose funds are used for the treatment and support of people suffering from HIV and AIDS, and for the prevention of the disease, in the world's most afflicted region, Southern Africa.

TAC is chaired by Zackie Achmat, himself living with AIDS and giving his active, total dedication to the TAC objectives: access to affordable treatment for people with HIV/AIDS, preventive education, and raising awareness of living conditions of poverty which exacerbate suffering and cannot provide the nourishment necessary to respond to treatment.

Achmat and the TAC have been nominated for the 2004 Nobel Prize, and in 2003, the organization won the prestigious Nelson Mandela Award for Health and Human Rights, as well as the National Press Club Award for Newsmaker of the Year. The group's unflagging efforts continue to mobilize not only countries in Southern Africa but the global community in awareness of disparities in treatment access; with the support of church groups, civic groups, and high-profile individuals, TAC has become South Africa's leading AIDS pressure group, and through Zackie Achmat, a most compelling world-voice for people with the disease.

The publisher's profits from the worldwide sales of *Telling Tales* will go to the TAC.

For further information, visit TAC at www.tac.org.za.